At the Drop of a Hat

Jenn McKinlay

BERKLEY PRIME CRIME, NEW YORK

THE BERKLEY PUBLISHING GROUP
Published by the Penguin Group
Penguin Group (USA) LLC
375 Hudson Street, New York, New York 10014

USA • Canada • UK • Ireland • Australia • New Zealand • India • South Africa • China

penguin.com

A Penguin Random House Company

AT THE DROP OF A HAT

A Berkley Prime Crime Book / published by arrangement with the author

For information, address: The Berkley Publishing Group,
a division of Penguin Group (USA) LLC,
375 Hudson Street, New York, New York 10014.

ISBN: 978-0-425-25891-0

PUBLISHING HISTORY
Berkley Prime Crime mass-market edition / February 2015

PRINTED IN THE UNITED STATES OF AMERICA

10   9   8   7   6   5   4   3   2

Cover illustration by Robert Steele.
Cover design by Diana Kolsky.
Interior text design by Laura K. Corless.

To Barbara Peters and the amazing staff
at The Poisoned Pen Bookstore in Scottsdale, Arizona.
I discovered this shop in 1991
when being an author was just a dream.
Little did I know then how incredibly supportive
you all would be when that dream became a reality.
Thank you for everything that you do
for authors and readers.
You are simply amazing and I am honored
to call you my friends.

Chapter 1

I stood at the counter of Mim's Whims, the hat shop my cousin Vivian Tremont and I had inherited from our grandmother Mim, and I gazed out the window. All I could see was gray.

Gray clouds, gray sheets of rain, gray fog filling the streets and alleyways, gray, gray, gray. Or as the Brits like to spell it, grey.

Our shop is nestled in the midst of Portobello Road and takes up the bottom floor of the three-story white building that our grandmother bought over forty years ago. I've always loved it and found the bright blue-and-white-striped awning and matching blue shutters on the windows above to be cheerful, but even they couldn't defeat the never-ending gloom that seemed to descend upon our section of London.

Having been raised in the States and hailing most

1

recently from Florida, I was being pushed just to the right of crazy by this late September weather.

Three solid weeks of rain will do that to a girl. Besides, I was quite sure I was going to sprout mold if I didn't get some sunshine, and soon.

"It's the last one," Fee said. "You should have it."

"No, no, I insist you take it," Viv said. She tossed her long blond hair over her shoulder as if the gesture added weight to her argument.

Fee is Fiona Felton, my cousin Viv's apprentice. She's a very nice girl with a tall willowy build, a dark complexion courtesy of her West Indies heritage and a bob of corkscrew curls that she likes to dye new and different colors. Currently, she was rocking green streaks, which I thought was pretty cool but would look hideous in my own auburn shoulder-length hair.

Viv is the mad hatter of our little trio. Growing up down the street, she trained to be a milliner beside Mim. My own attempts at millinery were encouraged, but it became readily apparent that I did not have the family gift for twining ribbons into flowers or shaping brims or anything artistic or even crafty.

Viv and Fee were standing on the other side of the counter, taking a break from their current creations in the workroom. They were pushing a plate back and forth between them which contained one rogue piece of Walker's Toffee, the last of the package we had been nibbling on all day.

"After such a large tea this afternoon, I couldn't eat another bite," Fee said.

"Fee, honestly, I insist you take the last piece of toffee," Viv said. She sounded very bossy about it.

"No, I couldn't possibly. You absolutely must have it," Fee said. She blew a green curl out of her eyes.

"Oh, for goodness' sake," I said. "I'll eat it just to end this."

I scooped up the last piece of toffee and popped it into my mouth. Viv and Fee both turned to look at me with wide eyes.

"What?" I asked while chewing.

"Nothing," Fee said and glanced away.

"It's fine," Viv agreed.

I stopped chewing. I knew the stone-sinking sensation of committing a social gaffe when I felt it. Scarlett Parker, boorish American, that's me.

"Aw, man," I said. "I messed that up, didn't I?"

"It's fine, honestly," Viv said.

Which was how I knew it really wasn't.

"What did I do?" I asked. "Did I not force it on you two enough?"

"You're making fun of us," Viv said.

I swallowed the last of the toffee. "No, I'm just trying to figure out how pushing something that you apparently really want onto others makes sense. If you want it, take it."

"That's not our way," Fee said. "There are just certain things we do out of politeness like saying 'Cheers' when you step off the bus."

"The toffee push could have gone on all day," I said.

"It probably would have," Viv agreed.

"See? You did us a favor," Fee said.

"And now you're trying to make me feel better for being a clumsy American," I said.

"You're half British," Viv reminded me. Like I could forget my charming mother, Viv's mother's little sister, that easily. The woman had all but demanded a vow of celibacy out of me after my last relationship implosion went viral on the Internet and had my dad, a pacifist, looking into buying a gun to shoot the rat bastard who hurt his baby girl.

"I still don't get it," I said.

"It's just one of the many idiosyncrasies of being British," Viv said. "You indicate you're longing for something by rejecting it. Repeatedly."

"Now I see why you're both single," I said.

"Was that nice?" Viv asked. "We're just very polite."

"One might say cripplingly polite," I said.

"Huh, enjoy that toffee, yeah?" Fee said.

I smiled. Maybe I was too brash and forward for my cousin's sensibilities, but at least I didn't spend my time pining or pretending I didn't want things that I actually did.

The doors to the front of the shop opened and in strode Harrison Wentworth. My heart did a little toe tap against my ribs but I refused to acknowledge it. Okay, so maybe I did pretend I didn't want something that I really did want just a little.

"Afternoon, ladies," he greeted us as he stood in the door and shook out his umbrella.

"Hi, Harrison," Viv and Fee greeted him in unison.

"Hiya, Harry," I said.

His bright green eyes glittered when they landed on me.

4

"It's Harrison, Ginger," he corrected me.

Little did he know I liked hearing him call me Ginger, especially in that swoonworthy accent of his. Although I had tried to get everyone to call me Ginger over the years, Harry was the only one who'd kept it up from childhood. Yes, I'd known him that long.

Most of my school holidays had been spent in Notting Hill in Mim's hat shop. My mother had insisted that I be well versed in all things British, and palling around with Viv was never a hardship. She was two years older than me, and given that we were both the only children in our families, she was the sibling I had never had.

Harry had been one of our brat pack, the kids whose families lived or owned businesses on Portobello Road, who ran amuck in the neighborhood. His uncle had been Mim's bookkeeper just as Harry was ours. Of course, I had recently come to find out that he had bought a share of the business and was now technically my boss. Yeah, I was still chewing on that one.

I couldn't fault Viv, though. She'd gotten into financial trouble over a haul of Swarovski crystals—yes, like me, she has impulse control issues. Unfortunately, I'd been so caught up in the drama that was my life at the time that she'd forged ahead and had Harry save the business when I should have been there to help. I still had guilt about it, but I was working through it.

"What are you doing here?" I asked Harry.

He raised his eyebrows at me and I realized my American rudeness was rearing its ugly blocky head—again.

"Sorry," I said. "Was that too abrupt?"

"One does generally start with a comment about the

weather," he said. "Then you slowly segue into a softly ped-aled interrogation."

I glanced at the window. "After three weeks of gloom, I am thinking any conversation about the weather would be redundant, but if it makes you feel better . . . ruddy wet out there today, isn't it?"

He grinned and then looked at Viv. "There's hope for her yet."

Fee snorted. "Not if there's toffee involved."

I was about to protest when the bells on the door jangled and a woman in a blue hooded raincoat entered the shop carrying a large plastic bag.

She stood dripping on the doormat, and I took it as my opportunity to escape the discussion of my manners or lack thereof. I left the group at the counter and crossed the shop.

"Hi, may I help you?" I asked.

"Oh, I hope so," she said.

She opened the dripping plastic bag and pulled out an old hatbox. It was white with thick blue stripes and a blue satin cord. On the top of the box in a swirling script were the words *Mim's Whims*.

I heard a gasp and realized that it came from behind me. I knew without looking that it was Viv, and I knew she was reacting to the same thing that I was. This box was an old one of Mim's before Mim had updated the shop's boxes in the nineties.

"Is there a hat in there?" Viv asked as she joined us on the mat in front of the front door.

"Yes, it's an old one that belonged to my mother," the woman answered.

She pushed back the hood on her raincoat and I was struck by how dark her hair was. It was an inky black color, thick and lustrous, the type you'd expect to see on a model. After I recovered from my spurt of hair envy, I noted that she was quite pretty with big brown eyes and an upturned nose. Mercifully, she was spared from being perfect as her lips were on the thin side and she wore glasses, a nerdy rectangular pair with thick black frames.

"I don't want to drip all over your shop," the woman said.

"No worries," I said. "Here, I'll take the bag and your coat."

She handed me the dripping bag and shrugged out of her coat, freeing one arm at a time as if afraid to let go of her hatbox. I hung her coat and the bag on our coatrack by the door. Usually we kept it in the back room, but so many people had been coming in with wet coats that we'd moved it out front for the interminable rainfest we had going.

I hurried after them as Viv led the woman over to the counter, where Fee and Harrison were watching the happenings with curious expressions.

"Ariana, is that you?" Harrison asked. He looked delighted to see the young woman, and I felt the prick of something sharp, like the spiny point of jealousy, stab me in the backside.

She looked up at him in surprise and then laughed. "Harrison, fancy meeting you here!"

He stepped around the counter and swept her into a friendly embrace. "I wondered why Stephen asked me about this place. Was it for you?"

This place? I turned to exchange a dark look with Viv, but neither she nor Fee was looking in my direction. Did they not see that Harrison had just insulted our shop?

"Yes, I knew you did the books for a hat shop on Porto-bello and was so hoping it was the same one, and then Stephen said that you bragged that it was the best in the city and that the girls who owned were—"

"Yes, well." Harrison interrupted her by coughing loudly into his fist.

He glanced at me and I narrowed my eyes at him. What had he said about us? I opened my mouth to demand to hear it when Viv spoke first.

"Do you know what year your mother purchased the hat?" Viv asked Ariana.

"I do. It was 1983, in fact," she said. "The hat was a bridal hat for her wedding."

"Oh, 1983 was a very good hat year. John Boyd was designing for Princess Diana. I loved the turquoise hat he made for her first foreign tour to Australia. It was a cap framed by matching ropes of silk with a net over the top and a matching flower at the back. I tried to re-create it during my apprenticeship but I could never match his artistry."

"He is a genius," Fee agreed. "I adore the red boater that she wore perched to the side with the matching jacket."

"None of us were even born in 1983," I said. "How is it you know what the hats looked like back then?"

"Every milliner studies John Boyd and Princess Diana," Fee said.

"That and I did an apprenticeship in his Knightsbridge shop," Viv said. "Mim loved his work. They were friends, you know."

I didn't, but I didn't say as much, mostly because I was too embarrassed to admit that although the name "John

Boyd" sounded familiar, I wasn't really up to speed on his work. The truth was I didn't know much about the millinery business. I had studied the hospitality industry in college and my gift was more with people, which brought my attention back to the woman in our shop.

"I'm sorry, Ariana, I didn't catch your last name," I said. I glanced meaningfully at Harrison but he didn't look embarrassed in the least.

"Oh, of course, forgive me," he said. "Ariana Jackson, these are the owners of Mim's Whims—Scarlett Parker and Vivian Tremont—and their apprentice, Fiona Felton."

"Ariana, what a pretty name," I said. I gave her my most winning smile. "It suits you. Do you and Harrison go a long way back?"

Harry raised his eyebrows, no doubt surprised that I hadn't used his nickname. Well, just like he didn't know that I liked the name "Ginger," he also didn't know that I considered "Harry" my personal name for him and I really didn't want to share it.

"Not at all, just a few rugby seasons," Ariana said. She and Harrison exchanged a smile. "My fiancé, Stephen, plays on the same league team, and when I said I wanted to get my mother's hat fixed for our wedding, Stephen asked Harrison about Mim's Whims. I was thrilled to find out you're still here."

She put the old hatbox on the counter. "I was hoping you might be able to help me. My mother's hat needs some refurbishing and since it originally came from this shop . . ."

"Let's see what we've got here," Viv said. She gestured to the box. "May I?"

Ariana gave her a quick nod and Viv eagerly pried the lid off. Nested amid layers of pale tissue paper was a wide-brimmed white confection. Viv carefully reached into the box and gently pulled the hat free.

I gasped. It was beautiful: a wide-brimmed, white silk hat swathed in tulle with a large silk bow and a lush organza rose nestled in the center. As Viv lifted it, a long organza train fell down from beneath the bow and spilled over the brim. Fee reached out and pulled the train free—it was long and delicate with embroidered edges. Even I could see our grandmother's handiwork all over it.

"Oh, Mim," Viv said. Her voice sounded wistful and I knew just how she felt. To hold something our grandmother had made over thirty years ago brought her right back to us.

The sweet scent of lily of the valley filled my nose. I glanced at Viv at the same moment she glanced at me. *Mim.* It was the distinct scent Mim had always worn. I glanced around the shop as if expecting her to appear, but of course she didn't. Still, she was here, or the essence of her was here. I was sure of it just as I was sure she wanted Viv to restore the hat.

"I'd be happy to try and fix the hat," Viv said. "No, I'd be honored."

Chapter 2

"Are you certain?" Ariana asked. "There's been some damage."

Viv examined the hat. A vee formed in between her eyes as she examined the fabric of the hat.

"Dupioni silk?" Fee asked.

"Yes," Viv said. She ran her fingers over the silk, examining the stitches.

"How is that different from other silk?" Harrison asked. I could have hugged him for asking what I wanted to know but hadn't asked because I didn't want to look dumb.

"Dupioni silk is a crisp type of silk," Viv said. "They use a fine silk in the warp and uneven thread from two different cocoons, sometimes in different colors, in the weft."

"And here I thought I'd understand what you were talking about," Harrison said with a shake of his head. "Please

11

excuse me, ladies, while I go play with numbers, which make much more sense to me. Ariana, give my best to Stephen and tell him I'll see him on the pitch."

"I will," Ariana promised.

Harrison turned and strolled to the workroom in the back of the shop. As I watched him walk away, I admired the broad shape of his shoulders under his sweater and the way his dark brown hair curled at the nape of his neck. He was an annoyingly handsome man.

"All right, Scarlett?" Fee asked.

I glanced away from Harrison to find all three of them looking at me.

"Absolutely. Why?" I asked.

"You sighed," Viv said. Then she grinned and added, "Longingly."

"Really?" I asked. I ignored the heat I could feel warming my face. "I must be hungry."

"But not for food, yeah?" Fee asked and then laughed. Viv joined her but Ariana gave us all a confused look.

"Ignore them," I said to her. I rolled my eyes. "They're just teasing me. I mean Harrison, really?"

"I don't know," Ariana said. "I may be getting married to his teammate in a month but even I can see he is quite dishy."

Now my face was flaming hot. Subject change now.

I forced a smile. "So you're getting married? Congratulations. Is that why you want the hat refurbished?"

Ariana's face grew somber. "Partly. You see, my mother passed away when I was in school. My father's new wife"—she paused and made a pained face—"gave away my mother's wedding dress to charity when she was clearing out her things, so this is all that I have of hers and I was really hoping to wear it at my own wedding."

A glance at Viv and Fee and I knew from their sympathetic expressions that they felt Ariana's sadness as deeply as I did.

Viv turned the hat around in her hands. "There are some tears and discoloring in the silk. In order to fix it, I may have to remove large sections of the original material."

"But you think it can be done?" Ariana asked.

Her hopeful expression had me holding my breath as I waited for Viv's answer. I so wanted Ariana to have her mother's hat on her special day.

"Yes," Viv said. She gave a decisive nod. "I can do it."

"Oh, that's wonderful!" Ariana cried, and she clapped her hands together. Then her face fell. "I am on a bit of a budget, however."

"Not to worry," Viv said. "Before I do any of the work, I'll get you an estimate. We'll make it work within your budget."

"Thank you," Ariana said. She glanced at the watch on her wrist and her eyes widened. "Oh, I have to go. I work for a solicitor in Kensington, Mr. Anthony Russo. He'll throw a wobbler if I'm late getting back."

"Here, give us your phone number and we can text you the estimate," I said. She was looking anxiously at the door and I didn't want to hold her up longer than necessary.

She quickly jotted down her number and I walked her to the door. I retrieved her coat from the rack and held it open for her.

"Thank you," she said. She glanced back at Vivian and the hat and asked, "You'll mind it well, won't you?"

"As if it were my very own wedding hat," Viv promised with a smile.

Ariana puffed a sigh of relief, cried her thanks one more time, and hurried back out into the lead-bottomed day. As the door shut behind her, a draft of cold and wet snuck in and splashed against my black tights. My black ankle-high boots and purple knit dress were no defense against the damp, and I hurriedly closed the door after her.

"She's going to make a lovely bride with this hat on, yeah?" Fee asked.

"I wonder what her gown looks like," I said.

I love weddings. I love everything about them: the brides, gowns, tiaras, flowers and all that goes with them, well, all except for the groom. As I mentioned, I was off men for at least a year and thoughts of men in tuxedos were not helpful, so I found it better just to focus on the bridal portion of things. Luckily, at Mim's Whims, we were mostly about the bride.

"We'll have to ask," Viv said. She was considering the hat, turning it over in her hands.

"Maybe she'll order all of her bridesmaid's hats through us," Fee said. She gave us a hopeful look as she left the front of the shop and headed back to the workroom to finish her latest project.

"Assuming she hires us to fix the hat," Viv said. She was still examining the inside, running her fingers over the stitching. She glanced up at me. Her smile was wistful. "I hope she hires us. I love the idea of restoring one of Mim's hats to its original glory."

I glanced down at the beautiful silk and organza and ran my fingertip over the same stitches Viv had.

"I get the feeling Mim wants you to," I said in a soft voice.

"Me, too," she whispered back. "No matter how much Ariana can afford, I think we need to make this happen."

"Agreed," I said.

Of course, everything seems like a great idea when you have no idea what you're getting yourself into.

Chapter 3

"It's the third message I've left for her this week," I said. "If the wedding is in a month, she needs to give you time to get the work on the hat done."

It had been several days since Ariana had been in with her mother's hat. Viv had done the estimate right away and I had called Ariana at the number she'd given us but hadn't gotten a call back. Viv had instructed me to be flexible with the cost, but since I hadn't heard from her, I hadn't even had the opportunity to haggle.

"Maybe she's caught up in so much wedding stuff, she hasn't had time," Viv said. "You know how brides are."

It was true. We did a lot of wedding hats, from the bride's veil to the bridesmaids' hats, the mothers and the guests. It was very lucrative. And yes, we had dealt with our share of hysterical brides. Ariana hadn't seemed like that. th~

"I'm locking up," Viv cried over her shoulder as she crossed the shop to the front door.

"Excellent," I said. "We have to be over at Andre and Nick's before the show starts. Nick said he's feeling inspired."

"I can't believe they have us watching *The Great British Bake Off*," Viv said as she came back. "Between us we can barely boil water."

"I think Nick is smitten with Mary Berry," I said. "Besides I am crushing ridiculously on the chef from Devon, what's his name—Trevor, no, Trey, no . . ."

"Travis," Viv supplied. "Travis Manfred."

"What?" a voice squawked from behind me. I turned to see Harrison standing in the doorway to the workroom. "Ginger, you're crushing on that mangy git? I wouldn't let him fry me an egg."

I smiled. I couldn't help it. I got a perverse pleasure in riling Harrison. I tossed my hair over my shoulder and tried to look nonchalant.

"I can't help it if he has the dreamiest blue eyes," I said. "Don't you think so, Viv?"

"Oh, no, you're daft if you think I'm getting in the midst of this," she said. She turned and narrowed her eyes at Harrison. "Correct me if I'm wrong, however, didn't you say you were only joining us because you thought the dark-haired girl was quite fit."

I frowned. I might be from the States, but even I know that when a British man calls a girl "fit," he is not talking about her exercise capacity; rather, he thinks she's hot.

"How very shallow of you, Harry," I said.

"Bloody double standard you're working there, Ginger," Harrison said.

I ignored him. I'm very good at that, just like I can pretty much tune out any words I don't want to hear or not see things I'd rather not. Probably that's why my last relationship was a CATASTROPHE, in all caps.

All joking aside, I was in no shape to date anyone possibly forever. No, it was much better to drool over an amateur chef as he baked his way into fame and fortune.

"Come on, you two," Viv called from the workroom. "We're going to be late!"

Our friends, Nick Carroll and Andre Eisel, lived several shops down Portobello Road from our hat shop. The lower half of their place housed Andre's photography studio and they lived in the two floors above much like Viv and me, except Nick and Andre are a couple instead of cousins. Oh, and Nick's a dentist.

Lucky for us, they love to entertain, because Viv and I do not. So it was understood that we would bring the wine and dessert when they invited us to dinner, which happened about once a week and usually on *Great British Bake Off* night.

It helped that Nick thought of himself as a great undiscovered chef, and in all fairness, he really was skilled. It goes without saying that he was the one who liked to watch *the show* the most. I half expected him to enter the running every time the applications were open.

The way he yelled at the bakers, "Bloody hell, use the

whisk! The whisk!" or "By all that is holy, how can you call that a reduction? It's reducing me to tears, I tell you," it was more fun watching him than it was the show.

"What did you pick up for dessert?" I asked Harrison as we walked down the street.

He was carrying a large bakery box, and just the sight of it made my stomach growl.

"Pecan tarts from Paul Rhodes Bakery," he said. "They are amazing."

"Hmm. Are you sure you don't want me to taste test one, Harry? It would be bad form to show up with a marginal dessert."

"I'm quite sure, thanks," he said. "And it's Harrison."

I gave him my best grumpy look. He did not appear swayed in the least.

"Do we know what Nick is cooking tonight?" I asked Viv.

"No, which is why you are carrying red wine and I am carrying white," she said. We passed the main entrance to the studio and stopped in front of a small side door. Viv turned the handle and it opened. Harrison held the door and waited for us to enter first.

"Hello? Anyone home?" I called up the stairs.

"Scarlett, is that you?" Andre's head appeared over the banister above. His smile was a white slash against his cocoa-colored skin. He was wearing a form-fitting periwinkle silk shirt, and the diamond stud he wore in one ear winked at me in the overhead light.

"Yes, it's me and I found two strangers and invited them to join us," I teased. "Is that all right?"

"Did they bring dessert?" he asked.

"And wine," I replied.

"By all means, show them up," he said. "Oh, and lock the door behind you, would you?"

"Done," Harrison called from behind me.

The three of us trudged up the stairs just in time to hear Nick in the kitchen.

"Three cups of broth? I only have two! Dinner is ruined!"

"Sounds like there's a drama happening in the kitchen," Andre said. "Make yourselves at home and I'll see if I can use my sous chef magic to calm him down."

We put the wine and the bakery box on the side table in the dining room and made our way to the living room, where the stereo was on and playing David Gray.

I glanced out the large windows onto the street below and noted that it was raining again. I followed the path of a raindrop down the window with my finger. I felt as if I hadn't seen the sun in forever.

"Why so glum, Ginger?" Harrison asked as he moved to stand beside me.

"I honestly don't think I can take much more of this rain," I said.

"It could be worse," Viv said. "It could be raining cats and dogs and then there'd be poodles everywhere."

Harrison snorted while I gave her my best unamused face. It really is a good one. I've practiced it in the mirror.

"They said it would keep raining for another week, but I drought it," Harrison quipped. This time Viv busted up. I refused and gave them both my frostiest look.

"Well, you are in merry ol' England," Harrison cajoled. "We are rather known for our precipitation."

"You're right," I said. Then I teased, "I'm beginning to think it was a pour choice."

They both blinked at me.

"Aw, now that was a good one. Get it? 'Pour' choice instead of 'poor' choice, you know, because it's pouring out."

Harrison patted my shoulder and Viv gave me a sympathetic look. I knew they were teasing me. It was a bit of a game between us, but it made me more determined than ever. One of these days I was going to unleash a pun that they couldn't help but laugh at.

"Crisis averted," Andre said as he rejoined us. "But I'm glad you brought two bottles of wine. We might need them."

"Is that a dig at my cooking?" Nick asked as he followed Andre into the room.

"No!" Andre quickly assured him. "I was referring to the tension in the *Bake Off*, you know, Scarlett is rooting for that Trevor fellow."

"Travis," Viv and I said together and I heard Harrison huff out a breath.

"Now don't be sullen just because he's more talented than what's her name," I said.

Andre and Nick both turned to look at Harrison and he lowered an eyebrow at me.

"Prudence Chatham," he said. "You know very well what her name is."

"Doubtful," I said. I took the wineglass that Nick proffered and kissed his cheek in greeting. "She doesn't have dreamy blue eyes."

"No," Nick agreed. He brushed the bib of his purple apron and used his ring finger to smooth one of his blond eyebrows. "I'd say she's a bit peaky looking, like a strong wind might carry her off."

"A bit ferrety if you ask me," Andre added. "All nose and teeth."

I made the mistake of sipping my wine when he spoke and started to laugh, making the wine almost shoot out my nose. I covered my face with my hand while I coughed and laughed and coughed.

"Laugh it up there, Ginger," Harrison said. "We'll see who's laughing when my ferret beats Mr. Dreamy Eyes."

"Oh." Nick rubbed his hands together. "Do I hear a wager in the making?"

Harrison's bright green eyes met mine. His gaze positively sizzled with nefarious intentions.

"What do you say, Scarlett?" he asked. "Do we have a bet?"

"That depends," I said. "What did you have in mind?"

My voice came out low and husky, inviting all sorts of midnight naughtiness. I watched Harry's Adam's apple bob when he gulped.

Damn it. I was at it again. I really needed to find the shutoff valve for my flirtatious streak. But honestly, I didn't want to. This celibacy thing was really beginning to cramp my style.

Harrison cleared his throat as Viv, Andre and Nick swiveled their heads between us like they were watching a tennis match. When Harry's gaze met mine, the look he gave me scorched. Wow!

Okay, so dreamy blue eyes had nothing on Harry's magnetic green gaze. I shook my head. It didn't matter. I was staying single and not letting Harrison or anyone else lure me into the miserable world of dating, bad relationship choices and heartbreak. Jaded much? Yes, I am.

I glanced at Viv, hoping to silently communicate my distress at the situation. Call it cousinly intuition or what have you, she got it right away.

"I suggest the wager be in line with what you're betting about," she said. "Since you're betting over a cooking competition, the loser has to make a meal for the winner."

"Oh, dear, I'm obliged to hope Scarlett wins then," Nick said.

"Why's that?" Harrison asked, looking offended.

"Because Scarlett can't toast bread, never mind cook. Truly, mate, I'm looking out for you by hoping you lose," Nick said and then he burst out laughing as if the idea of me cooking a meal was too preposterous for words.

"I think I'm offended," I said. I held out my hand to Harrison. "I'll take that bet."

The grin he gave me was pure mischief, and the feel of his large man hand closing around my smaller one made me go just the tiniest bit weak in the knees. I locked them in place, refusing to be swayed by any misplaced surge of hormones. It was only natural to react to a man since my libido had been on lockdown for longer than I could ever remember.

"Excellent," he said. He looked as if he thought victory was his, and then I realized that an intimate dinner for two was a victory for him in that it moved us into an area that was almost date-like. For me, it was a loss because it was going to test my strength of character on the whole staying single thing, which frankly was proving to be more challenging than I'd anticipated.

Before I let go of his hand, I looked him right in the eye and said, "Just to clarify, the loser makes dinner, at least three courses plus dessert."

"Agreed," he said, still smiling.

And then I lowered the boom. "For all five of us on a date to be determined."

"What?" Harrison gaped, but it was too late. Andre and Nick cheered the suggestion, and Viv looked at me with a knowing smile. Yes, I suspect she knew exactly what I was up to, avoiding being alone with Harrison for as long as I was able.

"You're not backing out now, Harry, are you?" I asked.

He narrowed his eyes at me. "No. I accept the wager."

We shook on it and he released my hand. I missed the warmth of his fingers against mine immediately.

"Since that is settled," Nick said. "I do believe it is time for dinner to be served."

Nick sashayed back to the kitchen while Harrison fell into step with Vivian and I walked beside Andre to the dining room table, which was already set with mismatched cobalt-blue-and-white Wedgewood plates and bowls. Andre had a passion for Wedgewood, but he bought miscellaneous plates instead of a whole set because he felt it was more visually interesting.

Looking at the blue-and-silver accents on the table, I noted that the place settings went well with Nick's Brierley Hill Crystal. I always felt like more of a grown-up when I dined at Nick and Andre's. Left on our own, Viv and I usually did takeout and ate in front of our television, and that was only if Viv wasn't caught up in some creative endeavor which left me eating alone.

I had been watching my cousin over the past few weeks, looking for any signs of interest outside of hats or our shop. As far as I could tell, she had none. Oh, there were designer friends she created hats for, and she had a loyal customer base that she was friendly with, but there was no one of any significance in my cousin's life. This disturbed me. Partly because I felt guilty for not noticing sooner and partly because it wasn't like Viv.

Viv had known from the time we were kids that she was going to follow Mim's lead into the millinery business. She was a natural at it, creating hats that were in demand from Paris runways to the Royal Family. Her work had been featured in fashion magazines and the wait to get a hat for Ascot from her was three years long.

Despite all that, Viv had always managed to have a life. She'd had friends in the neighborhood and friends from school. She was always a little flighty, being a creative genius, and disappeared from time to time without telling anyone, usually on some crazy quest for feathers or lace or hat forms, but still she had relationships outside the business. Since I had gotten back to London four months ago, however, I had seen no evidence of any sort of social life for my cousin.

She never talked about friends or men or anything really. I was worried about her, and while I tried not to badger her about her lack of a social life, I was definitely keeping an eye on her. Honestly, if I hadn't come back when I did, the only thing she would have in her life would be the shop, Harrison and Fee. And no, Harrison and Viv were just friends. Yes, I checked.

Andre held my chair while Harrison held Viv's. I was across the table from Harrison, which was nice but also distracting. Andre went to help Nick schlep the food to the table while the three of us settled in.

"So anything noteworthy happen at the shop today?" Harrison asked.

Viv and I exchanged a glance. Harrison was always good about asking about the business, and I got the feeling it wasn't because he was part owner but because he genuinely cared that things were going well.

She shrugged as she put her napkin in her lap. "Nothing dramatic. Hats were made and hats were sold."

Andre and Nick flitted back and forth with a variety of dishes that smelled divine.

"Nick, you've outdone yourself," I said. "It all looks amazing."

Nick flushed with pleasure and then waved his hands at the food. "Go ahead and start. It isn't any better when it's cold."

We each chose a dish and started serving and passing. Compliments were heaped on Nick's culinary prowess and I realized, duh, that he was lapping it up like a kitten did cream. I imagined he received fewer compliments for his dentistry, not that he wasn't a great dentist, but let's face it, you don't generally heap praise on the person who roots around in your mouth, nags you to floss and occasionally delivers the bad news bomb that you have a cavity or worse.

"So that's it?" Harrison steered the conversation back to the shop. "No gossip from any of the customers?"

"None," Viv said. She shrugged.

"Oh, but there is one thing you could help us with," I

said. "Ariana Jackson hasn't answered her phone for the past three days, and we really need to get in touch with her about her wedding hat."

"I can text Stephen and have him tell her," Harrison offered.

"I'd really like to talk to her directly," I said. If she wanted to haggle about the price, I wanted to be the one to do it and not have Harrison and his rugby buddy make a mess of it.

"Doesn't she work for a solicitor in Kensington?" Viv asked. "Could you get his number from Stephen?"

"Yeah, that should be no trouble," Harrison said. "Do remind me after dinner."

"I think his last name was Russo," I said.

"Anthony Russo?" Nick asked.

"Yes, that's right," Viv said.

"Ooooh," Nick and Andre said together. It wasn't a good sort of Ooooh. It was the sort of Ooooh someone said when there was a juicy story to be had. I was all in.

Chapter 4

"What do you know?" I asked. I looked back and forth between them, wondering who I could get to crack first.

"We only know what we've heard," Nick said.

"Unfounded rumors and gossip," Andre said. "All speculation really."

"So speculate," Viv prodded them.

Andre and Nick exchanged looks. I knew they were having a silent debate about how much to say and, more important, who got to say it. Andre gave Nick a small nod; it was his dinner party after all.

Nick dabbed the corners of his mouth with his napkin. I took a bite of my beef Wellington. It was melt in your mouth yummy, but I was betting that Nick's gossip would be just as tasty.

"Word on the street is—" Nick began but Andre burst out laughing.

"Word on the street?" Andre said. "You have been watching too many American cop shows."

Nick wrinkled his nose at him. "I can't help it if I find Nathan Fillion simply delicious, now can I?"

"Not at all," Viv said. "I quite agree."

"The point, people, could we get back to the sordid tale of Anthony Russo?" I asked.

"So eager for gossip?" Harrison asked.

"More like answers," I said. "What do we know about Ariana Jackson, really, other than she's marrying a friend of yours?"

Harrison frowned as if he had never thought about Ariana before as anything other than Stephen's fiancée.

What I didn't add was that of course I was eager for juicy gossip. Having done my time in the hot seat, I always enjoyed hearing about someone else's foibles so long as it wasn't mean in nature.

"Anthony Russo is known for being a womanizing, drunken, lascivious letch," Andre said. "And a gambler."

"How does he still have a career then?" Viv asked.

"He is also an excellent attorney," Nick said. "He works for people in the entertainment industry who find themselves in sticky situations."

"Such as?" I asked.

"The singer Shelley Martin was busted for drug use and sex with underage boys," Andre said. "Russo got her off without even an ASBO."

I lifted my eyebrows. An ASBO is an antisocial behavior order and was actually quite common.

"And then there was Mark Tracey," Nick confided. "Doped up on heroin and decided to take a naked stroll in front of Buckingham Palace. He was wearing nothing but his rubbers."

I burst out laughing. Rubbers having an entirely different meaning in the States, making Nick's comment even more hilarious.

"Got off with some charitable works, I believe," Nick said. "Reading to the blind or some such malarkey."

"I find it hard to believe Ariana works for such a man," Viv said. "She seemed very earnest and hardworking, not the sort who would be amused by the shenanigans of spoiled rock stars."

"It's a job," I said. "A good-paying job, and since she doesn't seem to have any family to lean on, it makes sense that she would work for whoever paid her the most. She strikes me as the type that would be very good at legal work. There is something very . . ."

"Dependable." Harrison supplied the word I was looking for.

"Exactly, dependable about her," I said. Then I frowned. "Except I really would have expected her to answer my texts or messages by now."

"It could be a severe case of bride brain," Vivian said. "Goodness knows we've dealt with worse. Remember the bride who showed up at our shop the night before her wedding completely pissed and wanted hats for her entire wedding party—the ones she had met in the pub that afternoon?"

I laughed. Pissed in this case meant drunk rather than angry and the bride in question had been sauced. She had left the shop with ten mismatched fascinators, adorable small hats worn mostly in front or on the side, and to this day I wonder what had happened and would love to see the pictures of this sordid wedding party.

"I suppose we're just going to have to pop in at her place of employment," Viv said. "That way we can speak with her directly about the options for her mother's hat."

I noted that everyone's gaze turned to me. Of course they did, because we all knew that when Viv said "we," she meant "me," not the two of us.

Kensington, the borough where Russo's office was located, was on the other side of Hyde Park from Notting Hill. I could have bussed the entire distance but I decided to catch the tube to Lancaster Gate and cut through the park instead because for the first time in weeks the sun had trumped the rain and the world was sparkly and shiny and new once again.

There was a crisp sweetness to the air as if I were breathing the first bite of a crunchy apple. The sun was warm on my face but the breeze was cool, tossing and teasing my hair as I made my way into the park.

Judging by the way the ducks were cavorting in the fountains of the Italian gardens, I wasn't the only one enamored with the beauty of the day. The grassy hill to my left was dotted with the striped canvas chairs that the park people put out so that visitors could rent a seat for one pound sixty pence per hour or eight pounds for a whole day. I was so tempted to sit and soak up the world for an hour or two. If I'd had a cheese-filled baguette, a hot cup of coffee, and a book, I would have been unmovable.

Sadly, I had to get back to the shop to help Viv. Manning the front of the shop was not exactly her gift, and Fee was in class this morning and not coming to work until later.

I took the path that ran along the north edge of the park. As I passed the Princess of Wales Memorial Playground, I stopped by the food stand to treat myself to a hot chocolate. They had food, but I didn't want to wait. I kicked myself for not stopping at the Pret A Manger outside Notting Hill Gate for a sandwich on my way.

While I waited for the girl to make my cocoa, I watched two young boys scamper across a huge wooden pirate ship complete with a crow's nest and rigging, the whole works. They had wooden swords and were apparently fighting off a takeover from a bloodthirsty pack of girls. I laughed when the boys decided that jumping ship was their best chance of survival. Amazing how the whole guy-girl thing doesn't really change as we mature.

I sipped my cocoa and stayed to the edge of the path as people on rented Barclays Cycles zipped by me. Viv and I had used the bike rental service a couple of times. They had a stand in our neighborhood and it was quite handy until you went to return it and found the rack to be full. Then you had to wait for someone else to rent a bike or go to the next stand, which could be a bit out of your way. Still, it beat the upkeep and maintenance of owning a bicycle of your own.

I took my phone out of my purse and checked the directions to Russo's office. I veered off the main path onto a side one that let me out of the park just past Kensington Palace. I had heard that Kate and Will had renovated the big, red-brick colossus and wondered, like everyone else I'm sure, what their life was like living in such a beautiful place.

I remembered my brief, very brief, stint with infamy and blanched. If I never had a photographer shove a camera in my face again, well, that was fine with me.

Stepping out of the park was like a punch in the nose. Buses, cars, pedestrians, sirens, horns, construction noise and voices all clamored to be heard. I sipped my cocoa, trying to maintain my Zen. I crossed the street and wound my way to a quieter section of Kensington.

According to the map on my phone, I needed to walk up a block and take a left on Edgemere Place, then two more short twists and turns and I'd be there. My inner compass, which is faulty, is always overriding the directions I've been given, causing me to spend a lot of time lost and backtracking. Today I was determined to follow the directions to the letter.

Townhouses with offices on the bottom floor lined the small side street that I turned onto. My phone vibrated in my hand and for a moment I thought it was congratulating me on finding my way, a cell phone version of a high five. But no, it was an incoming text from Harrison.

Ginger, I heard from Stephen. Ariana misplaced her phone.

That was it? No cute or pithy or flirtatious anything added

to the message? I have to admit I was a bit disappointed. Ridiculous, I know.

Here's the thing with me and Harry. We go back. Way back. We weren't just pals as kids; he'd had a crush on me. One day, he asked me to go for ice cream and I stood him up to chase some other silly boy. For the record, I was ten. Fast-forward seventeen years, and I am committed to my vow of celibacy, which Harry almost completely messed up by kissing me and making me see stars. Then he did the most unforgivable thing. He accepted my vow of celibacy and said he'd wait. Who does that, I ask you?

Mind you, there were extenuating circumstances to his kissing me, such as he'd just taken a blow to the head. Does that make the stars I saw null and void? Maybe the kiss would have been *meh* if we hadn't just been in a life-threatening situation. How was I supposed to know, since we were now apparently just waiting? Ugh, it was maddening, truly.

I debated texting Harry back, but then I decided not to since he'd really given me nothing to work with. My thanks could wait until after I'd met with Ariana, who did not at all seem the type to lose her phone.

I glanced down the street trying to figure which one might be Russo's office. They were mostly redbrick buildings with stern rectangular shapes and white trim on the windows and eaves. A few bore brass plaques stating the name of the business inside. I resigned myself to following the numbers and hoping I picked the right side of the street on the first try.

I did not. Halfway down the street I spotted the building I needed across the way. I looked both ways, to the right first, naturally, or rather unnaturally, as it takes me forever to get into this habit when I'm across the pond. Seeing the road was clear, I hurried across the street.

A shallow staircase with a thick white hand railing on either side led up to the front door. A brass plaque announced that I had indeed found the office of *Anthony Russo, Attorney.* I glanced at the windows on each side of the door. There were sheer curtains blocking my view, and I couldn't see if Ariana was inside.

I looked for a buzzer but couldn't locate one, so I chose to give the door three sharp raps with my knuckles instead. I stepped back waiting for the door to be opened. It was not.

Given that it was a business, I wondered if the door was unlocked and I was expected to just go in. I paused. For some reason I felt awkward. What if Ariana had forgotten about the hat? Or worse, had decided she didn't want to do business with us? I would have wasted a trip over here and I'd feel like an idiot.

Ah, well, I was here now and the walk through the park had been just the sunny boost to my rain-drenched spirits that I'd needed, so regardless of how this turned out, I was fine with it.

I decided to try the door this time, and if it was unlocked, I would assume that I was supposed to let myself in. The knob turned and I opened the door.

The first thing that hit me was how silent it was. For an office, it was eerily quiet. No voices, no tapping on a keyboard, nothing. It made the hair on the back of my neck stand on end and I had a mild moment of panic, wondering if I'd entered the wrong office. I took a small step onto the marble foyer and paused.

I was about to call out a greeting when an ear-piercing shriek ripped through the air, making me jump. What on earth had I just walked into?

Chapter 5

My heart clenched up like a fist and it took me a forced breath to get it to loosen its grip on my chest and start beating again.

Probably Ariana had screamed because of a mouse or a large bug or some other ew-making thing. I glanced at the floor by my feet but it was mercifully rodent and insect free.

"Help me!" a cry sounded. "Someone help me!"

The plea snapped my head up. It was coming from outside the back of the building. I jogged down the short hallway that appeared to lead deeper into the office space. I passed a bathroom and two more offices and then went down a short flight of stairs into a small kitchen. At the back of the kitchen a door was ajar, leading into the small yard at the back of the house.

I opened the door wider and dashed outside. Ariana was

crouched in the corner of the cobblestone patio with her hands knotted into fists in front of her mouth as if to keep in any more screams. It was partially working as she was only making whimpering noises. Her eyes were wide and looked wild as if she couldn't take in what she was seeing.

I glanced down and that's when I saw the man lying at her feet. Even from across the patio, I could see that the side of his head had been smashed in and his limbs were twisted at odd angles as if broken.

Bile splashed up against my throat as the metallic smell of blood and other pungent body odors hit my nose. I choked it down and held out a hand to Ariana, forcing myself to walk to her even as my legs wanted to buckle under me like useless noodles. I knelt beside her, grabbing her arm to steady myself.

"What happened?" I croaked. My voice was raspy with shock.

She began to rock back and forth. The distressed noises coming from her throat were becoming louder and more horrible.

"Ariana, speak to me," I said. "What happened?"

She opened her mouth to answer but the only noise that came out was a wail of complete horror. I glanced at the body and pressed a finger to the wrist of the hand lying closest to us. There was no pulse. I hadn't really expected one.

Ariana's keening was reaching a decibel level that was going to make my ears bleed. I had to snap her out of it. I tried to haul her to her feet but she was balled up and clenched tight with the density of a rock.

I stood and yanked her into a standing position. She was still wailing, so I grabbed her by the upper arms and shook her.

"Ariana, we need to call for help," I began but she was beyond reason.

"He . . . he . . . he . . ." she panted.

There was no help for it. I knew hysterics when I saw them.

"I'm sorry, Ariana," I apologized.

Then I slapped her. A good open-palmed thwack against the cheek, not enough to leave a mark but definitely enough to get her needle unstuck from its groove.

"Huh." The air went out of her in a puff and she sagged against me. "He's dead. My boss is dead. Oh, my God, how could this happen?"

"We need to call the police," I said. "They'll get it figured out. Do you know what happened?"

"I don't," she said. "I was making tea and then I saw him drop right past the window." She blanched and pressed her knuckles so hard against her mouth, she was going to bruise her lip.

I glanced up at the house. None of the windows were open; he must have fallen from the roof.

"He has no pulse," I said. "Was he like that when you found him?"

She nodded. It was then that I noticed the blood on her hand, streaks of it staining her palm and the cuff of her pale blue silk blouse. Her face crumpled and she pressed her forehead into my shoulder as she sobbed. "I can't believe he's dead."

I studied him over her dark hair. There was no rise and

fall to his chest. He looked shattered like a vase broken into too many pieces to be glued back together. The thought made my head spin.

"We'd better call an ambulance anyway," I said.

Ariana nodded and together we wobbled our way back into the kitchen.

Sadly, it occurred to me that I had more experience with discovering a dead body than any person ought to have at the age of twenty-seven. For a second, I desperately wished my friend Andre were here with me, as he had been on the last few occasions that my timing had been this crummy. Then I felt bad for wishing such a horror on my friend. Still, a buddy would have been nice.

Ariana was sobbing into a tissue, so I pulled out my cell phone and placed the call.

"Police emergency," a female voice answered.

"Hi," I said. I cringed. That sounded entirely too cheerful. "Er, I'm calling to report a dead man."

"Right, a dead man, you say?"

"Yes, he appears to have fallen off the roof of his office building," I said.

"What is the address?"

Of course, my mind chose that moment to go completely blank. I couldn't even remember my home address, never mind this one.

"Ariana," I said. "Where are we?"

She looked up from her tissue. Her eyes were red and swollen and her lips were trembling. Clearly, she didn't understand me.

"The address here, what is it?" I asked.

"Oh." She sniffled. "Thirty-one Taylor Place."

I related the address into the phone. The dispatcher was very kind and told me to wait on the line until she had verified that someone was on their way.

I paced while I waited. Ariana cried. I wished I knew what to say to comfort her, but truly I barely knew the girl, so I didn't want to say the wrong thing and make things even worse.

"I'm going to wait out front and flag them down," I said to Ariana.

She glanced over her shoulder at the backyard and said, "I'll come with you."

I couldn't blame her. I wouldn't want to wait with a dead man either.

We climbed the short flight of stairs back up the hallway. The furniture that had seemed lovely when I walked in now seemed overstuffed and ominous, and I decided that I would open the front door to be able to keep an eye out.

Still, it wasn't far enough away from the horror on the other side of the house, so I stepped out onto the front steps.

A siren blared and a yellow ambulance with green rectangles on it zipped up the street toward us. Ariana leapt to her feet and began waving her arms. The driver parked right in front of us.

"They're here," I said into the phone.

"Very good then," the dispatcher said.

"Thanks and . . . bye," I said. I ended the call wondering if everyone she spoke to was as awkward as I was. Then I shook my head and muttered, "Focus, Scarlett, focus."

Ariana hopped from foot to foot while the medics

grabbed their gear. It took only moments and they all rushed right past me, following Ariana back into the house.

I didn't want to go back there again. It was already going to take me more pints than I could afford to erase the image of that broken body. I gagged. Maybe not pints then; more like shots of Scotch or whiskey.

A panda car stopped right behind the ambulance. This I knew belonged to the Metropolitan Police, and was named for its markings. I had heard the term "panda car" every time I visited London since I was a child, and for years I always thought they were talking about a car that looked like a panda. When I finally figured it out, I was horribly disappointed that it didn't look anything like a panda. I glanced at the car, and yes, I still was disappointed.

A constable hopped out and I waved him over. There was no help for it. I would have to show him where the body was.

"They're back here," I said as he climbed the steps. I turned and hurried through the house. When we stepped outside, it was to see the medical personnel gently pulling a cloth over the man's body. I turned away from the sight of it, but the constable marched over to talk to them.

Ariana was standing pressed up against the back wall, looking lost and frightened. I crossed the cobblestones and took her hand in mine.

"Come on," I said. "We can wait inside."

The constable glanced over his shoulder at us and I gestured that we'd be inside. His eyes were compassionate and he gave me a brisk nod.

"Can I get you anything?" I asked as Ariana sat on the edge of a small black leather love seat in the reception room.

"No, thank you," she said. "Oh, I suppose I should be asking if I can get you anything. I'm all a muddle."

I sat on the armchair beside her. "That's understandable. Is he . . . er . . . he was your boss?"

Ariana looked up at me with red-rimmed, horror-filled eyes and nodded.

"Do you know what happened?" I asked.

"I was making tea," she said. I nodded encouragingly. We had covered that before. She waved her hands in the air. "Sorry, I know I said that before."

She sounded like she was going to cry again. I didn't want to be the one to cause her more upset, so I reached over and took one of her hands in mine.

"It's all right," I said. "We don't have to talk about it."

"No, it's not that, it's just I can't believe it, I don't understand how he could have fallen or from where . . ." Her voice trailed off and I got the impression that Ariana knew as much about what had happened as I did, which was a whole lot of nothing.

"Scarlett, did you come looking for me?" she asked.

"Yes," I said. "I have the estimates for your wedding hat, but we haven't been able to reach you by phone so I thought I'd pop over since it's, well, it was a nice day out."

"Oh," she said, nodding. We could hear someone coming into the house and she glanced down the hallway. "I lost my phone. Sorry, I should have called you from here and let you know."

"It's all right," I lied. Sheesh, I was beginning to sound as proper as Viv and Fee, saying things were fine when they clearly were not. I'd give fifty pounds to be anywhere but here, but since I was polite and all, I didn't say it.

The constable arrived back in the room. He'd removed his large hat and was kneading the brim like a cat trying to plump a cushion. He looked supremely uncomfortable and I couldn't blame him.

"Excuse me, Miss?" he asked. "I'll need to ask you both a few questions."

"Certainly." Ariana nodded.

"Of course," I said.

"Because of the nature of the situation, there will be some more investigators coming to determine the cause of the man's fall," he said. "You have identified the man as Mr. Anthony Russo, the solicitor whose office this is."

"Yes, sir," Ariana said. "He was my boss. I am his assistant, Ariana Jackson."

The constable paused to look at me. He didn't have to ask if I worked here as well; I could see the question on his face. I shook my head.

"No, I'm Scarlett Parker," I said. "I work at a millinery shop over on Portobello Road." How that was relevant, I had no idea, but I felt it took me out of the situation entirely, which was pretty much what I was going for.

"Miss Parker, we meet again." A man in a tweed jacket and dark trousers came through the front door and paused beside my chair.

I craned my neck up and got an eyeful of mustache and jowls and the recognition was immediate.

"Detective Inspector Franks," I said. "Good to see you again. No, that isn't right, is it?"

He smoothed his mustache as if considering. "Your meaning is clear but the circumstances do indicate otherwise."

"How do you do, Miss Parker?" Another man entered the room after Inspector Franks and I glanced past Franks at his partner.

"Inspector Simms," I said. The younger of the two with a bit of a unibrow issue, Simms was big and burly, and I'd previously seen him put away his body weight in tea and crackers. For all that, I liked him. I liked them both. They made me feel safe in a world that suddenly felt very tremulous.

I noticed Ariana and the constable were looking back and forth at us and I hastily added, "This is Ariana Jackson, she works here, and no doubt you know Constable . . ."

My voice trailed off as I realized I hadn't ever gotten his name.

"Brouillard," he said. "Constable Brouillard."

I nodded my head in greeting and watched as he shook hands with the inspectors. There was obvious admiration from the constable for the detectives so I sensed he had heard of them and approved, or he was hoping to rise up the police ladder into their corps one day, or both.

"If you'll take me to the . . . deceased," Inspector Simms said to Brouillard. "I'd like to inspect the area and talk to the first responders."

"Of course," Brouillard said and led the way down the hall to the back of the house.

"Miss Jackson, can you recall the events of the morning for me exactly as they happened?" Inspector Franks asked.

"I'll try," she said. "It was a hectic morning. Mr. Russo had several calls he had to place and I was working on some legal documents for an upcoming case of his."

She paused and bit her lip. Inspector Franks said nothing but just waited for her to gather her thoughts. I did not have his patience and felt like giving her a good thump on the back to get the story going.

"I was distracted," she said. "You see, I'm getting married . . ." She paused and gestured to me, and Franks turned to look at me in surprise.

"To you?" he asked. "She's marrying you?"

Chapter 6

"What?" I blinked. "Oh, no, we're not, we've only just met."

His eyebrows rose even higher.

"No," I said. "Viv and I are restoring her mother's bridal hat so that Ariana can wear it in her own wedding. That's why I stopped by, to give her the estimate for the repair."

"I seem to have misplaced my phone," Ariana said.

"So I came by to give her the estimates as the wedding is only a few weeks away," I said.

Inspector Franks nodded. I figured that was my cue to shut up.

"Please continue, Ms. Jackson," he said.

Ariana talked a little bit more about her office duties and then she mentioned that Mr. Russo had said he needed to go upstairs to his flat above the office. He resided in the two floors above, like Viv and I did at our shop. Ariana said he'd been gone quite a while and that she had decided to go and make tea. While she was in the small kitchenette, she heard a yell and then saw Mr. Russo plummet to the ground.

She twisted her fingers together as she said it. Her delicate features looked pinched and she paled with the grisly memory. She swallowed and I wondered if she was trying not to throw up. The thought of Russo's bent and twisted body made me feel like upchucking so I could hardly blame her.

"Of course, I ran outside right away," she said. "I realized that there was no way he could have survived the fall but I checked anyway. He was already dead."

I could see the bloodstains still on her hands and I glanced at Franks and saw that he was looking at her hands as well.

"I didn't want to leave him like that," she said. Her voice sounded small and scared and nothing like the confident girl I had met before. "So I hollered for help and then Scarlett arrived."

"I heard her cry just after I stepped into the office," I said. "I ran out back and then together we called 999."

Franks nodded. He paced on the rich Aubusson carpet with his hands clasped behind his back.

"Do you know why he went upstairs?" he asked.

"No, he just said he was popping up there for a minute," she said. "He did that sometimes if he forgot some paperwork, or wanted a different pair of shoes. I didn't think much of it."

"Except?" Franks prodded her and I assumed he heard the hesitant note in her voice, too.

"Well, he was odd when he left," she said. "He sort of stood in the door and stared for a moment."

"Stared?" Franks asked. "At what?"

"Me," she said. She pushed her glasses up on her nose and I realized this was a nervous habit of hers. "I got the feeling he wanted to say something but he didn't. He didn't say anything at all."

Franks blew a breath out of his nostrils. "We're going to want to have a look at his flat."

"Of course," she said. She gestured to the stairs on the far side of the room. "The door should be unlocked."

It made sense that it would be unlocked because he hadn't come back down through it, and while none of us said as much, I knew we were all thinking it.

The inspector called in a few people from the yard and they all disappeared up the stairs while Ariana and I were left to wait in the main room. A stiff breeze was blowing in through the open front door and I shivered, longing for the little bit of sunshine I'd gotten earlier.

"Do you want me to call someone for you?" I asked. "You could use my phone."

"Oh, thank you," Ariana said. "I'd like to call my fiancé, but I don't think I should use the office phone. Mr. Russo didn't allow personal calls on the business line."

"And you'd feel odd doing it now that he's dead," I said.

She nodded. I handed her my phone and she tapped in her fiancé's number. She didn't appear to be getting an answer, and when she spoke rapidly into the phone, it was clear she was leaving a message.

I glanced away to give her an illusion of privacy because, really, in such a small room I could hear everything she was saying. She sounded weepy but she didn't cry. When she was done, I turned back to her and she handed me the phone.

"Thank you," she said.

"Do you think he'll come right here?" I asked.

"I don't know," she said. "If he gets the message, I suppose he will."

I nodded. I wasn't sure how long I was supposed to stay. It felt awkward to leave her like this, but then again, it felt pretty darn awkward staying. I supposed I should ask Inspector Franks if he needed me any longer, but I couldn't help but feel as if I was abandoning Ariana if I left.

"Miss Jackson," Inspector Franks said as he came down the stairs from the flat above. "I'll need you to come down to the station to file an official report."

"What?" Ariana looked shocked. "Leave? But who will mind the office?"

"The crime scene investigators—" he began but Ariana interrupted.

"Crime scene?" she asked. I wouldn't have thought she could get any paler but she did. "Do you think someone did this to him?"

She glanced around the room as if looking for a bad man to be lurking in a corner, and I found myself doing the same.

"We can't determine that as yet," Inspector Franks said. The look in his eyes was gentle as if he understood how terrifying this all was for her. "It is highly unusual for a person to fall off the top of a three-story building, however, so our assignment will be to determine how he came to be on the roof and what caused him to pitch off of it. Perhaps he is a drinker?"

Ariana shook her head. "Not during work hours, at least, not so that I ever noticed."

Inspector Franks nodded. "If it's not an accident, then

we have to consider the likelihood of him being pushed, or whether he jumped."

"Murder," Ariana said. "Or suicide? I can't believe that. I just can't."

"Well, as you say, he wasn't a drinker," Inspector Franks said. "We'll need to determine how it happened that he fell to his death. I think it'll be easier for you to make a formal statement at the station."

Ariana glanced around the room, looking lost and uncertain.

"I'll go with you, if that helps," I said.

The words were out of my mouth before my common sense had a chance to filter them. Darn it. The last thing I wanted to do was spend my day at the police station, but the poor girl looked so undone by everything that was happening to her, how could I not go with her? It would be like letting a puppy play in traffic and not helping it to safety.

"Oh, I can't ask you to do that," she said. "You've already taken up so much of your day with this."

"A little bit longer won't make much of a difference then," I said. I glanced up and saw Inspector Franks studying me.

"What time did you say you got here?" he asked.

I liked Inspector Franks, I did, but I knew I looked like a square peg trying to fit in a round hole in this situation. I couldn't blame him for being suspicious.

"Judging by the fact that I stepped into the house and heard Ariana screaming, I'd say I got here just after he fell, so maybe half an hour ago," I said.

"Is there any other point of access to the roof?" Franks asked Ariana. "From outside perhaps?"

"None that I know of," she said. "I think there's just the one door on the third floor."

Inspector Franks smoothed his mustache as if considering her words. The gesture made me nervous, and judging by the way Ariana twisted her fingers in her lap, it made her nervous, too.

Inspector Simms chose that moment to rejoin us in the sitting area. He looked a bit green around the gills and I figured staring at a man's broken and bloody body would do that to even the most hardened police officer.

"Can I have a word?" Simms said to Franks.

"Excuse me, ladies." Franks led Simms out the front door. I could hear the low murmur of their voices but I couldn't make out what they were saying.

I glanced at Ariana but she didn't appear to be trying to listen to them. Then again, she was much closer to the situation than I was. I couldn't imagine what was going through her mind. One second she's making tea and the next she's standing beside the bashed and bloody body of her boss. Talk about a rough day at work.

The inspectors returned to the room and I noted that the fresh air had done Simms some good as he looked less pasty than he had when he'd left.

"If you'll come with us, Ms. Jackson," Inspector Franks said. "We'd like to continue our conversation back at the station."

Ariana gave me a helpless look and I stood up.

"I'm coming with you," I said. It was appalling how much I sounded like my mother when she'd made up her mind about something, but dang if it didn't work.

Inspector Franks frowned and his voice was grudging when he said, "All right then."

We followed the inspectors to their car, which was double-parked in front of the building. Traffic on the small street had become snarled and one constable was out in the road, trying to establish some order. Judging by the shouting and honking, he was failing spectacularly.

He looked relieved when he saw the inspectors open the back doors for us and gave a wave as the men climbed in and Inspector Simms maneuvered us through the tight street.

I had been to the Notting Hill Station—it's a long story and really doesn't bear repeating—but I'd never been to the Kensington Station. We hurried down Kensington High Street and worked our way toward Earl's Walk. I took it as a good sign that the inspectors didn't have the siren wailing as they drove.

We arrived at the redbrick building and Inspector Simms pulled over to the curb, letting us out. Inspector Franks gave him a nod as we climbed out and I assumed it meant that parking the car was the younger inspector's job.

Two bright blue pots with small evergreen shrubs sat on each side of the glass double doors. Given the barren appearance of the very flat redbrick building, I took the planters as a sign of eternal optimism.

Personally, my positive thought of the moment was the hope that Ariana's fiancé would arrive shortly and I would be spared spending the entire day in the station.

Inspector Franks led the way and we followed behind him like two good little ducklings. The station was a bustling box full of phones ringing, loud conversations and a drunk slumped in the corner who looked to have peed himself. Lovely.

Inspector Franks led us down a narrow hall, leaving the noise and chaos behind us as we went. I felt myself breathe a little bit easier as we went.

Glass-walled offices filled this section of the station and he led us to one of these. A wooden bench ran along the hallway and he gestured for us to take a seat.

"I won't be long," he said.

We watched him walk into the office area and talk to another man. I wondered what he was saying. Was it his superior? Was he reporting in? I really hated not knowing what was going on.

I turned to Ariana to ask her what she thought, but the words caught in my throat as I saw one fat tear slide down her cheek and drip off her chin.

"Ariana, are you all right?" I asked. Which really was the stupidest question ever, wasn't it? Her boss was dead, she'd found him broken and bloody, how all right could she be? Gah!

She wiped the tear away and sniffed. "I'm afraid they're going to think I did it."

"Oh, no," I said. "They won't. You'll see. I'm sure it was all just some horrible accident."

"But what if they find out?" she asked.

"Find out what?"

"That I wanted him dead," she said. She looked at me, and for possibly the first time in my life, I was speechless.

Chapter 7

"What? I—" I began but I was interrupted.

"Ms. Jackson, would you come in here, please?" Inspector Franks stood in the open doorway.

I rose to go with her, but Franks shook his head at me. "Not you, Ms. Parker."

I grabbed Ariana's hand before she left, and I hissed, "Do you want me to call someone?"

She shook her head, looking bereft, and turned and followed Inspector Franks into the glassed-in room.

The door had barely closed when I was calling Viv. I'd thought I was doing okay until Ariana had dropped that little word bomb on me. She wished him dead? What the hell did that mean? Oh, my God, were we working for a killer?

"Scarlett, where are you?" Viv answered on the second ring. "You should have been back ages ago. Please tell me you did not take it into your head to go shopping. Are you at Waterstones on Kensington High Street, faffing around browsing books while Fee and I work ourselves to death?"

"Not exactly," I said, knowing that Viv's faffing around meant procrastinating; otherwise I might have been offended. "Although I am still in Kensington."

"Oh, Barker's Arcade, is it then?" she asked.

"Honestly, Viv, I came here on business, do you really think I'm out shopping?" I asked. I was feeling just the teensiest bit put out.

"I can't think of any other reason why you haven't returned," she said. "Oh, dear."

"Oh, dear, what?" I asked.

"You haven't picked up a bloke, have you?"

"What?" I asked.

"Well, you are an incorrigible flirt, and according to Nick and Andre, Anthony Russo is quite the ladies' man."

"So you think I picked him?" I asked. "What do you think I'm doing now then, shagging him?"

Okay, I can admit it, I was outraged.

"Well, this is the longest you've ever gone without a boyfriend," she said. "You could be highly susceptible to—"

"A womanizer?" I asked. "Really? Because the last rat bastard I dated, the one who caused me to take my vow of celibacy, wasn't bad enough?"

"Good point," Viv said.

"I'll say it is," I snapped. "And even if I had been inclined to get tangled up with the man, which I am not, it would be hard to get anything started with him since he's dead."

"What?" Viv cried. "Scarlett, I must have misheard you. What did you say?"

"Anthony Russo is dead," I repeated very loudly and very clearly.

The line was silent for so long, I was sure we'd gotten cut off.

"Hello? Viv? Are you there?"

"Yes, I'm here. Explain."

So I did. I paced the hallway while I told her all about my arrival at Mr. Anthony Russo's place of business, the discovery of his body, the arrival of Inspectors Franks and Simms and my current location at the Kensington Police Station.

Viv waited until I was done and then asked, "Are you all right?"

"I'm fine," I lied. "But I'm very worried about Ariana."

"I'm going to call Harrison and send him over," Viv said.

"Oh, don't do that," I cried.

Harrison had been riding to my rescue since the day I arrived in London. I really couldn't bear it to have him find me in yet another pickle. At least this one was definitely not of my own making, but still, it was getting embarrassing.

"But that's why we have him," Viv insisted. "To sort out these types of situations for us."

"No," I insisted. "I'm sure I'll be long gone before he could even get here." Big fat lie. Judging by what Ariana had said, things were even more complicated than I had supposed.

"All right," Viv said. She sounded reluctant. "Keep me up to date on what's happening."

"Will do," I said.

I spied a Klix vending machine at the end of the hallway wedged in between two bathrooms. I strolled over and considered my options. It offered everything from hot soup to tea, but the thought of a hot cup of coffee soothed in ways that no tea or soup ever could. I dug through the bottom of my purse looking for the needed pence.

I had just chosen the Kenco smooth black with sugar when I heard the tread of heavy steps and raised voices coming toward me. I spun around and there he was. Damn it, Viv!

Harrison, looking annoyingly handsome in his charcoal gray suit with a burgundy tie loosened at the throat of his crisp white dress shirt, was striding toward me with two other men. All three were talking animatedly but hadn't seen me as yet, so I took the opportunity to turn back to the machine and pretend I hadn't seen him. My accelerated heart rate made a liar out of me, but I ignored it. How in the heck had he gotten here this fast? And what was he going to say about this latest kerfuffle I found myself in?

Putting off the explanation I knew I was going to have to make, I stared at the machine and waited for my cup to dispense. What was I supposed to say exactly? It was unreasonable that I should feel guilty, as if I'd had anything to do with Russo's falling to his death. My timing had just been its usual spectacular self, causing me to be at the wrong place at the wrong time . . . again.

When I turned from the vending machine, braced for the conversation to come, it was to find the hallway empty. I studied the empty space and took a sip from my thick paper cup. Okay, was I hallucinating Harrison? I mean, I knew our relationship was complicated, but if I was starting to imagine him there when he wasn't, well, maybe it was time to reconsider my current vow of celibacy.

A door was thrust open to my left and a familiar dark-haired, green-eyed man popped his head out.

"Ginger, there you are," he said. "Come along then."

Okay, so I hadn't hallucinated Harrison Wentworth's appearance. That was reassuring. My relief was short lived as my annoyance at his arrival took over.

"Harry, what are you doing here? Did Viv call you? She said she wouldn't. I mean, it's ridiculous. I really don't need any help."

He watched me rant for a moment looking amused—which was even more annoying.

"I had no idea you were here until Ariana just told me," he said. "Now would you care to join us or did you want to stay out here alone, stewing about everything?"

I lifted my coffee cup to my lips and studied him over the rim. The steam off the hot liquid felt good against my skin. I took a long sip before lowering the cup.

"I'll come," I said.

He pushed the door open for me and I strode past him into the office area. Desks were set all around the room, usually two together so that the people faced each other. Several offices lined the wall and it was one of these that Harrison led me toward.

The two men Harrison had arrived with were already in the room with Ariana. I didn't see either of the inspectors as Harrison pushed the door open and we joined the group.

"Oh, Scarlett, you're still here," Ariana said as she rose from her seat. "I'm so sorry. I had no idea that this was going to take so much time."

"It's no problem," I said. I did not mention my cranky talk with Viv.

"My fiancé got my message, and came straightaway with friends," she said. "Scarlett Parker, this is my intended, Stephen Whitcomb, and his friend Alistair Turner. And, of course, you know Harrison."

I shook Stephen's hand. It was a firm shake, dry and cool and perfectly appropriate. He glanced at me briefly, but his gaze stayed on Ariana and it was clear that he was worried about her. He was dressed casually in khakis and a pullover polo shirt. His straw-colored hair looked slightly mussed and he had a ruddy tinge to his cheeks as if the cold air outside had given him a good cheek pinch from a favorite aunt.

He took Ariana's hand and kept it in his, offering her steadfast support without being suffocating about it. I liked that.

I turned to Alistair to shake hands as well but he rejected that and instead brought my hand to his lips, where he kissed the back of it. Oh, wow. Not many men could pull that off nowadays and still come across as manly, and boy howdy, did he ever.

He was in a suit like Harrison's but his was black. He wore a pewter shirt underneath with a thin black tie. His dark hair was chin length in a side-parted blunt cut, giving him a roguish look that was only enhanced by his wicked smile.

"It's a pleasure, Scarlett," he said.

"I'll say," I said as I stared back at him.

"Your charm is wasted on her, mate," Harrison said to Alistair. "She's taken a vow of . . . er . . . not dating anyone for a year."

"Tragic!" Alistair exclaimed. He turned to Harrison. "Is that your fault?"

"My fault?" Harrison frowned at his friend. "How could it be my fault?"

"Did you break her heart?" Alistair demanded.

"No!" Harrison and I answered together.

You'd think this would cause us to have a moment of accord, but no. Harrison glared at me, obviously put out that I was so quick to answer in the negative.

"It's a long story," I said.

"Excellent," Alistair said. "We'll have to go out for pints so you can give me every sordid detail. Glad it's not your fault, Wentworth. I'd hate to have to mess up that pretty face of yours with a thrashing."

"As if you could," Harrison scoffed.

"Excuse me," Stephen said. "Not to take away from your manly crowing, but we have a situation here that needs tending, yes?"

"Quite right," Alistair said. He looked at Ariana and said, "Let me see what I can find out from the inspectors. I'll be right back."

He left our small room and walked out into the maze of desks. He seemed quite at home here and I gave Harrison a questioning glance.

"He's a barrister," he said. "What you in the States would call a defense attorney, I believe."

"Oh," I said. "Did Stephen call you?"

"No, the three of us were having lunch together when Stephen got Ariana's message from your phone. We hurried over to the office but she had already been taken here." He paused and studied me. His look was warm and approving and I felt it all the way down to my toes. "It was good of you to come with her."

"It was the least I could do," I said. I glanced over to where she and Stephen had their heads together. He was whispering in her ear and she was nodding. Her lips were pressed tightly together as if she was trying very hard not to cry again.

"She'll be all right," Harrison said. "Stephen is a good man. He'll get her through this."

I glanced back at him. "So Alistair and Stephen are both friends of yours?"

"Rugby mates," he said with a nod. "We've been playing together for years. You should come to a match sometime."

I looked at him. Was he inviting me as an old friend, a new friend, a woman he had recently kissed senseless? How was I to know? And, I scolded myself, why did it matter? I was not interested in him or anyone. Right?

"I'm sure Viv, Fee and I would love that," I said. My voice sounded stiff.

"Excellent. I'll let you know when we have our next match," he said. His voice was as starchy as mine.

What had happened to our easy friendship? Oh, yeah, he had kissed me and that now sat between us like a big hairy beast.

"Excellent," I parroted him. Yeesh, if the conversation

became any more wooden, I'd be picking splinters out of my tongue. Bleh.

Much to my relief, Alistair reappeared. He gave Ariana an encouraging smile. "The inspectors thank you for your cooperation and have said that you're free to go."

Ariana sagged in relief. Stephen kissed the top of her head and said, "Come on, love, let's get you home."

Harrison and I went to follow them but Alistair stopped me with a hand on my elbow.

"I'm sorry, Scarlett, but you're not dismissed yet."

Chapter 8

"What?" I asked. "Why?"

He gave me a sympathetic glance under very long thick curly eyelashes that made me positively green with envy. Such beautiful lashes were wasted on a man, okay, maybe not on him, because, well, wow. But still, I could really put lashes like that to use.

"The inspectors asked to speak with you particularly," Alistair said.

I drew my attention away from his lashes and focused on his words.

"I suppose I have no choice then," I said.

Ariana glanced around at me with horrified eyes. "Oh, no, I'm so sorry, Scarlett. Here, I'll wait for you."

"No," I said. "It's fine. Inspector Franks and I go way back. He's practically a favorite uncle. Go on ahead."

Stephen gave me a grateful smile but Ariana looked unsure. I stepped close and took her hands in mine. "You've had a terrible day. There's no need for you to stay for me. Truly, I'll be fine."

"I'll wait for her," Harrison said. "In fact, I'll even go in with her. Inspector Franks and I go a ways back as well."

"Are you quite sure?" Ariana asked.

"Absolutely," I said. "Tell you what—why don't you pop over to the shop tomorrow and we can discuss your hat in greater detail. All right?"

Ariana gave me a watery smile. Then she unexpectedly let go of my hands and hugged me tight.

"Thank you for everything," she said. "I don't think I could have gotten through this day without you."

I patted her shoulder and she stepped back. Alistair gave me a small smile and a wink before following after Ariana and Stephen.

Once they had disappeared, Harrison turned to me and asked, "Well, should we go see what the good inspectors want?"

"I suppose," I said. "I mean, it can't be as bad as last time, right?"

"Well, at least you're not a suspect this time," Harrison said. "So I'd say that's a leg up."

We worked our way down the corridor until we found a small office. *Detective Inspector Franks*, read the small sign beside the third door on the right. The door was closed so I knocked twice.

There was a window that looked into the office, which made me wonder why there was a door. To muffle the sounds of an interrogation? Or maybe the window was to monitor the activities of the good detective? Curious.

"All right," Inspector Franks called, and I turned the knob and opened the door. The small space was made smaller by the presence of both Inspector Franks and Inspector Simms. Harrison and I wedged our way in, standing behind the two chairs in front of the inspector's desk, while Simms leaned against the far wall.

"Ah, Ms. Parker, thanks for stopping by," he said. "I see you've brought Mr. Wentworth with you."

"No, I didn't," I said. As soon as the words came out of my mouth, I knew I sounded too defensive. How could I explain the turmoil that being in close proximity to Harrison caused me? I couldn't. I cleared my throat and tried again. "What I mean is that he offered to wait and I agreed."

"Very nice of you, Wentworth," Inspector Franks said.

"I'm known for it," Harrison said. I saw Inspector Simms smile.

As I took in the sparse appearance of Inspector Franks's office, I did notice he had a framed picture of Alan Jackson on the wall behind him. I remembered the first time I'd met him how he'd loved that I was from the States and assumed being from Florida that I would be a fan of country-western music. His personal favorite being Alan Jackson, he had sung a bit for me, and in all fairness he had a decent set of pipes.

"Still singing?" I asked him.

He smiled and the ends of his mustache turned up. "Every Tuesday evening at the Barmy Badger, you should come around."

I nodded. I had no intention of going but it seemed rude

to be so blunt. Then again, maybe I should go. It couldn't hurt to have a friend on the police force.

I turned to Simms. "Do you sing as well?'

"Oh, no," he said. He looked horrified at the thought. "I'm more of a darts and billiards man myself."

"Did you want to talk to Scarlett about something specific?" Harrison asked. It was an obvious attempt to get the conversation back on track and everyone nodded as if in agreement that it was time.

"If you'll have a seat, Ms. Parker—Scarlett." Inspector Franks gestured to the two available seats shoehorned into the corner of the cramped room.

I slid into one and Harrison followed, folding himself into the other.

I put my hands in my lap and tried to look composed. I was definitely feeling like a kid sent to the principal's office, but that was ridiculous since I really had done nothing wrong.

"About this morning," Inspector Franks began. "I had a few questions for you."

I nodded.

"How long were you in the house before you heard Ms. Jackson scream?"

I blew out a breath. I tried to think how long it might have taken me to walk into the house, assess the empty room and hear a scream.

"No longer than thirty seconds," I said. "I'd just gotten my bearings and found the building when I entered and *bam*. Ariana screamed and I followed the noise out to the backyard and found her crouched over his body."

"She was crouched, you say?" he asked.

"Yes, she said she had just checked for a pulse." The image of his lifeless body, broken and bloody, flashed through my mind and I shuddered.

"And he was dead?" Simms asked.

"Yes, I checked him as well," I said. "There was no pulse, no rise and fall to his chest, nothing."

"But you didn't see or hear anything before the screams," Inspector Franks asked.

"No, sir," I said.

"So you have no way of knowing how long she may have been sitting with that body?" Inspector Franks asked.

I frowned. "What do you mean?"

He stared at me, waiting for me to put it together.

"You think she was waiting for me, so she could pretend to have just found him?" I asked. "But that's crazy."

Inspector Franks's mustache twitched up on one side while Simms's unibrow lowered ominously.

"I don't think crazy is exactly what you meant there," Harrison said. He looked alarmed by my lack of tact. Really, you'd think he'd be used to it by now.

"No, of course not. What I mean is that Ariana didn't know I was going to stop by her office today," I said. "Your question implies that she knew I was coming and was waiting for me, but since she lost her phone, I couldn't call her and tell her I would be by. It was a complete coincidence."

Inspector Franks rubbed his mustache as if considering what I'd said.

I sincerely hoped that they realized I had nothing to do with anything and let me go home soon. Apparently my gross-out of the morning had passed and I was now hungry enough to eat black pudding, an acquired taste, and I'd even ask for seconds.

"Thank you, Scarlett," Inspector Franks said. So we were back to my first name. I took it as a good sign. "You've been most helpful."

"I'm free to go?" I asked.

"Yes," Inspector Franks said. "But, of course, we may have follow-up questions."

"Of course," I said. "Anything you need."

He glanced from me to Harrison. "Can we still reach you at the same address?"

I felt my face get warm, which was ridiculous since Harrison and I had nothing going on. We were just business associates and friends of a sort. It was the inspector's implication that we might be more that had me flustered. Could he tell that I had a thing for Harrison? And if he could, could Harrison? That was mortifying. I had tried to keep things very casual between us over the past few months.

"Yes, same address," I said.

"Thank you for your time," Simms said. "We appreciate it."

He pushed off the wall, and Harrison and I rose from our seats.

"Anything to help," Harrison said. He shook hands with both inspectors and we were on our way.

We had just cleared the building and were outside when I realized what had been a gorgeous day was now gray again; not only that but judging by the wind, we were about to get a soaking.

"Come on, Scarlett." Harrison grabbed my hand and began

to run. I hurried after him and we jumped onto a red double-decker bus just in time.

We both used our Oyster cards to pay the fare and then Harrison took my hand and led me deeper onto the bus. It was crowded so he gave up on seats on the lower level and we climbed the very narrow staircase behind the driver to the next level. The top was mostly empty so we took a small bench at the front overlooking the roads.

I watched the rain trickle down the large flat window. My mood went with it. It could have been hunger but I felt downright surly.

"You look like you want to tear the mickey out of someone," Harrison said.

"More like I want to tear the ham out of a sandwich," I said. I sounded whiny and didn't even care.

"We can grab a bite on the way," Harrison offered.

"No, I'd better get back before Viv has a conniption," I said. "In fact, I should text her right now."

I opened my purse and searched for my phone.

"Although what I am going to say to her, I have no idea," I said. "I mean, honestly, what the heck could have happened to Anthony Russo? A person doesn't just fall off a roof. And what was he doing up there anyway?"

These were the questions that had been dogging me ever since the police had shown up.

"There must be some logical explanation," Harrison said. "We've had a lot of rain. Maybe his apartment had a leak and he went to check it out."

"Wouldn't he call a handyperson for that?" I asked.

"Maybe," Harrison said.

"Also, if it was a leak, he would have mentioned it to Ariana, don't you think?" I said. "That's the sort of thing you say to someone, and as his assistant, it seems likely she would have called a repairman."

The bus tipped just a little as the driver took a sharp turn. I slid ever so slightly into Harrison and it reminded me of the first time I had seen him since we were kids, when he picked me up upon my arrival in London and we shared a cab to the shop on Portobello.

Just like then, I was a bit too aware of him as a man. The urge to bat my eyelashes and say something flirty was almost more than I could stand. Instead, I puffed out my cheeks as I blew out a breath and righted myself.

"Well, if he didn't fall, then what are we left with?" Harrison asked.

"Suicide?" I suggested. I hated to say it but throwing yourself off a building was definitely one way to go.

"No note left behind," Harrison said. "At least, if there was, the inspectors are keeping it to themselves."

"Maybe someone pushed him," I said.

"Wouldn't Ariana have seen someone in the house?" Harrison asked.

"She didn't mention seeing anyone, and I'm sure the inspectors must have asked her if anyone else was there," I said. "According to Nick and Andre, Russo was quite the playboy so maybe he had a visitor up in his apartment, you know, one who spent the previous night."

"So he went upstairs to have a little afternoon delight and instead she pushed him to his death?" Harrison asked. "He was dressed, wasn't he?"

"Yes," I said. "Believe me, it was bad enough as it was. Naked and dead and I'd require therapy."

"So no hidden lover then," Harrison said.

He turned to look out the window. He was drumming his fingers on the windowsill and his lips were pursed, obviously sifting through the different possibilities that had led Russo to his death.

I was relieved as it gave me a minute to get myself together. Sitting so close to Harrison while debating another person's love life made me think of Harrison in ways I should definitely not be.

I was only a couple of months into my "no men" lifestyle, which was hardly anything to brag about at this juncture. My cousin Viv, however, seemed to be a master at it. As far as I knew, she hadn't been involved with anyone in years. At first I had thought she and Harrison had a thing, but no. They were best buds but that was it.

It certainly wasn't for lack of male attention. I had seen several men over the past few weeks show a marked interest in Viv, and while she was always charming and polite, she was also aloof and impossible to pin down. I think she managed to get away with it without hurting anyone's feelings because, well, she's beautiful, but also she plays the mad hatter part, marching a bit too much to her own drummer for regular guys to manage.

"What are you thinking?" Harrison asked me. "Have you solved the how and whys of Russo's fall to his death?"

"Actually, I was thinking about Viv," I said. "I have yet to figure out why she's been so steadfastly single over the past few years. Every time I think she's going to tell me what's going on, she wriggles off my hook like a very crafty fish."

"Viv as a fish," Harrison said. "I don't think she'd thank you for that comparison."

I laughed and Harrison grinned. We leaned close to each other in the way of friends but, yeah, there was definitely the same spark of attraction between us. Then my stomach gave a rumble that sounded over the rain on the window and the engine of the bus. Harrison frowned.

"Up, up, let's go," he said.

"What?" I asked.

The bus was still in motion. Harrison didn't care but took my hand and led me down the stairs to stand by the door. The bus pulled over and I noted we were on Bayswater Road on the north end of Hyde Park.

"Let's go grab a bite," he said. As if sensing I was going to argue, he added, "The shop will be fine. They ran it before without you; surely they can manage one day."

I would have argued but I was too hungry. The rain was pelting down hard. Harrison grabbed my hand in his and we ran down the wide sidewalk until we came to a crosswalk.

As soon as the signal changed, we dashed across the street to a large two-story white building tucked under some very large trees. The Swan, an old coaching inn turned pub, beckoned us inside with a dry warmth that felt like a welcoming hug.

As the door shut behind me, I turned to look at Harrison to assess the damage. He looked like I felt, as if I had swum there. Water was dripping off his nose, his jacket was drenched and together we were forming a small puddle around our feet.

The place was packed and I figured we'd have to wait for a table to open up. Harrison must have been thinking the same because he looked at me and said, "I'm pretty sure they'll let us have a table out on the patio."

I laughed at him. The smell of food cooking hit me low and I said, "I'll eat standing up so long as they feed me."

He glanced over my head while I tried to ring the excess water out of my hair.

"Table open," he cried and he grabbed my hand and led me over to a small table in a dark corner. Thankfully, the warmth of the pub was bringing back the feeling in the tips of my fingers.

"Do you see anything you fancy?" he asked.

He gestured to the large board on the wall over the bar. I saw that today's special was beef stew in a bowl of Yorkshire pudding. No need to look at anything else.

"I'll have the special," I said.

"Sounds good," he agreed. "A Fuller's, too?"

I nodded. I'd had a rough morning. Surely, I deserved a pint with my lunch. I opened my purse but Harrison waved me away.

"It's on me," he said. Ordering drinks and food took place at the bar, so I stayed in my seat and waited.

I watched as a waiter walked by carrying food up the short stairs to the diners above, fish and chips and bangers and mash, and it all looked so good I could have tackled the poor guy and swiped the food.

Harrison came back and placed my pint in front of me.

He also set down a wooden spoon with the number 21 scrawled on it.

"That's our order number," he explained. "They deliver your food by the number."

"Ah," I said.

More food went by—two shepherd's pies—and I turned my head to watch them go.

"All right, Ginger?"

I turned back to Harrison. I could feel my lower lip pooch out in a pout that I was unable to stop.

"Crazy hungry," I said.

"Let's talk about something else," Harrison said.

"Read any good books lately?" I asked.

"*Why Nations Fail*," he said. "It's about—"

"Politics and money," I interrupted. "Any good gossip in there?"

"Such as?" he asked, looking amused.

"Did two wives of opposing nations wear the same dress to a global event and spark a war?" I asked. I was teasing him, but seriously, I knew people in the fashion industry who would not think that was out of line in the least.

He laughed. "Er, no."

"Not my cup of tea then," I said. "How about movies?"

"Movies are a date sort of thing," he said with a shake of his head.

Now he had my attention. Movies were for dating? And he hadn't seen any? Did that mean he wasn't dating? Not at all? I mean, I knew he had made some comment about waiting until I was back in the dating game, but we were looking at the better part of a year to go and I really didn't think he would go that long without asking someone out.

I needed more information but how to get it? I took a long slow sip of my beer while I mulled it over. I didn't want to be too blunt and ask straight out if he was waiting for me, because there was no way I could ask that without sounding full of myself.

I ran my fingers through my hair in an effort to help it air dry. I tossed it over my shoulder and then fixed my gaze on him. He was watching me but his expression was inscrutable.

"So if you don't watch movies with your dates, what do you do?" I asked.

Yeah, I might have wanted to put a little more thought into that question. His eyebrows rose and he propped his chin in his hand and studied me across the table.

"That didn't come out nearly as cleverly as I thought it would," I confessed.

Under his green gaze, I could feel an embarrassed warmth heat up my face, which was disconcerting because that sort of thing never happened to me. I was the queen of meaningless flirtatious banter; what was happening to my glib tongue? Then again, I had seen a dead body just a few hours before, so I wasn't at my best.

"Now I'm in a quandary," he said. "I can think of a whole host of answers to your question but I'm not quite sure they're appropriate lunch conversation."

Now what was that supposed to mean? Was he dating? What was he doing on his dates? All sorts of images of

Harry in various states of debauchery flitted through my head. I opened my mouth to interrogate him right as the waiter set my beef stew down in front of me.

Harrison smiled at me and I knew that he had seen the waiter coming and had said what he did just to be provoking. The truth made me smile. I was well matched in Harrison Wentworth.

I put my napkin in my lap and tucked into my beef stew. It was the finest meal I had ever eaten in my life. Okay, yes, I was starving, but still the Yorkshire pudding with beef stew was amazing. I could have written a poem to its deliciousness. We didn't talk for the rest of the meal, and I realized Harrison must have been as hungry as I was.

The rain let up and Harrison walked me to Lancaster Gate, where I caught the train back to Notting Hill, and he headed off to a business meeting in East London. Once on the train, I wondered how Ariana was doing. I supposed it was inappropriate of me to think it, but since I never got to ask her if she wanted us to refurbish the hat or not, I realized my entire day had been for nothing.

Well, not completely nothing. I did have a very nice lunch with Harrison. I was walking up the steps out of Notting Hill Gate when I froze in place. Oh, no! Harrison had bought lunch and I had let him. Did that constitute a date?

A man slammed into me from behind, knocking me up the next step and getting me back in motion.

"Sorry, Miss," he said as he hurried around me and out of the hole in the ground.

As I strode toward the shop, I pondered all of the things that made it a date and all of the things that made it not a date. I was leaning pretty much in the not date direction when I passed by my friend Andre's art studio. I peeked inside and saw him handing a big, brown wrapped package to an older couple.

Since the shop was empty aside from them, I pulled the handle on the door and entered. Surely, ten more minutes away from the shop would not make a difference.

The couple passed me on their way out and we all smiled at one another in the greeting of strangers who'd most likely never see each other again but wanted to be considered pleasant regardless of the lack of a future relationship.

"Scarlett, what brings you here?" Andre asked.

He opened his arms wide and we hugged and gave each other an air kiss on each cheek.

"I'm in crisis," I said.

Andre's eyes went wide and he gestured for me to sit down on his very unforgiving modern furniture. It was pewter gray and as hard as granite. It did not encourage lingering.

I took a seat and said, "I'm not sure but I think I had a date with Harrison."

"No!" Andre gasped and clapped a hand over his mouth.

Chapter 9

He looked at me in shock, and I nodded and said, "I know!"

Then he frowned. "Wait. How do you not know if it was a date?"

"Well, it was after we left the police station—"

"What?" he cried. "Why were you at a police station?"

"Because of the dead body—"

This time he interrupted me with a scream.

"Scarlett Parker, that is not funny!" he said.

"I'm not joking," I said. "I went to see Ariana Jackson about the estimate for her bridal hat, and when I got there, she was crouched beside the body of her boss, Anthony Russo, and he was dead."

Andre blinked at me. He didn't yelp, or cry, or scream. He just sat there, blinking.

"Are you okay?" I asked.

"I think I might be in shock," he said.

"I know. I spent most of the day like that," I said. "And poor Ariana is a wreck. Would you like some tea or a glass of water?"

"Sparkling water, please," he said.

He sat unmoving while I walked over to the wet bar they had installed in a corner of the studio. I opened up his mini refrigerator and grabbed one of the little bottles of Badoit carbonated water, to which I knew he was partial.

"Glass?" I asked.

He shook his head and I twisted off the top and handed him the bottle without a glass. He downed about a third of it before he lowered the bottle and let out a delicate burp.

"Beg pardon," he said.

"Not at all," I said.

"I can't believe Anthony Russo is dead," he said. "The tabloids are going to go mental."

"They hadn't gotten wind of it when we left the scene and no one showed up at the station," I said. "Must be a busy news day."

"Perhaps, but when they do catch the scent, it is going to be ugly," Andre said. "How did he die? Drug overdose? Alcoholic coma? Stabbed by a jilted lover?"

"He fell off the roof of his building," I said. "Splat."

Andre gasped. "And you saw him?"

"Only afterwards. It was pretty awful," I said. I shivered as if I could shake off the image of his squashed melon, but no. I had a feeling it was imprinted on my brain and would likely come a-calling in the wee hours of the morning when I couldn't sleep.

Andre threw an arm around me and hugged me close. "Oh, Scarlett, love, I'm so sorry, but I'm also terribly grateful."

"Grateful?" I reared back to stare at him.

"That for once I wasn't with you when you found the body," he said.

It was true. Andre was sort of my dead body buddy, having stumbled upon two corpses with me in the past.

"You're welcome," I said. I wasn't sure that was the most appropriate response but in this situation was there a proper thing to say? Darned if I knew.

"How did he fall?" Andre asked. "And what was he doing up on the roof?"

"No idea," I said. "And if the police have a clue, they're keeping it to themselves. Harrison and I kicked around the possibilities over lunch, but we didn't come up with anything for sure."

"Ah, yes, Harrison," he said. He leaned back and studied me through narrowed eyes. "I'm going to assume your preoccupation with whether lunch with Harrison was a date or not was part of some crazy coping mechanism over seeing Russo . . ."

"Dead," I said when his voice trailed off.

He nodded, obviously relieved not to have to say it.

"Maybe," I said. I definitely appreciated the thought as it made me seem less shallow. "But I am worried that lunch was a date. It can't be a date. I made a vow, a commitment to singledom, that I take very seriously."

"Well, don't get your knickers in a twist," Andre said. "Probably, Harrison was just being kind and buying you lunch because you were in a strop."

"I was not in a bad mood," I protested. "And forgive me, but Harrison and kind don't exactly go together in my head."

"No, I imagine when you think of Harrison, it's more along the lines of a top shag."

Now it was my turn to gasp and give him my most outraged expression.

"I have absolutely no interest in Harrison in that way whatsoever," I lied.

"Oh, stop, you're embarrassing yourself," Andre said. "You two practically light the room on fire when you're in it together. And just so you know, you and Harrison may have a wager on who will win *The Great British Bake Off*, the ferret or the dreamy blue eyes, but Nick and I have a bet on when exactly you two will get together."

"What?" I cried. "But I'm not dating anyone for at least another eight to nine months, and by then, Harrison will probably be engaged to someone else."

"No, he won't."

Andre said it so confidently that I wondered if he knew something I didn't know. I knew I should pretend not to care but my curiosity got the better of me.

"What do you know?" I asked.

"Nothing," Andre said. He tipped the bottle of water, finishing it.

"Aw, come on," I said. "You're holding out on me. I'd hate to have to call Nick at his office and tell him all about Russo, thus denying you the pleasure of a good tell-all."

"Scarlett, I am shocked," Andre protested. "That you would think that I would be so heartless as to look forward to gossiping about a poor man's death, well, I . . ."

I pulled out my phone and started thumbing through the contacts until Nick's name appeared. Andre peeked over my shoulder. I pressed Nick's name to bring up his information. When his number appeared, I moved my thumb to press the phone icon and place the call.

"Wait!" Andre cried before I hit Send. "All right, fine, I do want to be the one to tell Nick what happened today. Can you blame me? It's a tasty bit of goss, although I do feel quite horrible about the poor man's death."

"Of course," I said. "It's a horrible tragedy for a man to lose his life like that."

We were both silent for a moment. I wasn't sure how long our moment of silence lasted but Andre finally heaved a sigh and said, "All right. Have I repented enough for being a heartless bastard?"

"It'll do," I said. "Now tell me what you know."

"And you won't call Nick?" he haggled.

"No, I won't," I said.

"I really don't know anything," he said. "Except Nick and I both agree that Harrison is totally smitten with you. You should see how he looks at you. I don't think his twelve-year-old boy has ever gotten over his crush on your ten-year-old girl."

"Aw," I said. "That is so sweet, but that's terrible. Then today's lunch probably was a date. I'm ruined, Andre, ruined."

"Don't panic," Andre said. "If you play it off as two friends having lunch, then that's what it is."

"You think?" I asked. I really did not want to have to deal with things being awkward between Harrison and me.

"Yes, besides, once you get over your transference and start focusing on what's really bothering you, the dead body, then all of this will be beside the point."

"I suppose you're right," I said. I glanced out the window. It was raining again.

"Can I borrow an umbrella?" I asked. "I really need to get back to the shop before Viv sends out a search party."

"Of course," he said. "There are several in the stand. Pick whichever strikes your fancy."

Andre walked me to the door and I grabbed a bright pink umbrella out of the batch.

"Yours or Nick's?" I asked.

"Would I be caught dead in that shade of pink?"

"Right, so it's Nick's." I smiled. "Tell him I will return it promptly."

Andre studied me closely for a moment. "Are you sure you're all right?"

"No," I admitted. "But I will be."

Andre gave me a quick hug then pushed open the door for me and I popped the umbrella up as I stepped out. The wind had picked up and was pelting the rain at an angle. I tipped the umbrella to get the most coverage possible but my ankles and shoes were still soaked.

"Bloody hell," I muttered. I was beginning to feel more like a resident than a visitor and the cursing helped my mood.

As I trudged toward the shop, I considered Andre's words. I knew he was right. I was transferring my upset over seeing Russo broken and bloody into relationship angst. It was stupid but effective. Besides it was so much nicer to ponder the possible unspoken meaning in Harrison's green gaze when he looked at me than it was to consider what the shape of the puddle of blood pooling under Russo's cracked head resembled.

The wind whipped under the umbrella and slapped me in the face with its cold wet fingers. Thankfully, I had arrived at Mim's Whims. I snapped the umbrella shut while pulling the door open.

Viv was standing behind the counter assisting a customer, and I could tell by her body language that the encounter was not going well. It was not a big surprise since the customer was Leann Littleton—or as I called her, Lame Leann, because she was, you know, in slang speak, lame. To be clear, I'm not talking about a bum leg here, more like a bum personality.

I plopped Nick's umbrella into the stand by the door and shrugged out of my jacket, which I hung on the coatrack. I trudged across the shop, but I wasn't moving very quickly. My belly was full; I was cold and wet and completely emotionally drained.

"But I specifically said I wanted a burgundy hat, whilst this is quite obviously oxblood," Lame Leann complained. She did it with just the right amount of disdain, the right amount to make you want to punch her in the mouth, that is.

She was middle-aged with fine lines around her eyes and jowls just beginning to appear on her jawline. Her mouth was screwed up in a dissatisfied moue, and I got the feeling she really enjoyed being a whiner.

"Mrs. Littleton, here is my cousin Scarlett," Viv said as I approached. She looked at me as if I were a life raft appearing in shark-infested waters. "I'm sure she can assist you."

Digging deep, I searched for my inner people-pleasing, customers-first, can-do attitude and found—nothing.

Chapter 10

I glanced from Viv to Leann and back. Viv's blues eyes, so like my own, were pleading for me to take this miserable woman off her hands. I glanced back at Lame Leann and glowered.

"If you don't like it, don't buy it," I said. "The personal shopper for Lady Fownes was in the other day and wanted to buy that very hat in that particular shade of *burgundy*. We'll just sell it to her and you need not be bothered purchasing it. All right?"

Lame Leann started sputtering but I ignored her. I really did not give a flying feather if she bought the damn hat or not.

"I'm going to make tea," I said to Viv. "Want some?"

"Love some," she said. She looked bemused by my outburst.

As I walked away, I heard Lame Leann insist that Viv sell her the hat. I smiled. Maybe my surliness was a customer service skill I needed to employ a bit more frequently.

In the workroom, Fee was sitting on the large wooden worktable with her legs crossed and a pile of ivory chiffon in her lap. With her usual tiny, precise stitches, she was fastening a beautiful lace trim to the edge of a wedding veil.

I went over to watch her work, finding the movement of her nimble fingers soothing. Not for the first time, I envied the other's ability to make something magical out of plain cloth and odd bits of feathers, lace and trim.

"It's coming out beautifully," I said.

Fee glanced up. Her smile flashed bright white against her brown skin then she frowned and tipped her head to the side as she studied me.

"All right, Scarlett?" she asked. "You're looking a bit peaky."

"I'm fine," I said. I walked over to the kitchenette and put the kettle on. "I'm better than Anthony Russo at any rate."

"I heard," Fee said. "What sort of crazy accident was that, falling off the roof of a building?"

"That was genius, cousin!" Viv said as she strode into the kitchen. "Mrs. Littleton pitched an absolute fit when she thought we might sell her hat to Lady Fownes's personal shopper."

"Wait until she finds out Lady Fownes doesn't have a personal shopper," I said and cringed. "We may lose a customer there."

"Pish," Viv said with a dismissive wave of her hands. "Good riddance."

Fee glanced between us while I dropped a couple of Earl Grey tea bags into the waiting pot. Contrary to what my friends thought, I could actually boil water and my tea-making skills were coming on strong, too.

When the kettle whistled, I poured water over the tea bags in the pot and then covered it with a cozy to allow the tea to steep. I saw Fee glance at the clock and knew she'd be on top of letting us know when it was ready. Fee is a stickler for the three-minute rule when it comes to steeping a black tea, of which Earl Grey is one.

"So did you want to talk about what happened this morning?" Viv asked. "I told Fee what you told me."

"I think I'm talked out, between the police and Harrison, oh, and Andre," I said.

"Harrison and Andre?" Fee asked.

"Explain," Viv ordered.

Fee gestured at the teapot with her hand and Viv took over preparing the tea. I told them about going to the station with Ariana and how her fiancé, Stephen, had shown up with Harrison and Alistair in tow.

I prepped a plate of Tesco's all-butter, dark chocolate ginger cookies, which are amazing, even though I was sure I couldn't eat another bite. I was wrong.

Fee had pushed aside the veil and was nibbling a cookie and sipping her tea while listening to me describe the questioning by Inspectors Franks and Simms.

"And how are the dear inspectors?" Viv asked.

"The same," I said. "I think of them as the big mustache and the unibrow, but very kind for all that."

"What do you suppose they think happened?" Viv asked.

"I haven't the foggiest," I said. "But when talking to me, they did seem focused on Ariana being near the body when I got there, which as I explained, was complete happenstance since she didn't know I was stopping by."

"Good thing for her," Fee said. "You've become her witness, yeah?"

"I suppose," I said.

"So what did Harrison have to say about all of this?" Viv asked.

"We kicked around several ideas, but I think he's just as stymied as anyone," I said. "Thankfully, Stephen also brought his friend Alistair Turner. He's a barrister who specializes in criminal defense."

"Will Ariana need him in that capacity?" Viv asked. She looked worried.

"I don't think so, but it sure was handy to have him there today," I said. "Also, he's very easy on the eyes."

"How easy?" Fee asked.

"Like jam on toast easy," I said.

"Scarlett, must you always talk about me when I'm not in the room? Honestly, you're going to start rumors about us."

I whipped my head around to see Nick peering at us from the doorway.

"Hi, Nick," I said. I put my cup on the table and hurried across the room and into his big bracing hug. "What are you doing here?"

"Andre called me as soon as you left and told me everything, so I had to stop by on my way home and check on you." He released me and stepped back to study my face.

"You don't look shocky or trembly. So our boy Harrison tended you well then?"

"Andre told you about that, too?" I asked.

"Yes, and for the record, the answer is no, it wasn't," he said.

"What answer is no?" Viv asked. Her eyes were narrowed in speculation as she watched us. I so did not want to have the "Did lunch with Harrison constitute a date?" debate with her, mostly since I knew she'd say yes just because she'd made it clear that she liked Harrison and me together.

"I wanted to know if I would be overreaching if I made beef, ale and parsnip pudding for my dinner bet with Harrison in the unlikely event that I lose," I said.

"And you said no?" Viv asked Nick. "Well, there's a note of confidence."

"Yeah, you might want to turn it back a bit and stick to food that only requires reheating, yeah?" Fee asked.

I gave them both a sour look but squeezed Nick's hand to let him know his message was received. Now you'd think I'd be happy that he was telling me that, no, it wasn't a date with Harrison, and I was. All except for my inner girly-girl, who truly felt if she didn't get to go on an honest-to-God "buy me dinner, take me dancing and try to make a move on me" date sometime in the very near future, she was going to shrivel up and die. Did I mention she is a bit of a drama queen?

"Well, with any luck, Nick's ferret-girl will lose the competition, and he'll be doing the cooking," Nick said.

"Would you like some tea?" I asked.

"That would be lovely," he said.

Viv poured him a mug while I offered him a cookie.

"Dark chocolate ginger, divine," Nick said as he took one. "So have you heard anything about Anthony Russo?"

"Not a word," I said. "As his only assistant, I imagine Ariana is going to have her hands full informing his clients of the situation."

"They will all have to retain new counsel," Viv said.

"I wonder if she will cancel the wedding," Fee said.

"Oh, no," Viv said. "I hope not."

I looked at the sad little downturn of her lips and I knew Viv was thinking of Mim's hat. If Ariana canceled the wedding, then Viv wouldn't get a chance to restore it.

"It's still a few weeks away," I said. "I doubt she'll cancel it. Stephen was very kind to her at the police station. They seemed strong together."

"Still, we have no idea what she wants to do, do we?" Viv asked.

"No, I never got the chance to talk to her about it," I said. "Sorry."

"Hardly your fault," she said.

I nodded. I knew it wasn't and yet I felt the same way that she did about Mim's hat and wanted it to be fixed. It was more than just a job for us; it was a way to have Mim here again in the hat shop, a way to keep her legacy alive.

"Have they reported Russo's death on the news?" Nick asked. "That'll give you a good indication of how this is going to play out."

"Meaning?" I asked.

"If the reporters swarm like locusts onto every girlfriend he's ever had, then you'll know they're treating it as a homicide," he said. "But if they are all very hush-hush and somber faced about it, then it would seem more likely an unfortunate accident."

"I know this is ghastly of me to say, but do you suppose it was suicide? Then again, of all the ways to do yourself in, why would you throw yourself off of a building?" Fee asked. "That wouldn't be a decision made lightly."

"Poison," Viv said. "That would be my method of choice."

I frowned at her.

"Not that I've ever given it any great thought," she said. "But you hear about other people's choices and it's only natural to think what you would do."

"Agreed," Fee said. "Poison would be my choice as well."

"Not me," Nick said. "If I'm taking myself out, it has to be done in a dramatic fashion like jumping off the London Bridge, wearing nothing but a purple feather boa."

"Looking to make a splash, are you?" Viv asked, and they all laughed.

"No, he just wants to make waves." Fee snickered.

"Water you talking about? You can't wear a purple boa; you'd need to have something sparkly," I said.

No one said anything.

"Don't you get it?" I asked. " 'Water' instead of 'what are'?"

All three of them gave me sympathetic looks, but I saw the corner of Nick's mouth turn up.

"You thought that was funny," I said and pointed at him.

"No, I think *you* are funny; there's a difference," he said.

"So are you laughing at me or with me?"

"At you, most definitely," he said.

I gave him a dark look but he just winked at me.

"So, Scarlett, you haven't answered the question," Nick said. "How would you punch your own clock should the need arise?"

I sighed. Having recently come out of a bout of global public humiliation, I'd be a liar if I said ending it all had never occurred to me. It had. Only briefly and only in my very dark moments, but in my defense, an Internet video of me lobbing cake at the man I thought I loved had gone viral. So not only did I find out the rat bastard was married but the entire world, or so it felt at the time, got to find out with me.

"The one time it crossed my mind very, very briefly," I said. "I was driving down a dark stretch of road in Florida and it all felt like it was just too much, you know, the heart-break and the humiliation, and for just a second, a nanosec-ond really, I thought about cutting the wheel into a bridge abutment."

The three of them stared at me, and I suddenly felt naked and exposed.

"Oh, were we not sharing actual life moments?" I asked.

"Sweetie," Viv said. She put down her teacup and hugged me close. "I so wish I had been there so I could have slapped that man until my arm gave out."

"Hear, hear," Nick said. "I don't have much of a punch but I give a hell of a knee to the crotch."

"And I am a very good hair ripper outer," Fee added.

"And as for me, I would have happily busted his jaw."

I turned and glanced over my shoulder and there stood Harrison, looking at me with such fierce protectiveness I felt it all the way down to my toes. Something lifted in my chest at the sight of him, but I tried to convince myself it was just the combo of ginger and dark chocolate cookies and Earl Grey tea giving me heartburn.

"Well, it's a good thing you all weren't there," I said. "Else you'd all be in jail now."

I tried to make light of it, but honestly, it felt so good to know I had such wonderful friends. I was actually a bit choked up. Shaking it off, I looked at Harrison and gave him a warm smile.

"What brings you by so early, Harry?" I asked.

To my surprise, he didn't correct the nickname. Instead, his countenance darkened and he said, "It's Ariana. She's being held as a person of interest in the murder of Anthony Russo."

Chapter 11

"What?" I gasped. "When? How? Why?"

"Speaking of locust-feeding reporters," Nick said.

I swatted his arm to hush him.

"I don't have all of the specifics," Harrison said. "Alistair just texted me that Stephen called him when the police arrived at Ariana's apartment with a search warrant and again when they arrested her."

"Oh, no," I said. "This is bad, isn't it?"

"It's not ideal," Harrison said.

"What will happen next?" Viv asked.

"I guess that depends upon what the police find," Harrison said.

"Poor Ariana," I said. I thought about the wide-eyed girl, crouched beside her boss's body, looking horrified and lost. "She didn't do it."

I thought it spoke well of them that no one contradicted me. I'd been ready to put forth an argument, but there was no need. It wasn't this crew that needed to be convinced of Ariana's innocence.

"Oh, no," I said as I looked at Nick. "The reporters."

"It will have started by now," he said.

Together we raced for the door. He was fumbling with his phone as we hit the stairs to our apartment at a jog. I entered first and switched on our flat-screen television, flipping through channels until I found the nightly news on BBC One.

"Andre is coming over," Nick said. "He wants to know if you need anything."

"Tell him to bring dinner," I said. I watched as a montage of Anthony Russo in various states of drunken disorderliness with a bevy of beauties on his arm flashed across the screen. "This is going to be a long one."

We kept up our vigil through the eight o'clock and the ten o'clock news. The reporters had missed Ariana's arrival but it didn't deter them from camping outside Notting Hill Station, which is where the custody suites for criminals arrested in the Kensington Borough of the Metropolitan Police Service were located. Nick, Andre and Fee departed before the ten o'clock news, but Harrison stayed with Viv and me. When they were rehashing the story for the umpteenth time, Viv took the remote and shut it off.

"Enough," she said. "I can't listen to another word."

"Agreed," I said. "I kept hoping there would be a new suspect announced."

"Seems unlikely on the first day," Harrison said. I appreciated that his tone was regretful.

"Well, Harrison, always a pleasure, even under poor circumstances," Viv said. She stepped forward and kissed his cheek. "See him out, won't you, Scarlett? I'm dead tired."

She didn't wait for an answer but disappeared into her bedroom before either of us could offer so much as a good night.

"I have a key," Harrison said. "You don't need to walk downstairs. I know you've had a long day."

"No, it's all right," I said. "I always do the final sweep of the shop before we lock up for the night. It gives me peace of mind."

He led the way down the narrow staircase. The store was dark with just the emergency lights on. I glanced at the wardrobe in the corner with the large wooden raven carved in the top. I had named him Ferd the bird and we frequently conversed when I did my nightly rounds. Okay, I conversed as his beady wooden eyes followed me around; still, it was our routine.

All was quiet and there was a certain intimacy to walking through the deserted shop with Harrison at my side. I tried to tell myself it was the one-two punch of the enormous amount of spaghetti and meatballs I'd eaten, which was Andre's go-to meal for impromptu events because he could pick up all of the ingredients at the Tesco up the street, combined with the late hour, but it wasn't.

Like it or not, I felt a closeness to Harrison that defied any past experience I'd shared with a man. Usually, if I liked a guy, I started dating him immediately. The passion tended to burn out pretty quickly when I discovered his inability to use a hamper or wash his dishes, or, you know, actually divorce his wife, and so the relationship would fizzle after a few months.

But Harrison was different. By consciously not dating him, despite finding him extremely attractive, I was forced to build a different sort of relationship with him, a friendship with sizzle, if you will.

Call me crazy but it felt infinitely more dangerous than any of the relationships I'd thrown myself into after ten minutes of thinking the boy was cute. I wasn't entirely sure this was such a good thing, but I'd set my course and I was determined to stay it.

At the front door, Harrison paused and turned to face me. It felt too cozy in here with the lights mostly out and the room warm against the chilly air outside. I pretended to be scanning the room to see that every hat was in its place, but I could feel Harrison's gaze on my face.

"Ginger." He said my name, his voice a deep gruff growl with his very precise British accent making the "r" disappear in the most delightful way. It positively made me dizzy.

"Hmm, yes?" I said, still checking out the shop.

"Are you going to be all right?" he asked.

"Me? Oh, yeah, I'll be fine," I lied.

"I don't believe you," he said. "You can always call me, you know, anytime, day or night."

"Good to know." I looked over his shoulder at the shelves on the far wall. Nope, nothing out of place.

He captured my chin with his hand and gently turned my

face toward his. He stared at me for a long moment while I felt the blood rush to my ears and my breath stall in my lungs. It was dangerous, being this close to him. I closed my eyes, thinking it might be best if I didn't look at him.

When I felt his mouth brush ever so gently against my cheek, I almost turned toward him like a sunflower turning its face to the sun, but I resisted even though it about killed me.

I felt him move in closer, the heat of his body pressing and mingling against the heat of mine. He was so close, so wonderfully, magically close, I actually trembled.

The soft pulse of his breath brushed against my ear when he whispered, "Good night, beautiful."

Hard to say how long I stood in that same spot—seconds, hours or a few blissed-out weeks, I have no idea. The man hadn't even kissed me properly and I was completely undone. It had to be the accent, I assured myself. How could a girl not feel stirred by such charming elocution?

I shook myself out of my trance and glanced at the door. Not only was it shut, but he had also locked it. I crossed the floor into the kitchen to check all of the windows and doors, and on my way back, I passed the wardrobe. I glanced at Ferd and I was pretty sure he was smirking at me.

"Don't say it," I said to him. "Don't even think it."

Maybe it was the events of the day making me see things, but I was pretty sure he bobbed his head in a silent laughing fit.

I stomped up the stairs to our flat. Viv's door was shut and her light was off. I took that as a sign that she didn't want to be disturbed. That was fine with me—I was pretty sure I wasn't up to conversing with anyone, and I definitely didn't want to answer any questions even indirectly about

Harrison's departure. In fact, I didn't even want to think about it.

As I tugged on my flannel jammies and climbed into bed, I resolutely shoved aside any thought of Harrison and whatever the heck that, wow, was between us at the door. Instead, I thought about Ariana. How must she be feeling being arrested for the murder of her boss? She had to be terrified.

I sifted through the events of the day. Russo dead. The police station. Even then, the police had been looking closely at Ariana. I tried to make it work in my head. She had said she wanted her boss dead. Was it a confession? No, it hadn't felt like it. Instead it had sounded as if she knew she was going to be a suspect and felt that wishing ill of her boss made her culpable.

Ariana Jackson, a murderess. I couldn't see it. I couldn't believe it. There was something so refined and orderly about Ariana. In a nutshell, she seemed too smart to be a killer. Besides, what could she possibly have to gain by killing her boss? She'd be out of a job—how was that a good thing when she was about to be married?

Tomorrow, I promised myself as I began to fall into the sweet abyss of sleep, tomorrow I would find out as much as I could about Ariana Jackson and Anthony Russo.

"I don't think Harrison is going to like this idea," Viv said.

We were standing in the shop putting on our jackets. I glanced outside to see if I needed my umbrella or not. It was pale gray and chilly looking. I supposed I'd better bring it just in case.

"Why should he like it?" I asked. I could feel my face get warm at the mere mention of his name. Gah, this would not do! I had to get a grip on myself. "It has nothing to do with him so I don't know why he'd have any say about it one way or another."

"You really think he isn't going to find out that we went to see Ariana?" Viv asked.

"Oh, no, I'm sure he'll find out," I said. "But since it's about the business, I don't really see that he can complain."

"About the business?" Viv laughed. "That's a stretch, isn't it?"

"Not if we inquire about the hat, it isn't," I insisted. "I mean, we don't know what to do with it or what she wants us to do or even if she's going to forge ahead with the wedding."

"Perhaps we shouldn't mention that part of it," Viv said. "Awfully depressing to have to postpone your wedding because you've been arrested for murder, and if she did kill her boss—"

"She didn't," I interrupted.

"How can you possibly know that?" Viv asked.

"I just do," I said. And no, I didn't mention the part about Ariana telling me she had wished him dead. I wanted to talk to Ariana first.

"All right," Viv said. She had that tone she used when she thought I was being bullheaded. Normally, I would balk and argue that I wasn't, but I had a feeling this time she might be right.

"Let me know how it goes, yeah?" Fee asked from the front counter of the shop.

"We won't be long," Viv said. "Please tell Mrs. Hodges

that I'm sorry I couldn't be here, but I know you'll do an excellent job with her."

Fee looked pleased with the praise. "I'll call you if there's a problem."

Together Viv and I pushed through the door out onto Portobello Road. Despite the gloomy weather, there was a fair amount of foot traffic. I saw the white-breasted flash of a black-headed magpie as it winged overhead with something snazzy in its beak. It looked quite pleased with itself and I smiled.

I knew some people considered the magpie to be a pest, but I'd always thought they had a lot of personality. Plus, that whole attraction to shiny things, well, I thought it made them quite smart, but that could be my own attraction to shiny things doing the talking.

The fastest way to get to the Notting Hill Police Station was to walk through the neighborhood. It was a solid half-mile hike down Ladbroke Grove, and Viv and I had both dressed warm to ward off the early autumn chill. We crossed Ladbroke Road and approached the imposing weatherworn brick building that I had first gone into to report Viv missing several months before. I could have lived without a repeat visit.

Viv strode forward as if she stormed police stations every day. I was trying to be a little less conspicuous. I didn't particularly want to be noticed, especially by Inspectors Franks and Simms if they happened to be around.

It was too much to hope that the station would be quiet and we would be able to slink on in and ask the constable at the front desk if we could visit with Ariana. Oh, no.

A frothing pit of reporters and photographers filled the

lobby to bursting. Viv and I were pushed back against the wall as the reporters fired questions at the woman behind the desk. She wore a black-and-white-checked cravat with a white shirt and dark pants. From the tight expression on her face, I could see she was feeling harassed.

"What should we do?" Viv asked. "I don't see how we can get through this."

"We'll have to pull rank. Follow me," I said. I pushed my way through the crowd. It took a few shoves and one sharp elbow, but I finally made it to the desk.

Chapter 12

"When will the inspector be available to answer questions?" a female reporter asked the constable.

"I haven't received a schedule from him," the constable answered. "But I'll let you know when I do."

She glanced at me and her expression changed from one of annoyance to one of concern. "Can I help you?"

"Yes, could you let Inspector Franks know that Scarlett Parker is here to see him," I said.

"What's it regarding?" she asked.

I leaned close so that the reporters couldn't hear me and whispered, "The Russo murder. I was on the scene."

The constable straightened up. She gestured for me and Viv to follow her. Protests sounded from the reporters behind us, but the officer didn't show any interest in their whining. Instead, she led us through a door into a waiting area.

"Have a seat," she said. "I'll tell him you're here."

Viv sat next to me, looking as if she was afraid to touch anything. I couldn't blame her. Although the place seemed clean, it wasn't the cream of society passing through here, was it?

"What do you suppose he's in here for?" Viv whispered.

I followed the line of her gaze toward a man down the hall sitting on a hard wooden bench like ours. He was talking to himself and would occasionally give himself a good slap across the face. The cheek being smacked was a vibrant shade of red, so whichever one of his personalities was doing the slapping, it really didn't pull any punches.

"Domestic violence," I said. "Or does it not count if you're smacking yourself?"

"Well, if you feel you deserve it, I don't think it can be considered abuse," she said.

We watched as the man rocked back and forth and then hugged himself.

"Oh, that's nice," Viv said. "They've made up; maybe now he'll get to go home."

"I wouldn't bet on it," I said.

"Scarlett!"

I turned at the sound of my name to see Alistair Turner striding down the short hallway toward us. Today he was wearing an impeccable navy blue suit with a crimson necktie. It was definitely a power suit.

"Alistair," I said as I rose to my feet. "Good to see you. Is Ariana still here? Is there any way we can go and see her?"

Alistair had stopped in front of me, but his attention was one hundred percent captured by Vivian. He looked like he'd been frozen in place and I was pretty sure he hadn't heard a word I'd said. I sighed. Viv was known to have this effect on men.

Wearing a darling knee-length pale blue Jenny Packham day dress, with her long blond curls hanging down past her shoulders and her makeup applied lightly but effectively, Viv was stunning. Alistair looked like he'd swallowed his tongue.

"Oh, I'm sorry," I said. "Alistair, this is my cousin Vivian Tremont. Viv, this is Alistair, a friend of Harrison's and Ariana's barrister."

"Nice to meet you," Viv said. She glanced at him briefly and then away as if she was uncomfortable under his scrutiny.

"I assure you, Ms. Tremont, the pleasure is mine," he said. I glanced between them. Alistair looked like a dog shaking water off his coat when he turned back to face me. "I'm sorry, Scarlett, I was preoccupied, what was that you said?"

"We were wondering if we could see Ariana," I said. "I imagine she could use the support."

"That's very kind of you," he said. "They haven't told me that she isn't allowed visitors. In fact, Stephen is with her now."

"Excellent," I said. "Could you take us to her?"

I felt the need to get moving before Inspector Franks appeared and I had to admit that I had lied about wanting to see him.

"Certainly," he said. "Follow me."

We stopped at the custody desk, where they checked us

over and made us turn in our personal belongings. I assumed it was so we couldn't slip Ariana a hacksaw to file her way out. Viv looked less than pleased at leaving her purse in the gray plastic tub. Behind the desk, I saw another room through a glass window. The walls had six television screens and I realized the video feed was from the cells. Only four of the televisions showed occupants and I recognized Ariana's dark hair in one of them.

I nudged Viv with an elbow and pointed. Her eyes went wide and then she looked horrified. I followed her gaze to a different monitor and saw that the person in one of the cells was throwing up.

"Oh, gross," I said.

The uniformed officer in the monitor room didn't look thrilled either.

We were buzzed through a security door and then led into another hallway that had several dark blue metal doors. I saw Stephen standing in the open door of the one nearest to us with an officer at his side.

"Come on," I said to Viv, and we rushed past Alistair.

"Scarlett, Vivian, you're here," Ariana said. Her face was red and splotchy, her eyes puffy from crying and her nose chapped from blowing.

The custody sergeant held up his hands to slow us down. "There's too many of you. Someone has to wait up front."

"I'm her barrister," Alistair said.

"I don't care if you're her sister," the officer said. "Only two visitors at a time."

"We'll just be a moment," I said to Stephen when he seemed reluctant to leave. He nodded.

Alistair jerked his head in the opposite direction to indicate that Stephen should follow him.

I watched as the two men walked away. Alistair's voice was low and I couldn't make out what he was saying over the din around us

"Hi, Ariana," Viv said. "We thought you could use a little support."

"Oh, that's so nice of you," she said. "I'd offer you a cup of tea or another beverage, but . . ."

I felt my heart pinch at her attempt at humor. The tiny closet-sized room behind her contained a steel commode in the corner with a sort of sink built into the top of it. *Ew.* The only place to sit was a hard-looking bed with a thin blanket and a pillow.

Viv put her hand over Ariana's. "It's going to be all right."

The compassion made Ariana's flip demeanor crack, and she bowed her head and nodded. I could tell she was fighting back tears so I went for a distraction.

"We wanted to check in with you about your wedding hat," I said.

Ariana's face lit up for just a second but then she frowned. "I don't know that there's much point in fixing it. I don't know if I'm going to be released in time to get married."

"Have they formally charged you?" I asked. "Or are they just holding you as a suspect?"

"No, there's been no formal charges but Alistair said they can hold me up to ninety-six hours with a magistrate's approval without formally charging me," she said. "I suspect this will be the longest ninety-six hours of my life."

"Ariana!"

We all turned to see a middle-aged woman bearing down on us. She was dressed in an ankle-length skirt that rode up a little bit higher in the back due to her rather large posterior. She paused to hug Stephen and thump him on the back but then kept on coming. Her intent to get to Ariana was clear, and both Viv and I backed up to give her room.

"Oh, my dear, this is awful, just awful," the woman cried. "How could this have happened? What can they be thinking? Who is in charge? I want to talk to them."

"Trudy, it's all right." Ariana gave the woman a smile that was full of affection.

"All right? It bloody well is not all right," the woman said. She had broad features and her gray hair was twisted up into a knot on the top of her head. Her hands were big and looked like they knew their way around a toolbox if need be. This was no shrinking violet. I liked her immediately.

She looked us up and down and frowned. I could tell she was the sort of person who did not tolerate screwups. "Beg pardon, that was rude of me. And who might you two be? You're not detectives, are you?"

"No!" Viv and I said together. The anger in the woman's glare demanded a quick response of the negative.

"We're milliners," Viv said.

The custody sergeant looked like he was about to step in and enforce his rule of two. Trudy froze him with a look before she turned back to us.

"Goodness gracious me, you don't say," Trudy exclaimed. "Whatever are you doing here?"

"Ariana commissioned a wedding hat from us so we came to make sure she still wanted it," Viv said.

"You must be the girls from Mim's Whims. Ariana was so excited to find someone to fix her mother's hat," Trudy said. She paused to sniffle a little bit into a tissue. "She is going to be such a lovely bride. But I have to say, coming here under the circumstances, well, that is impressive customer service."

"Indeed. Ms. Tremont, Ms. Parker, a word, please."

I turned around to see Inspector Franks standing right behind us. Uh-oh.

"Inspector Franks," I said. "Just the man we were looking for. Right, Viv?"

"We were?" she asked. I stared hard. "Oh, yes, of course, we were about the . . . uh . . ."

Viv glanced at me in a panic. Of the two of us, she really wasn't the quickest on her feet. Me? I could lie to get out of a jam before I even realized I was fibbing. Truly, it was a gift.

"We are thinking of stocking cowboy hats," I said. "And since you are such an Alan Jackson fan, we thought you might want to know. What size head do you have anyway? Have you ever been properly measured? I'm quite sure if you pop into the shop, Viv can measure you."

Franks stared at us for a moment. I knew he didn't believe a word I said, but he looked like he was deciding to play along. He rubbed his mustache. "An authentic Stetson would really add to my karaoke set."

Viv was looking at me over his shoulder. She mouthed the word "Stetson?" I ignored her because I'm good at that, too.

"Oh, we also came down to see how our customer and friend Ariana is doing," I added. "We're working on her wedding hat, you know."

"So you said," Franks said. "Brown or white?"

"Excuse me?" I asked.

"The hats," he said. "Will they be brown or white?"

"Both," I said. It was impetuous, no question, especially when Viv started jumping up and down behind his back like she was having a fit, which, of course, she was. I had a feeling Viv wanted to carry cowboy hats about as much as she wanted to chew tobacco and learn to spit.

"Excellent," he said. He gave me a broad grin under the mustache. "Let me know when they're in."

"Will do," I said.

He turned his attention to Ariana. "We're going to be taking you in for another round of questioning in a few moments." His voice was sympathetic when he spoke. "You'll want to advise your counsel to come with you."

"I'll go and get Stephen," Trudy said. She squeezed Ariana's hand with her fingers. "Chin up, my girl. We'll get through this."

We watched her walk down the hall. She was clearly a woman on a mission.

Ariana gestured to the custody sergeant standing near us and then asked Franks, "May I have a few moments alone with my friends? Girl talk."

"There really is no place to receive visitors," Franks said, looking around the custody area with a frown. "All right, if the three of you want to chat in private, you can go in there."

He waved toward the cell behind us. I glanced at Viv and

felt myself start to balk but then I looked at Ariana and realized she had many more hours to go in the tiny room on her own. If she wanted to talk to us in private, surely, I could handle it since I would get to leave.

We piled into the skinny room and Inspector Franks gave us all a nod and then he headed back down the cell-lined hallway. The officer closed the door after us.

I stood a good half foot away from the wall and folded my arms over my chest. I was determined not to touch anything.

"Is it just me or does it seem like Franks isn't really going after Ariana?" Viv asked.

"It's not you," I said. "We've seen him when he's fully engaged. This isn't that."

I shifted to stand beside Ariana. She was wearing jeans and a fleece and a pair of slip-on boots. They were the sort of clothes you threw on in the middle of the night when you were called for an emergency such as comforting a broken-hearted girlfriend, suffering a death in the family, or being brought in for questioning in the murder of your boss.

"How have they been treating you, Ariana?" I asked.

"Other than the harsh accommodations," she said, "the inspectors have been very kind. They've brought me tea and a hot breakfast from the station canteen and they let me use the lavatory out there instead of this manky thing."

"Have they been accusatory at all?" I asked.

"No, not really," she said. "Which given that they brought me in late yesterday, I figured I was in for a much rougher time of it."

"Do you know why they brought you in?" I asked.

"They haven't said." Her voice was low and weighed down with worry. "But I think there must be something, some sort of evidence, that they think ties me to the murder."

"What could it be?" Viv asked. "Either you pushed him or you didn't."

I glanced at Ariana. She met my gaze, and I knew she was thinking about the same thing I was—her confession that she had wanted Russo dead.

"Did you and Russo have a fight?" I asked.

"No, nothing like that," she said. "It was more that I was ready to leave his employ and he preferred that I didn't. He . . . he made it very difficult, no, he made it impossible for me to leave."

"In what way?" I asked.

Ariana glanced at the door as if she expected Stephen and his mother to enter at any moment.

"He said if I tried to quit, he would go public with pictures of us," she said. "Pictures of us in a compromising situation."

Chapter 13

"Oh." Viv gasped and put her hand over her mouth.

"It was a long time ago when I first started working for Anthony," Ariana said. "I was young and stupid and I was completely dazzled by him and all of his celebrity clients, but when I figured out how he really was, well, I ended it."

"But you kept working for him?" I asked. Clearly, I was mystified: I, too, had been misled by my boss but I had chosen to pelt him with cake rather than stay in his employ.

"I had no choice," she said. "He wanted to reconcile, but I refused, and then when I tried to give my notice, he showed me pictures that he'd taken of me and him—of us. He had a camera built into the headboard of his bed, and I had no idea. I suppose I should be glad it wasn't video, but still. He said he would go public with them and ruin my reputation if I quit."

"That's horrible," I sputtered. I wanted to use much stronger language but we were in public, a police station no less, so I curbed the impulse but barely.

"The price of being young and stupid," Ariana said. She looked thoughtful. "I was afraid he would use the pictures to force me to sleep with him again or whatever other perverted thing he thought up in his head. But surprisingly he didn't. And working for him over the past couple of years hasn't been that bad, well, except for the gambling, drinking, drug use and womanizing."

"Well, I guess that's something," Viv said.

"I know it sounds crazy," Ariana said. "But despite how awful he was to everyone else, he was mostly civil with me. Still, I always felt trapped and sometimes I thought . . ."

"What?" I asked.

She shrugged. "Just that I thought he enjoyed feeling like he had power over me."

We were all silent for a moment. Then a horrible thought occurred to me.

"Do you think the police found those pictures?" I asked. "Is that why they brought you in for questioning?"

"They didn't say." Ariana closed her eyes. "Oh, God, if Stephen finds out that I slept with Russo, I don't know how he'll take it."

"But it was before you met Stephen, right?" Viv asked.

"Yes, but Russo was such a notorious pig," Ariana said. "Stephen hated him. He thought Russo was reprehensible not only for the way he lived his life but also for the sleazy clients he defended. Stephen couldn't wait for us to be married, so I could quit. Promise me you won't tell any of them—Stephen, Alistair or Harrison—about the photos."

"Oh, Ariana, these things have a way of coming out," Viv said. "We won't say anything, of course, but it is better if you tell Stephen so he can be prepared."

"What if the photos never surface?" Ariana asked. I could hear the desperate note of hope in her voice and I felt like I was squishing a bug under my shoes when I answered.

"They will surface," I said.

"These things always do," Viv agreed.

Ariana bowed her head, and I got the feeling she was trying to find a place of peace, or maybe she was praying. Either way I bit down on the millions of questions I felt bubbling up inside me.

Viv glanced at the closed door. "What do you think Stephen will do if he finds out about the pictures?"

Ariana opened her eyes. Her expression was bleak. "I don't know."

Viv and I both reached out to squeeze her hands. Just a few weeks shy of her wedding and this poor girl was watching it all crumble like a sandcastle under a strong wave. I wished I knew of a way to make it better, but I didn't.

"You'll get through this," Viv said. Her voice was fierce and reminded me of when she called me after my ex had devastated me. Viv was good for a solid boot in the behind. "You're an intelligent, lovely young woman, and even though it looks grim, the truth will out."

Ariana stared at Viv and then she nodded. "You're right. I haven't done anything wrong. It'll be all right. They'll figure out what happened and I'll be released."

"Atta girl," I said. Although honestly I wasn't sharing their optimism. Something felt wrong about the entire situation, but I couldn't put my finger on it. There was a bell inside the cell to alert the custody sergeant that he was needed. I rang the bell. I was more than ready to get out of the boxlike room. The door swung open and I glanced out past the sergeant who was waiting for us to exit.

Down the hall Alistair was pacing back and forth. He looked agitated and I could tell that whatever news he was getting it was bad. I fervently hoped it was for a case other than Ariana's. When he jammed his phone into his pants pocket, I noticed Alistair's usual cheerful demeanor was grim. He gestured for Stephen and Trudy to follow him and they strode toward us.

He stopped in front of Ariana. I glanced between them and knew that this was official business. Stephen and Trudy must have sensed it, too, because they moved in close as Viv and I stepped back to give them room.

"There can only be—" the custody sergeant began and I interrupted.

"Yes, we know, only two visitors," I said. "We're going."

"Please don't," Ariana said. She gave Alistair a wary glance. "Something tells me I'm going to need all of the friends I can get right now."

Alistair rubbed a hand over his eyes. "I've just learned that the police will be moving forward with pressing charges against you in the murder of Anthony Russo."

"What?" Stephen roared. "That's preposterous. It's a trumped-up charge to get media attention. What do they need—a bigger budget to get new panda cars or something?"

The custody sergeant stiffened and opened his mouth to protest but Alistair didn't give him the chance.

"Easy, Stephen," Alistair said. He rested his hand on his friend's shoulder as if trying to calm him down. Stephen shook it off. He balled his hands into fists and glared around the station as if looking for someone to take his temper out on. "Losing your cool won't help Ariana at all."

"Bloody hell, I know that, but this whole thing is a lot of tosh," he said. "The man was a drunkard, everyone knows that. He probably climbed up on the sodding roof and fell."

"Perhaps," Alistair said. The tone of his voice led me to believe that the police had evidence to suggest it was not that simple.

"What did they find?" I asked. "If you tell us, maybe we can help somehow."

Alistair looked uncertain but Trudy pressed forward. "Please, let us help."

"You might as well tell us all," Ariana said. "It's sure to be on the news, whatever it is."

"The crime scene investigators found a tiny bit of fabric in Russo's fingers," Alistair said. "The lab has matched it to the shirt you were wearing yesterday."

The color, what little there was, drained from Ariana's face, leaving her just a pale shadow of herself.

"But how?" she asked. Her eyes scanned all of our faces as we stood in different levels of shock, watching her. She pushed away from the door. "I didn't do it!"

The custody sergeant moved in between her and us. "Time for you people to move along now."

No one spoke for a moment. The evidence was damning. There was no question about it.

"There's more," Alistair said, ignoring the sergeant who

was now shooing us like we were a flock of ducks waddling in the street. "The detectives found your phone in your flat. There were several threatening texts on it from you to Russo."

Ariana blinked. "But that's impossible. My phone has been missing for days."

We were all silent as we took in this damning bit of news.

"I never threatened him," Ariana said. "Never."

"Of course you didn't," Stephen said. He stepped forward. "Listen, I know you, and I know you could never harm anyone. Now, there has to be a logical explanation for this and we'll find it."

"He's right," Trudy said. She put her arm around her son and reached out to Ariana. "Don't you worry, dear, we'll get this sorted."

"All right, then," the custody sergeant said. "These two can stay but you three go. Now."

"Ariana, we have to go back to the shop," Viv said. "But I am going to work on your wedding hat, and you are going to spend your time in here meditating on your special day. This is all just a load of codswallop and I expect it will be cleared up shortly."

"Thank you," Ariana said. "But I need to pay you."

"Nonsense," Viv said. "It's our wedding gift to you. Right, Scarlett?"

"Absolutely," I agreed. "If you need anything, have Stephen or Trudy call us. I'll be back to visit as soon as I can."

"Thank you." Ariana choked out the words. I could tell she was going to cry, and being the world's foremost sympathy crier, I felt my own throat get tight.

"I'll be in touch," Stephen said. "Thank you."

Trudy was dabbing at her eyes and nodded her thanks as well.

Alistair, Viv and I backed away. It was clear from the frosty expression on the sergeant's face, we had pushed this meeting as far as it could go.

"I'll walk these two out and be back," Alistair said.

Ariana, Stephen, and Trudy nodded. Their faces were a picture of shock and bewilderment. I felt awful for them and the miserable situation they found themselves in.

Alistair glanced at the three of them, and while his face showed no emotion, I could see him clenching his jaw repeatedly. I wondered if he had told us everything he knew or just the important parts. His expression was inscrutable but I saw him glance at Ariana and away and I got the feeling he knew about the pictures.

Given that Stephen was his rugby mate, I wondered if the pictures changed things for him. I glanced at Viv and saw her watching Alistair as well. I knew she was thinking the same thing I was.

She fell into step beside Alistair, catching his attention. "Is there anything we can do?"

He studied her. His lips turned up in one corner in a self-deprecating smile, as if he knew she was only paying attention to him because of the desperateness of the current situation.

"Thank you, but no, I can't really think of anything," he said.

Viv met his gaze and I could see she was working her magic, making his brain turn to mush by giving him her full attention. It was an amazing thing to watch.

"I know I don't need to tell you that things are seldom as they appear," she said.

Alistair's eyebrows rose. He looked from Viv to Ariana and back.

"Talk to her alone," Viv said. "It will make sense, trust me."

Alistair nodded. Viv and I paused by the front counter to retrieve our things.

"If there is anything we can do to help just let us know," I said.

"I will," Alistair said. His gaze lingered on Viv. "I'll be in touch."

Viv and I made our way up the hallway, and I felt as if I were leaving a puppy at the pound. I didn't care what the crime lab had found. There had to be an explanation as to why Russo had a bit of Ariana's shirt clutched in his hand and it was not because she'd pushed him to his death. Of this, I was sure . . . mostly.

We were almost out. The pig pile of reporters was still filling the lobby, but I figured we could squeeze our way around them.

"Ms. Parker, Ms. Tremont, this way."

I glanced to the right to see Inspector Simms standing in a nearby doorway. He waved us over.

"You'll never get through that mob," he said. He glanced at me. "And if they recognize you, it'll be even worse."

I nodded. My notoriety had pretty much faded over the past four months, but I wasn't sure I wanted to risk being the center of attention again.

"I'll show you out the back way," he said. He gave us a small smile. "It's used by all the celebrities."

We followed him down another narrow corridor past several offices, which had their doors shut. I wondered what went on behind the closed doors and then was sort of glad that I didn't know. I'd never been arrested and I wasn't really looking to add that to my curriculum vitae.

"Here you are," he said.

We stopped in front of a door that had a big warning sign on it. It said it was for personnel only and it appeared to be heavily alarmed.

"Are you sure?" Viv asked.

I knew she was thinking the same thing I was, that the last thing we needed was to get busted for trying to commit a jailbreak.

"Sure, just let me deactivate the alarm for you," Simms said.

He pressed a code into a panel beside the door and then popped it open. He stuck his head out and scanned the area, stepping back inside and giving us the all clear.

"Thank you very much," Viv said.

She led the way out and I followed. I don't know what made me do it, but I thought that Simms might be the softer of the two inspectors since he was younger and had gone out of his way to help us out.

"Not for nothing, but Russo was quite a womanizer," I said. "It seems to me there'd be a lot of women with an axe to grind."

Inspector Simms's unibrow moved into the shape of an annoyed vee in between his eyes.

"You don't say," he said.

"I do say," I said. I saw Viv pacing at the bottom of the steps but I ignored her. "I think a jilted lover would have much more reason to do a man harm than a woman who is in love and getting married and about to leave his employ to go and start a new life, don't you?"

"Do you really think this is a matter you should be concerning yourself with, Ms. Parker?" Simms asked. His voice wasn't unkind so much as it was firm.

"I just—" I began but then I rethought it. I had been planning to go for a plea on Ariana's behalf but now I felt the need to sound more decisive. "Ariana is innocent."

"And your extensive experience as a homicide detective has caused you to deduce this?" Simms asked. Now he sounded straight-up exasperated. I couldn't really blame him.

"No, but I do know people," I said. "I've worked in the hospitality industry for ten years. You get to be a good read of people in the service industries."

"You don't say," Simms said. Now he wasn't even trying to hide his sarcasm. Fine, I was going for broke then.

"Just tell me this," I said. "Did the CCTV cameras pick up anyone on the roof with Russo right before he died?"

Pretty much all of London is on CCTV. Some people think this is a shocking invasion of privacy, but given all of the security cameras, traffic cameras and people with cell phone cameras that cover the world, there really aren't any civilized places left that aren't being monitored in some fashion.

Simms looked like he was debating telling me something. I widened my eyes, giving him my most innocently inquisitive look.

"Fine, then," he said. "The press will know soon enough as will the rest of the bleeding world. The portion of roof that Russo fell or was pushed from was a narrow corner that was not visible on any of the area cameras."

Damn. To have footage of someone else up on the roof with Russo would have been the alibi Ariana needed. It couldn't be coincidence that he fell from the one spot on the roof not under surveillance, could it?

It didn't seem likely. So it had to be someone who knew that section of the roof wasn't monitored. And the persons most likely to know that would be Russo, I sighed, and his lone employee, Ariana.

Chapter 14

"Exactly, Ms. Parker," Simms said. Obviously, he saw the concern on my face. "You can see the problem."

I nodded. Oh, yeah, it was crystal clear.

"Thank you," I said.

He nodded. "We'll be in touch if we have more questions for you."

I turned and heard the door shut behind me. Viv was waiting at the bottom of the short flight of steps.

"What was that all about?" she asked.

"I felt the need to point out Ariana's innocence," I said.

"And how did that go?" Viv asked.

"Not good," I said. I told her what Simms had told me as we hiked around the side of the building and back to the main road.

The stiff breeze blowing the traffic fumes at us sent her

hair across her cheek. She hooked her finger around it and pulled it away, tossing her head in the direction of the wind to keep the rest of her hair out of her face.

"Scarlett, I hate to say it, but . . ." Her voice trailed off and I knew she wanted to say the same thing that I had been trying not to think.

"What if we're wrong?" I asked.

She nodded. "Ariana has motive. If Russo was blackmailing her and making her stay on the job, she might have gotten frustrated and shoved him off the roof."

"But why did she tell us about the pictures?" I asked. "I mean, if you were going to kill your boss, wouldn't you make sure you had the incriminating evidence, in her case the naughty pictures, before you killed him?"

We crossed Ladbroke Road and headed back to Portobello Road, passing the three hectare garden that made up Ladbroke Square. Surrounded by wrought iron fences and full of large trees, the communal garden was one of the largest in the area and open only to residents.

"You know, it could have been a crime of passion and Ariana didn't think to get the pictures before she accidentally shoved him to his death," Viv said.

I paused to take in the tall trees, still leafy and green despite the cooler days, as I considered what Viv had said. Her point was valid. A crime of passion would explain why Ariana had told us about the pictures as a preemptive move toward declaring her innocence with what seemed like transparency, but it didn't work for me.

"A crime of passion would indicate that she shoved him off the roof without thinking, meaning that she wouldn't have thought to maneuver him to the one spot where no cameras would see what happened. That seems premeditated to me. Also, why would she tell us about the pictures at all?" I asked. "It makes her look guilty. Why would she do that?"

A woman pushing a double stroller turned into the gate that led into the park. The two girls in the stroller burst out of it as soon as she stopped and began to run across the green grass, chasing a soccer ball that the mother had lobbed out there for them.

Vivian leaned against the wrought iron rail, turned to me and asked, "What do your instincts tell you?"

"That she's innocent," I said.

"Mine, too."

"So we go with that until proven otherwise?"

"Yes," she said. "I think that's best and I'm still going to fix up her hat. If she's innocent like we think, she'll need something to cheer her up and get her through this ordeal."

When we arrived at the hat shop, it was to find a reporter waiting outside. I stopped half a block from the entrance, recognizing the man as one who had accosted me when I first came to London and was still grist for the tabloid mill.

He was paunchy with a gut that hung over his jeans like a loaf of half-baked bread. His curly black hair reached his shoulders and his face was covered in bushy whiskers with no visible effort at grooming.

"Scarlett Parker." He cackled when he saw me. "In the news again."

Before I could respond, he lifted his camera up and aimed it at me. I stood gaping like a boob, but before he could snap a picture, a large black suit appeared in my line of sight. Standing in front of us with his jacket held wide open was Harrison.

"Head inside, ladies," he ordered as he shielded us from the photographer.

"Oy, that's not right," the pudgy-fingered photographer bleated. "You're cutting into my ability to make a living, you prat."

"Make it somewhere else," Harrison said.

I heard the photographer snap a few pictures but he wasn't getting anything but Harrison's coat. Viv and I scurried into Mim's Whims with Harrison right behind us. The reporter was left to stomp out his frustration on the sidewalk outside.

"Get away from the window," Harrison ordered. "I don't trust the little toe rag not to try to get pictures through the glass."

I led the way and glanced back over my shoulder to check that Viv was following. Viv had two bright spots of color on her cheeks and I could tell by the way her eyes were narrowed that she was furious.

Fee was standing behind the counter, watching us with wide eyes.

"All right, Viv?" she asked.

"No," Viv said. "Not at all."

"Watch the shop, Fee," Harrison said. "If that git out there tries to come in, call for me."

"Done," Fee said. She blew a stray curl out of her eyes and

I tried to give her a reassuring smile as we all trooped into the workroom in back, but I didn't think she was reassured in the least.

Viv was banging around in the kitchen so I took a seat at the worktable and waited for her to calm down.

"Can you believe the audacity?" she cried. "He literally jumped us in our front yard. I wish I'd been close enough to knee him where it hurts."

Harrison cringed. "Trust me, it's better that you didn't, assault charges being rather messy and all. He won't linger. Your connection to Russo's murder is tenuous at best. He's just trying to play a different angle than all the rest."

"And dredge up my past in the process," I said with a sigh. "Thanks for blocking him."

"My pleasure," Harrison said. There was something in his voice—affection, protectiveness, I wasn't sure what exactly, but it wrapped around me like a warm fuzzy blanket and I was grateful.

Viv continued smacking cups onto a tray while waiting for the kettle to boil. She was muttering and grumbling and causing no small ruckus with the silverware and dishware. I watched her in silence, knowing that the storm would pass pretty quickly after the first downpour.

When Viv seemed calmer, Harrison turned his gaze on me.

"All right, Viv?" he asked.

She nodded. "Getting there. I can't believe you were ever subjected to that sort of boorish behavior, Scarlett."

"Times ten," I said. "Believe me, that just now was nothing."

Harrison frowned and I found it sweet that it bothered him that I'd been dogged by the paparazzi before.

"It should be a crime to harass people like that," Viv said.

She plunked a plate full of cheese and crackers and apple slices onto the table. I realized I was starving and tucked into the food while she poured boiling water into the teapot. She covered it and brought it over to the table and took the seat beside me.

Harrison sat across the table from us, watching while we ate. I got the feeling he was waiting for something. Viv poured out tea, but he waved off her offer. That was my first clue that something was amiss.

Naturally, he chose to speak right as I took my first sip of tea.

"Would either of you care to tell me what you were doing at the jail today?" he asked.

I choked and sputtered in surprise while Viv gave me two strong thumps on the back.

"Gees, Harry, could you hold the interrogation until after I've swallowed?" I asked.

"I'm not interrogating, I'm just asking a question," he said. He looked at Viv. "Alistair sent me a message that you two were there. He thought it was very kind of you."

I watched Viv over the rim of my cup. Whatever she was thinking, she was keeping it close to the vest. Her eyes stayed down and her expression didn't alter. There was no tightening of the lips, no eyelid flicker, nothing. She gave away not the slightest bit of how she was feeling.

"It was business," she said. Her voice was brisk as if using a bossy tone would make it inarguable. "Ariana's wedding is coming up fast, and if she wants her mother's hat, I needed her approval."

"I see," Harrison said. He watched her but said nothing. Not for the first time I wondered at their relationship. Not whether one of them was pining for the other romantically but more that there was a closeness, a level of understanding, between them that I didn't have with either of them.

In their own way, Harrison and Viv were closer than Viv and I. After Mim had passed away, I had a very difficult time coming back to Notting Hill, quite simply because I missed her. It had put an unfair burden on Viv to keep our business up and running, which had caused her to lean on Harrison. They had forged a close friendship over the past few years, and I occasionally felt very much like the third wheel on a bicycle built for two when it was just the three of us.

Yes, I felt guilty that while I was in Florida cavorting with a married man, who in my defense I thought was separated, Viv had been here dealing with the loss of Mim all by herself. It was incredibly selfish of me not to realize before how hard it must have been for her to lose her mentor and be thrust in charge of the shop she had loved since we were girls. Maybe that was why my life had imploded, to help me get my head out of my butt and be a better person. Harsh but effective.

"Alistair seems very competent," Viv said.

I looked at her like she had conked her head on something hard.

"Competent?" I asked. "There are loads of words that leap to mind when I think of Alistair Turner and competent is not the first one."

"Is that so?" Harrison asked. "Do tell what other adjectives spring to mind?"

"He's handsome, intelligent, handsome, kind, handsome—" I would have continued but Harrison interrupted me.

"I get it," he snapped. "You think he's handsome."

"Not only that," I protested.

"Clearly, it's his most remarkable feature in your eyes," Harrison said. "You mentioned it three times."

He sounded a teeny bit jealous, which made me want to smile, although I didn't.

"No, I'd say his most remarkable feature is that he seems quite smitten with Viv," I said.

Harrison raised his eyebrows and I nodded. "He looks at her like she's afternoon tea and he's parched."

"He does not," Viv protested but I noticed she looked embarrassed and pleased at the same time.

Harrison looked at me and said, "So you remarked on his handsomeness three times not for your benefit but . . ."

"To make sure Viv noted it," I said. "She can be very obtuse sometimes."

"Not when she's sitting right here listening to you, she can't," Viv said. She gave me an exasperated look.

"What happened at the station today?" Harrison asked.

Viv and I exchanged a look. I knew she was wondering what I thought about telling Harrison what Ariana had told us. I shook my head, pretending I was shaking out my hair, and Viv glanced away. I knew she had received my message. No, I didn't want to tell Harrison because how could he not tell Alistair and Stephen? I got the feeling she didn't agree but she didn't say anything.

"I'm sure Alistair told you everything that happened," I said.

"Maybe," Harrison said. "But I'd really like to hear your perspective."

The boy was cagey. I had to give him that.

"We think Ariana is innocent," I said. I figured it was best to lead with a strong sentiment.

Viv nodded. "Yes, we do. We both felt it."

"Felt it?" Harrison asked. He looked like he wanted to roll his eyes but he didn't. Instead, he helped himself to an apple slice and a cheese slice, put them together and bit into them.

"Instincts shouldn't be dismissed," I said. "Both Viv and I feel that Ariana is innocent."

"Russo was a drunken, womanizing letch," Viv said. "There had to be scores of jilted lovers who would happily shove him off a roof if the opportunity presented itself."

"Andre also said he was a gambler," I said. "That can get a person a broken arm or leg. Maybe he couldn't pay his gambling debts and the person who came to collect thought that a fall off of a building would teach him a lesson but he died instead?"

Harrison looked thoughtful. "I suppose anything is possible."

"I have every confidence in Inspectors Franks and Simms," Viv said.

"But?" Harrison asked.

"No buts," Viv said. She looked serenely about the workroom. "Scarlett, it occurred to me the other day that we should probably consider hiring some models to do a fashion shoot of the spring hats."

Harrison shook his head as if a fly were buzzing in his ear.

"Spring is eight months away," he said.

"Yes, but Fee and I are already working on the spring line and we could use the boost of publicity," Viv said.

This was a conversational segue out of nowhere. I couldn't imagine why she was thinking about this now. Unless . . .

"We really can't afford anyone who is cutting edge," I said. "We'd have to find people whose careers are more waning than waxing."

"You're really talking about business now?" Harrison asked. "You've spent all day at the jail, talking to a client who might very well be convicted of murdering her playboy boss . . . oh."

Viv and I both looked at him.

"No," he said. "Absolutely not. I forbid it."

Chapter 15

"Forbid it?" Viv repeated. She blinked at him as if he had belched and not excused himself.

"You heard me," he said. His voice was a low, gruff growl. Why are men so attractive when they are being bossy and pigheaded? It really puts a girl at a disadvantage.

"Lucky for us, you're in no position to forbid anything," I said. "Viv's idea is top notch. We can canvass Russo's clients under the guise of hiring them to model for us and maybe one of them will let something slip."

"No, no, no," Harrison said. "That's not how it works. Assuming it was one of Russo's clients, what do you think they're going to say when you badger them into modeling for the shop?"

"I expect they'll say, 'Oh, and by the way, I did it, I pushed Russo off of a building,'" I said without smirking.

Harrison let out a pent-up breath as if he were exhaling hot air in order to keep his internal temperature from reaching full-on combustion.

"You can't stick your nose into the investigation," he said. "Aside from the fact that you could hamper the actual detectives' work, if one of his ex-girlfriends is Russo's killer, then you're making yourself a target by nosing around too much."

Viv and I looked at Harrison for a moment and then Viv looked at me.

"So I was thinking we could start with the most recent girlfriend and work our way backwards," she said.

"Excellent," I said. "I'm sure a simple search on the Internet will give us a good starting place."

Harrison shoved his hands into his hair. "This is madness."

"Maybe," I said. "But this is your friend's bride. I would think you'd want to help him out by proving his future wife is innocent."

"If she is," Harrison said. "Let's look at the facts, shall we?" He lifted a hand and ticked them off on his fingers as he spoke. "She was alone in the building with Russo when the tragic event occurred. He fell from a spot only a person familiar with the building would know was not under surveillance. He was clutching a piece of her blouse, the very one she was wearing on the day he died, in his cold dead hand."

"Heard about that, did you?" I asked.

"Yes," he said.

"It's circumstantial," Viv said. "There's no way to know how he got that scrap of fabric in his fist."

"Sure there is," Harrison said. "He probably made a mad grab for her shirt trying to save himself when she lured him to the rooftop and pushed him to his death."

"Does Alistair believe that it means she pushed him?" Viv asked.

"He believes in his client," Harrison said. "But that's his job as her defense attorney. We're not her defense and need to view this situation through logical, rational reasoning of the facts."

"This isn't a math equation," I argued. "There is no two plus two equals four. Human beings are involved and human behavior is rarely logical or rational."

He looked at me and pursed his lips in a way that I knew meant he was unhappy. "You can say that again."

"Listen, Harry," I said. He frowned at me.

"Harrison," he corrected but I ignored him.

"All we're going to do is talk to some of Russo's exes and see if they know of anyone who wanted him dead," I said. "That's not going to mess up any investigation or put us on anyone's list to be rubbed out."

"Exactly," Viv said. "I'd say we're actually helping the inspectors, you know, by sorting their suspects for them."

Harrison groaned and put his head in his hands.

"Aw, chin up, Harry," I said.

He looked so beaten down that I couldn't help but throw my arm over his shoulders and give him a bolstering half hug. He lifted his head and I realized I was too close. Too close to the lovely bay rum smell of him, and too close to his bright green eyes, which seemed to see deeper into me than I was comfortable with.

"Harrison," he corrected me again. His mouth curved up in one corner in an irresistible smile.

I dropped my arm and scooted back a few steps. That made his smile deepen into a full-on grin as if he knew I was too aware of him.

"All right, I can see I've lost this battle," he said. "But there will be conditions."

I glanced at Viv. I hadn't really thought we'd win Harrison over, and I could tell by the look of surprise on her face, she hadn't thought so either.

"What conditions?" she asked.

"You don't talk to anyone alone," he said. "In fact, if it can be managed, I think I need to be in on all meetings."

"Won't that seem odd?" I asked.

"Given that I'm part owner in the shop, no," he said. "We'll explain that I'm taking an interest in the business. I can always portray a batch who just wants to flirt with the pretty models, if need be."

"Oh, I like that," Viv said.

I did not.

"Please try to schedule these things in the evening," he said. "I do actually have to show up at the office, or they might give my corner spot away."

"I doubt it," Viv said. "You're far too clever for Carson and Evers to let go. You could work from the back of an elephant in India and I'm sure they'd be okay with that."

Harrison shrugged. I knew he was a financial genius and worked for the same company that his uncle had. Essentially, they were business consultants who were hired to come in and help businesses increase their profit margins.

I had always assumed that the businesses he helped were like ours but I was beginning to see that Harrison operated on a much bigger scale than our modest millinery. Viv seemed to understand so much more about what he did than I did. Again, I got the feeling that Harrison and Viv knew more about each other than I knew about either of them, and I didn't like it.

"All right, Ginger?" Harrison asked.

I realized they had been talking and I had missed the entire conversation.

"Sorry, I drifted there for a bit," I said.

Harrison looked sympathetic. "I imagine the memory of finding Russo like that will pop up on you now and again."

Great, now I felt like a heel. Here I was mulling over the hierarchy of our friendship, and Harrison thought I was thinking about the dead body I'd seen just twenty-four hours before. And there was no way I could deny it without seeming like a horrible person.

"Yeah," I said. See? I am a horrible person, aren't I?

Viv and I spent the rest of the afternoon checking out Russo's list of exes. It was impressive, to say the least. His dating laundry list ran the gamut from lower royals to lingerie models and anything with a pulse in between.

Some were easy to dismiss since they were out of the country and a few seemed more like friends than girlfriends and then there was Mariska Kravchuk. An off-again, on-again lover, she and Russo lit up the tabloids every time they got back together and every time their relationship imploded. Accusations of cheating, public intoxication and vandalism riddled their breakups. It made for some very juicy reading.

I was working in the front of the shop, searching for articles on my tablet computer, while Viv and Fee worked on hats in the workroom. For what had to be the fifth time in the past two hours, I popped my head into the workroom to share what I'd found.

"Listen to this," I said. "According to the *Daily News*, attorney to the stars Anthony Russo and Russian model Mariska Kravchuk were splitsville following a nasty spat on the roof of the Shoreditch House."

"I thought you had to be a member to get into the Shoreditch House, yeah?" Fee asked.

"You do, but I'd be willing to bet Russo is a member since his client list is pretty much filled by their membership roster," Viv said.

"Really not the point," I said. "I think we need to talk to Mariska. And because she's a model, we could absolutely use the front that we want her to model hats for the shop."

Viv nodded. "It could work."

"Great. How do we go about that?" I asked.

"I don't know," Viv said. "Usually, when I'm working in high fashion, the designer hires me to work up hats to complement their clothes, and they already have their models picked out."

"Who would know how to do this?" I asked.

We were all silent for a moment and then the lightbulb over my head flashed. It must have been bright enough for the others to see because as one all three of us said, "Andre."

* * *

"My reputation is at stake," Andre said. "Whatever you do, do not tick off Mariska. I can't have her complaining about me."

"You hate fashion photography," I said.

"Yes, but I don't want to burn any bridges there," he said. "It's lucrative and you never know when you'll need to diversify your income streams."

Viv and I exchanged a scandalized look.

"You have been spending entirely too much time with Harrison," she said.

Andre waved her off.

"I don't need to tell you that fashion people judge you by what you're wearing, so dress appropriately," he said.

I glanced down at my outfit, a pretty soft brown wool skirt with a moss-green cashmere sweater and my favorite knee-high brown lace-up boots.

"No, you're not wearing that," he said to me. He looked at Viv. "You're fine, better than fine. That's perfect."

"What's wrong with my outfit?" I asked. I glanced at Viv's royal blue A-line dress with black patent knee boots and a snappy black trilby.

"Nothing if you're a first-time schoolteacher. Lose the Peter Pan collar," he said.

I fingered my collar. "I thought it looked cute."

"You were wrong. Besides, cute is for baby ducks," he said. He turned back to Viv. "Fashion models like gifts, so you should bring her a hat from the shop."

"Go change," Viv said. She actually waved me away. "I'll pick a hat whilst you're dressing."

I stomped up the stairs to our flat like a high school girl being forced to change into something more appropriate. As I walked into my room, the retina-searing pink walls mocked me. My room was stuck somewhere in 1999, and now that I looked in my full-length mirror, I think it was causing my fashion sense to go backward, too.

I ditched the pullover sweater and Peter Pan–collared shirt and went for a sophisticated sheer floral top in reds and browns with a fitted red jacket over it and kept the boots and the skirt. Take that!

I jogged down the stairs, fluffing my hair as I went. As I skidded into the shop, Viv was just boxing the hat of choice up and Andre turned away from her at the counter and looked me up and down.

"That's my beautiful girl," he said.

Given his faultless sense of style, this was high praise and I beamed at him.

"Which hat are we giving to Mariska?" I asked.

"The black cap with the black blusher and three long black pheasant feathers on it," Viv said.

"Oh, I like that one," I said.

"Me, too, but if Mariska is planning to play the grieving ex-girlfriend, and I'm betting she is, the hat will win her over, for sure," Andre said.

"Right then," Viv said. She looked at me. "You need to wear a hat."

"Why?" I asked.

"Because you're representing the shop," she said. Her critical gaze moved over me. "Oh, I know just the one."

She thrust the hatbox at me and then darted across the

room to the shelves on the opposite wall. Opening the cabinet below the shelves, she dug through the hats in there until she found a floppy-brimmed linen hat in the same rich brown shade as my skirt.

"Perfect," Andre said. "It makes you look like a seventies fashion model."

"Would that be a model in *her* seventies or a model in the *nineteen* seventies?" I clarified.

Andre laughed. "Hippie chic, darling. You've got it going on."

I glanced at my reflection in the nearest mirror. The brown hat did frame my red hair in a flattering way.

"Come on," Viv said with a glance at the clock on the wall. "We're going to be late."

"You'll stay until Fee gets out of class?" Viv asked. "She should be here in fifteen minutes."

"No worries," Andre said. "I bet I sell a ton of hats."

Viv and I gave him little finger waves as we dashed out the door and down Portobello Road.

The rain had lifted and today the sky was blue with big, rolling puffs of white. I inhaled a deep sweet-smelling lungful of air. A few of the trees looked ready to change color and there was a bite in the air that promised fall was on its way and there would be no going back to summer.

I didn't mind. Maybe because my hair matches the temperamental months of autumn, I have always felt a kinship with the season and therefore it's my favorite. I loved the riot of color, the shorter days, and spending time reading by the fire with a hot cup of tea.

"Which of us should do the talking?" Viv asked. "I mean,

I can talk about the hat and modeling, but I'm not sure I can segue into discussing Russo as skillfully as you can."

"I'll handle that part," I said. I had been mulling it over and knew much of it would depend on how we were received by Mariska. I'd dealt with a lot of diva types in the hotel industry so I felt like I was in good shape to take on a past-her-prime Russian model.

We caught the train at Notting Hill Gate and took the District Line back to the Kensington area. According to the directions on Viv's smartphone, Mariska lived in a posh apartment in the Kensington Chelsea area. Walking through her neighborhood, I was suddenly grateful that Andre had told me to change from my frumpy outfit.

"Here it is," Viv said. She stopped in front of a creamy white five-story building that towered over us. "I wonder which one is hers."

A scream rent the air and we snapped our heads up in the direction of the sound. A third-floor window was thrust open and more shouting commenced, punctuated by a water-fall of clothes that came raining out the window to splat on the ground at our feet.

"Wild guess," I said. "That one."

A woman's voice, yelling in what sounded similar to what I had studied in my one semester of college Russian, drowned out the noises of the street around us.

"Come on," I said. I had a feeling whoever she was yelling at was going to be chasing their clothing out the door, and if we stood nearby, we could slip right in without having to ring the buzzer.

Viv and I hustled up the walkway to the shallow steps.

Sure enough, a man wearing just a towel, and looking unshaven in an artistic rather than a homeless way, burst through the front door. I grabbed it before it could swing shut. He glared at me but kept on going, muttering to himself and waving his hand, which clutched the remainder of a cigarette, emphasizing his words like a symphony conductor's baton.

Viv followed me inside and I looked at the mailboxes on the right. Sure enough, 3B had the label *M. Kravchuk* on it. I glanced up at the stairs.

"You don't think she's going to roll any furniture down on us, do you?" I asked.

Viv glanced back out the front door. "No, I think it was just his clothes, which he is trying to put on. I expect he'll be leaving once he's dressed."

"Excellent. I don't want to be taken out by an armchair."

I led the way up the stairs, which wound up in a square. I was winded on the second level. Don't judge. Being a shop owner doesn't leave me as much time to exercise as I'd like. I took comfort in the fact that Viv was as winded as I was. They were very steep stairs.

We were halfway to the third floor, leaning against the wall and gasping, when Viv asked me, "What did Harrison say about our visiting Mariska?"

"Huh?" I asked. "I thought you told him."

"Me? Why would I tell him? You're the one with the special relationship with him."

"It's not special," I protested. "We're just friends."

"Oh, please, I see the way you two look at each other," Viv said. "There is definitely something there."

"Well, obviously, I'm aware of him," I said. "But you know I'm not dating anyone until I've been single for one year. So there is nothing special there. Besides, if anyone should have told him, it's you because you're such old friends. If anyone has a special bond, it's you two."

I wondered if Viv heard the note of jealousy in my voice. Then I wondered if I was jealous of Viv for having something special with Harrison or jealous of Harrison for being closer to my cousin than I was.

"What a lot of tosh," she said. "Harrison and I do not have a special bond. We've just known each other for a long time and he was very supportive right after Mim died."

"Did the two of you ever . . ." I knew the answer was no but sometimes a girl just likes to hear it anyway.

"Surely you are joking," Viv said. "Do we really seem like we've ever been a thing?"

Viv was as scatterbrained an artist as I'd ever met and Harrison was a buttoned-down businessman so, no, I couldn't really see it between them.

"No, but you do have a closeness," I said.

Viv gave me a look of understanding. "You have a lock on Harrison's affections. You don't need to worry about him and certainly not with me."

"Maybe not, but he knows you better than I do," I said. "I get the feeling that you tell Harrison things that you don't tell me."

So it was that I was jealous that Harrison was closer to Viv than I was, I realized with a blast of ill-timed self-awareness.

"No, I don't," she said. She was blustering. Whenever Viv blustered, she was fibbing.

"He does know more about you than I do," I accused. "It's so obvious in the way you two communicate without saying anything."

"Now you're just being absurd." Viv panted. We were on the last set of stairs and still climbing.

"Then tell me what is going on with you," I demanded. "Are you secretly seeing someone? Is that why you seem to have no interest in dating? I mean, Alistair practically drooled on your shoes and you didn't even bat an eyelash."

"Bloody Nora!" Viv cried. She stopped as we reached the third-floor landing and glared at me. "Do we have to do this now?"

I crossed my arms over my chest. "It's as good a time as any since we're both going to be in hot water when Harrison finds out about this, much like he knows everything else apparently."

"Oh, no you don't. Do not try to manipulate me with guilt," she said.

"Oh, my God," I cried as a horrible thought smacked me right upside the head. "You're involved with a married man, aren't you? That's why you don't talk about him."

Viv threw up her hands, which made the hatbox dangle precariously over the railing. "You have lost your mind!"

"She is not only one," a thickly accented voice spoke from the door to our right. The woman standing there glanced at the hats on our heads. "You are Vivian and Scarlett, the hatmakers."

Interrupted in mid-tiff by one of the most stunning women I had ever seen, I was rendered speechless, a rare event, to say the least. Given that the woman was wearing nothing but a see-through chemise and high heels, not only was I vocally impaired but I didn't really know where to look either.

Viv runs a pretty tight emotional ship so it wasn't surprising that she didn't react at all to the half-naked woman before us, but I noted that her gaze was on the door frame over the woman's head and she seemed incapable of conversing as well.

Finally, I nodded and Mariska gave us a small amused smile.

"Won't you come in?" she asked, and without waiting for our answer, she turned and strode into her apartment.

Chapter 16

"Well, this looks promising," I said to Viv.

She glowered and strode past me into the lavishly decorated apartment.

A mishmash of animal print upholstery on ornately carved, gilded furniture was the first thing that registered, followed closely by the realization that the walls and plush carpet were purple. It was sort of like walking into Barbie's house of horrors. My eyes started to water and I recommitted to getting my pink bedroom back at our flat painted posthaste. I did not want anyone to react to my room like I was reacting to this, as in I felt a bit queasy, which could have been the climb up the stairs, and cross-eyed, which was definitely because of the décor.

A man's shout sounded from outside. Mariska dashed over to the open window. A shouting match ensued between her and the man below, presumably the one who'd gone out in just a towel. Viv and I stood awkwardly in the sitting area.

I was about to offer to come back another time, when Mariska turned away from the window and stormed into another room. She came back carrying a lone boot. It looked to be very expensive, a black suede ankle boot with a patent leather toe. Yeah, and she tossed it right out the window.

There was a yelp from outside so her aim had been true. She gave a vicious laugh that was definitely not the laughing with you so much as the laughing at you sort and then she slammed the window shut while the man was still shouting.

"How you say in English?" she asked us. Then she said, "He is asshat!"

"That works," I said.

She strode out of the room again. This time she returned with a purple robe over her sheer gown. She tied the belt and gestured for us to sit down on the zebra-striped love seat. She took the leopard armchair across the glass table from us.

"Jean!" she cried.

A woman in a black housekeeper's uniform came through a door at the far end of the room. Before the door swung shut behind her, I could see that it was a kitchen.

"Yes, Miss?" she asked.

"Tea, please, for me and my guests," Mariska said.

"Yes, Miss," Jean said and disappeared.

"Please excuse." Mariska paused as if searching for the right words. "My lover and I had strong difference of opinion."

It took every bit of self-control for me to keep my eyebrows from rising up on my forehead. Seriously? If that was a difference of opinion, what did an actual argument look like and were weapons involved?

"We understand," I said. Viv's face remained serene and I suspected she was working to play it as cool as I was.

Now that we were all seated, and the drama appeared to be over, and Mariska was dressed, somewhat, I took a moment to study her. She had a thick mane of chestnut-brown hair that stopped at the middle of her back, her figure was amazing with long legs and lush curves, and her face was beautifully sculpted with a square jaw, full lips, a tiny nose and large eyes framed by thick lashes and arching brows. If ever there was a woman to give a girl low self-esteem, Mariska was it.

When I looked more closely, however, I could see that the corners of the eyes had the beginnings of crow's-feet and that her jawline had the tiniest bit of droop to it. Her looks were beginning to fade. Modeling was not going to be an option for her much longer even if she got the mandatory nips and tucks. There were too many young, beautiful women out there who didn't need to be enhanced, and they were going to take over her runways and magazine covers.

What an awful moment that must be for someone who'd spent her life getting by on her looks, to realize that in the end, she was just like everyone else. I imagined the only reason Mariska was willing to meet with us was because Viv's reputation as a milliner was up there with the big names, and because the tide was turning and she was desperate for work.

I noted that the enormous pictures on the walls were all of Mariska and her fashion magazine covers. This was a good indicator that the best way to get to her was through her own vanity. No, I was not above it.

"We are so very honored to meet you," I said. I put both of my hands over my heart and bent forward a little in obeisance.

Out of the corner of my eye, I saw Viv move. Thankfully she was facing me and not Mariska because her appalled look was hard to misinterpret even to the most self-deluded.

"My cousin has brought you a little something as a token of our appreciation," I said. "We know you are very busy being a worldwide celebrity and we so appreciate your time."

"Give it here," Mariska said.

She held out her hands like a child in anticipation of a present. Vivian handed over the hatbox and Mariska plopped it onto her lap and ripped off the lid. She plowed through the tissue paper and lifted out the black hat.

"It is not purple," she said. She twisted her lips as if considering whether this was okay or not.

I saw Viv press a fingertip to her right eyelid and I suspected she was trying to push back an eye twitch. I ignored her.

Mariska rose and strode over to one of the many mirrors in her apartment. I hopped up and followed her. She put the hat on her head and turned her face from side to side to study the effect.

"I don't know," she said.

"If you'll allow me," I said.

Used to people dressing her and doing her hair and makeup, Mariska waved her hand for me to go ahead. I knew Viv's designs almost as well as she knew them herself, so I was confident I could place the hat on Mariska to its best advantage.

I moved the hat off the center of her head and lowered

the blusher so that it draped becomingly across Mariska's face, ending just under her cheekbones, thus the reason it is called a blusher. The long black feathers curved around the back of her head in a wicked arc, and when Mariska turned her head, I saw her smile in approval.

"I like it," she announced.

She kept it on her head and strode back to where Viv was still seated, but thankfully, no longer holding her finger to her eye.

Jean reappeared with a tray. She set it down on the glass table and I glanced at it in confusion.

"Would you like me to pour, Miss?" Jean asked.

Mariska waved her off. "I will do it."

Mariska leaned forward over the tray. I exchanged an alarmed look with Viv. This was not tea, at least not any tea that I had ever partaken before.

Mariska took the stopper out of a pear-shaped crystal decanter of clear liquid. She poured a healthy amount into a very thin, heavy-bottomed shot glass.

"What sort of tea is this?" Viv asked.

Mariska gave us a wicked grin. "Russian."

"Is that . . . um . . . vodka?" I asked.

"Of course," Mariska said. "I call it tea to be polite." She made a *bleck* face. "I loathe that weedy-tasting stuff. This is good potato tea."

She laughed and then handed us each a shot. She raised her glass to us and said, "*Za milyh dam.*"

"*Za milyh dam,*" Viv and I repeated.

To be clear that I wasn't drinking to my own demise, I asked, "What does that mean?"

"To lovely ladies," Mariska said. Then she downed her shot and laughed.

Viv sipped hers and I did the same. It was icy cold but it still burned my throat and my eyes watered as I tried not to choke.

I glanced at the tray to see if there was anything to help put out the fire. A shallow round bowl sat in another bowl filled with ice. Black globules filled the bowl and I felt a sigh well up inside me. Caviar, naturally.

Mariska took a small plate and scooped the caviar onto it and then added several toast points. She added a delicate mother-of-pearl caviar spoon to each plate. She handed one to Viv and another to me.

I put my shot down on the table and mimicked Mariska as she put a tiny amount of the caviar on a toast point and nibbled at it. The expression on her face was pure bliss.

I'd have eaten a deep-fried cockroach if it would have helped assuage the fire in my throat. I put a dollop of caviar on my toast and bit into it. It was like taking a bite out of the sea. The delicate beads burst in my mouth with just a hint of salt and fish. Delicious. I took another sip of my vodka and felt it warm me from the inside out so I downed the whole shot. Mariska immediately refilled it.

I glanced over at Viv and noted that she was enjoying her "tea" as much as I was and Mariska refilled her glass as well. Maybe it was the vodka, but I was beginning to like the Russian model. She had style.

"Your lover," I said. "What did he do?"

Mariska licked a fish egg off her thumb. She lifted the

blusher of the hat off her face but didn't take the hat off. She made an impatient face.

"He is a man," she said as if that was explanation enough. Truthfully, it was.

"Toilet seat up?" I guessed.

Mariska looked at me in surprise and then she laughed. "More his zipper down."

Viv got it before I did and cried, "Cheating bastard!"

"Yes!" Mariska said and then downed another shot of vodka. She smacked the glass on the table and looked at us expectantly. Viv and I downed our shots.

I shivered as the alcohol hit like a punch to the gut. Then I loaded up a toast square with caviar and stuffed it in my mouth. If this was how Russian women dealt with heartbreak, count me in.

"Men are pigs!" Viv declared.

Mariska liked that and she filled Viv's glass again as well as her own. I kept mine in my hand, sensing that this could go very badly if the warm fuzzies I had going on were about to cut loose. I had been known to sing very loudly when I imbibed too much, and I didn't think that would be very professional, now would it?

Viv and Mariska toasted each other again. Viv was weaving on her seat with a silly smile plastered on her face. I had the feeling our window to gather information was rapidly closing.

"Speaking of pigs, how about that Anthony Russo?" I asked.

Mariska lowered her glass as if in slow motion. Her eyes snapped with temper and I felt the first stirrings of uh-oh.

"Why do you say that name to me?" Mariska asked.

I gave a careless shrug, paying more attention to my caviar than her.

"He's been on the news, and a client of ours is in jail for his murder," I said. "From what I've heard, he was a very bad man."

Mariska looked directly at me as if trying to take my measure. I gave her what I hoped was a tipsy smile but it felt more like one made out of fear, you know, when you're trying to humor the crazy person so they don't use their mother-of-pearl spoon to scoop out your innards.

"He was a wicked man," she said. "This I know."

"How?" I asked.

"He was my lover," she said. "Before . . ." She gestured to the window so I assumed she meant before the towel guy.

"Oh," I said as if this were news.

I glanced at Viv. She was being a glutton with the caviar. Etiquette dictates a person should have no more than two full teaspoons. Viv looked like she was about to start licking the bowl. I nudged her with a well-placed elbow to the ribs.

"What happened?" I asked Mariska.

She munched some caviar and then waved her spoon in the air. "Drugs, alcohol, gambling, he owed Bruno O'Malley a small fortune."

I pretended to know who Bruno O'Malley was when really I had no clue. Instead I filed the name away for later.

"Did he cheat on you, too?" I asked.

"Worse!" she yelled and slammed her glass down on the table. I jumped but she ignored me.

"He was in love with someone else," she said.

My foggy brain tried to slap itself sober. This could be important. Must get more details.

"Who?" I breathed. I tried to make it sound as if we were girlfriends sharing confidences, but Mariska was a wily one.

"No, no, no," she said. "That information is valuable."

"You would sell the person's name to the tabloids?" I asked. "How do you know they'll pay?"

Mariska poured herself another shot. She offered the decanter to both Viv and myself but Viv was reclined on the seat with her head back, looking like she was going to slip down the zebra-striped upholstery into a puddle on the floor and I shook my head, not wanting to end up on the floor beside her.

"I cannot say," she said. Obviously, pleased with herself, however, she leaned forward and said, "The expression, a picture is worth a thousand words? I think it is wrong. I think a picture is worth a million pounds even if it is of a dowdy little secretary, yes?"

She laughed and poured herself another shot of the ice-cold vodka. She tossed it back and went to pour another, offering the decanter to me. Again I shook my head. My insides were feeling icy cold, and no amount of fiery vodka was going to thaw me.

Chapter 17

I wanted to grill Mariska for more information. Was she talking about Ariana? Did she have a photograph? What did she know? How did she know it? My head was spinning with questions and alcohol.

Unfortunately, Viv chose that moment to reject both her caviar and her vodka. Clapping a hand over her mouth, she scrambled to her feet and ran across the room, banged through the door that Jean had come from and threw up in Mariska's kitchen sink.

I sat frozen on the couch. I had been in a lot of awkward social situations in my lifetime, but listening to my cousin puke while our hostess sat calmly sipping her vodka was a new one.

"Probably I should go check on her," I said.

Mariska waved her hand in a shooing motion, dismissing me.

I hurried after Viv and found her, pasty pale and shaking like a leaf. Jean stood beside her, wiping Viv's mouth with one cloth and holding another one to the back of her neck.

"How're you doing there, champ?" I asked.

Viv muttered something unintelligible that I suspected was not flattering toward my person.

"I think she's knackered," Jean said, giving Viv an assessing look. "Best to go home and sleep it off."

"Thanks, Jean," I said. "I haven't had to clean up after a drunk since working in a hotel back in the States."

Yes, this was me trying to build a rapport with the staff.

"You were in the service industry?" Jean asked.

"For years," I said. "The things people do. Oh, do I have stories."

"I have a few myself," Jean replied and laughed. The wrinkles in the corners of her gray eyes deepened. "I'm a cook and a housekeeper, so you could say I service all of the rooms in the house."

Our gazes met and I smiled. I liked Jean. She was built sturdy but with curves that weren't completely hidden by her serviceable plain black dress. Her ash-blond hair was in a knot on the back of her head, which was fashionable instead of dowdy.

She looked to be close to forty, and there was a faint scent of tobacco on her clothes. I got the feeling that she had been in the service industry her whole life and that nothing people did really surprised her anymore.

"Please tell me that my cousin isn't the only guest of

Mariska's this has happened to," I said. Yes, I was fishing. Since I couldn't grill Mariska, maybe I could glean some information from Jean.

"No, I've been with Miss Kravchuk for eight months now, and I've seen a fair few making pavement pizzas," Jean said.

Ah, yes, "pavement pizza," a euphemism for "hurl."

"Mariska can hold her alcohol," I said. I shook my head, still trying to get the effects to wear off.

"Just as well since she can't hold a man," Jean said. She clapped a hand over her mouth. "Oh, forgive me, that was unpardonably rude."

"But funny." I laughed. Jean visibly relaxed. "Mariska told me that very thing about herself so you're fine. She said the man before this last one was in love with someone else. I can't imagine that was easy to take."

"Anthony Russo," Jean said with a nod. "The one that took a dive off of his roof; he was a piece of work. Made your cousin here look as sober as a parson."

"I'd heard he was a ladies' man," I said.

Jean nodded. "Oh, they fought about that more than anything else. He started coming around again, though, over the past few weeks. Miss was devastated when she heard about his death. I think they might have been trying to reconcile."

"Did this new guy know that?" I asked. "He might have been jealous."

"Pish!" Jean waved a hand. "That one is a useless git. Likes Miss for her money, he does. He's just an arm charm for her so she doesn't have to go to events alone."

"What's his name?" I asked.

"Jarrett Reichs," Jean said. "Fancies himself an artist."

It was clear from her tone what she thought of his art.

"Jean!" Mariska called from the other room.

We both jumped with a guilty start. I reached out and squeezed Jean's arm. "It was a pleasure talking to you."

"Likewise," Jean said. "Excuse me."

I watched her hurry through the doors. I glanced down at Viv, who was resting on the edge of the sink. She looked like she'd been stretched on a hat form and left to dry.

"Ready to go?" I asked.

"More than," she said.

"Can you walk?" I asked.

Viv pushed up off the counter and gave me a half-lidded stare. "I'm drunk, not incapacitated."

It seemed one and the same to me, but I knew better than to argue the point.

"After you then," I said.

As we breezed through the living room, Jean was tidying up the remains of the food and drink, while Mariska reclined on a divan in the corner with Viv's hat pulled down over her eyes.

"Thank you for your hospitality," I said.

Mariska looked half asleep and waved at me, although again, it seemed to be more of a shooing motion.

"We'll be in touch about the photo shoot," I said.

Mariska's hand dropped and she emitted a loud snore. I met Jean's gaze briefly as Viv led the way out the door. I gave her a cheery wave and she waved back.

As I closed the door, I raced forward to help Viv down the stairs, fearing that she might misstep and bounce all the way down to the bottom. She did not. She did, however, start singing "Chain of Fools" at the top of her lungs. Have I mentioned that Viv can't carry a tune in a bucket?

We reached the second-floor landing, where a woman poked her head out of door 2A and yelled, "Quit your cat-erwauling! Ten years I've lived in this building and never have I heard such goings-on."

"Sorry," I said. Viv was still singing. "So very sorry."

I hoisted Viv's arm about my shoulders and hustled her down the steps. The last thing I needed was for the lady in 2A to call the police. I pushed through the front door, drag-ging Viv with me. As soon as I got to a busy street, I glanced about for one of the city's black cabs. It was worth the expense just to get back to Notting Hill as fast as possible without having to drag Viv.

Near the bus stop a black cab was parked. Its yellow taxi light on the front was illuminated so I hailed it and the driver zipped right over. I shoved Viv into the back and the driver looked from her to me and I shrugged.

"Tea didn't agree with her," I said.

He shot out into the traffic as if terrified that Viv was going to be sick in his cab. She wasn't. She was still singing, an excellent sign that she was feeling better but was still drunk.

The cabbie dropped us right in front of Mim's Whims. I paid him while he opened the door. I took Viv's arm and steered her to the shop. Fee was behind the counter when we entered and her eyes went wide at the sight of Viv.

"What happened?" she asked.

"Too much fermented potato," I said. "I'm going to get her upstairs to sleep it off."

"Need a hand?" Fee asked.

"I think I've got it," I said.

"Home sweet home," Viv cried. She broke out of my hold and wobbled across the room to hug Fee. "You're gorgeous, Fiona, did you know that? Isn't she gorgeous?"

"Yes, she's beautiful," I said. "Now will you please go pass out?"

My patience was getting sliver thin as my potato juice had worn off ages ago and now I just wanted to lie down and nap for a day or two. Of course, I couldn't do that because I needed to get in touch with Alistair immediately and warn him about Mariska's ominous comments about a picture being worth a million pounds.

Of course, I hadn't really worked out how I was going to tell Alistair this without letting on that Viv and I had sought Mariska out. As Ariana's defense attorney, he would undoubtedly be less than thrilled with our information gathering and, like Harrison, would probably call it meddling, which it most definitely was not.

"You might want to hustle her upstairs, yeah?" Fee said.

"I'm trying," I muttered. I caught Viv by the arm and tried to lead her to the door. She got distracted by a display of hats that she felt the need to rearrange; honestly, it was like trying to herd a cat.

I gave Fee an exasperated look, but she jerked her head toward the door. Her eyes were wide with warning. I glanced over and there was Harrison, pulling the door open, with Alistair right behind him.

Chapter 18

"Uh-oh," I said. "Viv, move it."

This time I grabbed her hand and pulled her across the shop.

"Scarlett, what is wrong with you?" she cried. "Ugh, I feel dizzy."

She stopped and dug in her heels. She bent over at the waist and I was afraid she was going to be sick again.

"Fee, trash can!" I cried.

Fee lifted the round steel can we kept behind the counter and raced it over. She plopped it on the ground in front of Viv, who stood up and laughed.

"Gotcha!" she cried. Then she clapped her hands and laughed. It was my turn to have a nervous twitch in my eye.

"Viv, you need to go upstairs and sleep it off," I said. My voice had the growl of a junkyard dog and still she ignored me.

"Sleep what off?" Harrison asked as he joined us.

I sighed. I had a feeling the cat was out of the bag or more accurately the drunk was out of the bottle.

"Hello, Harrison," Viv said with a sotted smile. "Oh, and look, it's the handsome Alistair."

Alistair nudged Harrison with an elbow. "See? I'm the handsome one."

"Oh, you're both handsome," Viv said with a flirty vivacity that was atypical of her. "It's just that Harrison is spoken for."

"Are you now?" Alistair asked Harrison.

"Yes, by Scarlett," Viv said.

"Oh. My. God." I closed my eyes but I couldn't stop the feeling of my face burning with embarrassment.

"Yes, er, ah, are you feeling all right, Viv?" Harrison asked.

I opened my eyes to see him looking at her and not me. Thank goodness.

He looked at her in concern and she giggled, which made his eyes narrow. "Oh, wow, you're pissed."

"No, I'm sotally tober," Viv said. She swayed on her feet. Alistair laughed and Viv grinned at him. "We were at a business meeting."

My shoulders slumped with relief. Viv hadn't outed us with her liquor-loosened tongue. If Harrison thought this was just a business meeting that had gotten out of hand, then I would be spared the lecture because, boy howdy, could he ever lecture, and even with his charming accent, it tended to run unpleasantly long.

Harrison turned to look at me. His green eyes were studying me closely. I was too relieved to be embarrassed any longer.

"And how are you, Scarlett?" he asked.

"Sober as a virgin Bloody Mary," I said. "Mostly."

"Oh, sure, don't include me in the good meetings," Fee muttered. The door opened and two customers walked in. She gave me a pouty look before going to help them.

"It was Mariska's fault," Viv said.

I cringed and Harrison crossed his arms over his chest in his inquisitorial stance.

"Mariska?" Alistair asked. "Please tell me it was not Mariska Kravchuk."

"All right," Viv said. She stepped in front of Alistair and walked her fingers up the front of his crimson necktie in a decidedly provocative move. "It was not Mariska Kravchuk."

"Oh, good, that would be problematic," Alistair said.

"Really?" I asked. "In what way?"

Harrison's electric green gaze was still boring holes into my head, so I tried to ignore him and concentrate on Alistair, but he was looking smitten with Viv's sotted charm.

"She's Russo's ex," Alistair said. "She's critical to determining who else might have wanted Russo dead. If you and Viv went there and talked to her, the investigation could be compromised."

"And that would be bad?" I asked.

"Terrible," Alistair said, and then he giggled as Viv's fingers tickled his neck.

"Compromised," Viv said. "That sounds like a bit of naughty, doesn't it?"

I gave Viv a disgusted look. I was never letting her drink vodka again. Ever.

"Tell him, Ginger," Harrison said. To his credit, he gave me a sympathetic look.

"Tell me what?" Alistair asked.

"It was Mariska Kravchuk," I said. I clapped my hands over my face and peered at him through my fingers.

Alistair gave Viv a horrified look. "You told me it wasn't Mariska Kravchuk."

"Because you told me to tell you that," she said.

"I'm getting a headache," Alistair said.

"Me, too," Viv said. Her lower lip pooched out but I wasn't feeling an ounce of pity for her.

I lowered my hands. "It's my fault. It was my idea to try and get some information out of her under the guise of hiring her to model hats for the shop."

Alistair walked Viv over to a nearby chair and helped her sit down. He gestured for Harrison and me to join them.

"Sit and tell me everything," he said.

And so I did. I spared no detail, including the naked artist lover in the towel, Viv's puking into the sink, my talk with Jean, Mariska's knowledge of Russo's gambling debt to Bruno O'Malley and her insinuation about Ariana and a photograph being worth a million pounds.

Alistair was quiet for the entire story. He listened so intently I had a feeling he was even hearing the pulse of quiet in between my words and extracting as much information from those as he was the story itself. When I finished, everyone was silent except for Viv, who was snoring.

"You know," Harrison said. "I have a feeling the girls got more information out of Mariska than any detective or attorney would."

Alistair rubbed his chin with the back of his hand.

"You might be right," Alistair said.

He glanced at Viv and his eyes softened and a smile played on his lips.

"She is something else, your cousin," he said to me.

Viv's hat was askew, her long blond curls draped across the back of her seat. There was a faint flush to her flawless skin, and her eyelashes fanned across her cheeks, thick and dark. Her hands were folded demurely in her lap while her feet were crossed at the ankles. She was a beautiful woman and I could see that Alistair thought so, too.

If she wasn't my cousin, I was pretty sure I would dislike her intensely. As it was, I adored her. I always had and I always would, which was probably why I was feeling very hurt that she was shutting me out of her personal life.

"I suppose it's bad form to let her sleep it off down here," I said.

"I'll carry her up," Alistair volunteered.

He stood and scooped Viv into his arms before either Harrison or I could react. I glanced at Harrison and he shrugged. I tried to give him the look that asked if this guy was okay. But he just gave me a confused look in return. Men are so dense.

"If you'll follow me," I said to Alistair.

I walked across the shop to the door that led upstairs. I opened it for Alistair and then followed behind him. Had it been me, I would have huffed and puffed and stopped every other step to catch my breath and shift Viv in my arms and most likely would have dropped her and then left her to sleep it off in the middle of the steps.

Alistair, however, strode up the steps as if Viv were no heavier than a sack of groceries—pretty annoying actually. Once we reached our flat, I led him through the sitting room and the great room to her bedroom. As I opened the door, I hoped it was neat. I had no wish to embarrass her. But I needn't have worried. This was the grown-up Viv's room. The bed was made, there was no clutter, no underwear on the floor or clothes strewn on the furniture. I made a quick mental note to go clean my own room later.

Alistair set her gently down on the bed. He carefully took the hat off her head while I slipped off her shoes. I dropped the shoes on the floor and took her hat from him and put it on her dresser. When I turned around, it was to find Alistair pulling up one side of the blankets and covering Viv with it.

His face was very kind and I felt myself liking him even more than I already did, which was quite a lot actually. He had an honesty and empathy about him that I didn't see in many men his age. Living in an urban environment, most men seemed to be preoccupied with acquiring the best job, the most money, the hottest girl, the fastest car and the most expensive flat.

While handsome and a snappy dresser, Alistair reminded me of Harrison, who also seemed to have more depth to him than other men in his demographic. It made sense that they were mates.

I hoped Stephen was cut from the same cloth. If what Mariska had said was true, and a photograph did come to light with Ariana and her boss, then he was going to have to be a very strong man to stand by his bride, especially if she remained suspect number one. Since the police already had Russo clutching a bit of the fabric of her shirt, a photo like that would box her up for good.

We slipped out of Viv's room and I closed the door behind us. As we were crossing the flat, Alistair cleared his throat. I took it to mean he had something to say.

"Yes?" I asked.

"Beg pardon," he said. "This is awkward but I can't help wondering and Harrison is utterly useless . . ."

"If Viv is seeing anyone?" I asked. I paused in the sitting room. I decided to take his measure. "Tell me, what exactly are your intentions?"

"My what?" he asked. He looked caught off guard as if he suspected I was teasing but didn't want to be wrong and offend me.

"You heard me," I said. "Exactly how many dinners does a girl get out of you before you expect her to come across?"

Alistair goggled at me. "Well, I . . . that is . . . I suppose it would depend . . ."

"Upon?" I prompted him.

"If she wanted to or not," he said.

Good answer. I crossed my arms over my chest and walked around him in a circle, studying him from the back of his head—no sign of a bald spot—to the heels of his shoes—just as shiny as the front—and everything in between.

"Where did you study?" I asked.

"Cambridge," he said.

"Not Oxford then," I said. "Huh."

Yes, yes, I know the Oxford-Cambridge rivalry is as big

as the Harvard-Yale rivalry in the States, but I wanted to see if he could take it. To his credit, he looked a bit miffed but said nothing. I continued to circle him.

"What would you say your earning potential is?" I asked.

He glanced at me with one eyebrow raised. "Better than a milliner's at any rate."

"Fair enough," I said. "How about your last relationship? How long did it run?"

"How is that . . ."

"It speaks to your ability to have a long-term situation," I said.

"Oh, I don't know," he said. He tossed back his chin-length black hair while doing his mental math. "Nine months."

"Hmm, the gestational period for a baby," I said. His eyes bugged out, and I had to glance away to keep from laughing. "Speaking of, do you have any—"

"Offspring?" he interrupted. "No!"

"You're quite sure?"

"Yes!"

"Do you own or rent your residence?" I asked.

"Ginger!" Harrison boomed from the doorway.

I held up my wait-a-minute finger at him and looked at Alistair. He was grinning now. He had caught on that I was teasing—mostly.

"Own," he said. "It's a charming flat just down the block from Harrison's place."

"Good to know," I said.

"Ginger, what are you about?" Harrison asked.

"Job interview," I said. I looked at Alistair and smiled. "You'll do."

He tipped his head at me. "Well, thank you, I think."

"Unfortunately, I can't answer your question," I said.

"Does anyone want to tell me what's going on?" Harrison asked. He glanced from Alistair to me, but we ignored him.

"You can't?" Alistair said. He sounded surprised.

"No," I said. "And it's very aggravating to me that I don't know the answer because it's not for lack of asking."

"Curious," Alistair said.

"Not off-putting?" I asked.

"No, 'intriguing' is the better word," Alistair said.

"If you find out the answer, you will let me know?" I asked.

"If you give me a good reference," Alistair said. He was grinning now.

"Done," I said. I held out my hand and we shook on it.

Harrison stood there looking at us as if we were both mental. I figured if Alistair wanted him to know he'd been asking about Viv, he would tell him.

Alistair didn't say anything but moved past Harrison to go back downstairs. "I'd best be off. I want to see Ariana and talk to her about what Mariska said. If there is going to be some nasty press, she's going to want to warn Stephen and I need to know how to combat it."

"Please give her our best," I said. "Tell her that I'll try to visit her as soon as I can."

"I know she'd appreciate it," Alistair said. "I imagine things are about to get pretty rocky."

Alistair led the way down the stairs, and Harrison and I followed. I wondered if I should have left a glass of water and some Nurofen tablets on Vivian's nightstand. Then

JENN McKINLAY

again, it served her right if she had a headache. What was she thinking, trying to go shot for shot with Mariska?

"I'll call you later," Harrison called to Alistair as he headed for the door.

Alistair waved at us and at Fee, who was ringing up a sale, before striding out the door. As soon as it swung shut behind him, Harrison turned to me.

"All right, Ginger, I've been more than patient. Start explaining," he said.

Chapter 19

"Of course," I said. I began straightening the display of floppy-brimmed linen sunhats in front of me. "What did you want to know?"

"For starters, why did no one inform me that you were going to talk to Mariska today?" he said. "We had an agreement."

"Oh, that was an accident," I said. "Viv and I figured it out when we got to Mariska's. I thought she had called you and she thought I had called you."

"But neither of you did," Harrison said.

"Sorry about that," I said. "But it was an honest mistake."

"All right, I'll give you that but just this one time," he said. "And only because nothing horrible happened to you. Did it not occur to you that the man in the towel, what was his name—Jarrett Reichs—could have been dangerous?"

I gave him a rueful glance. "Well, there really wasn't any need for a weapons check, if you get my meaning."

He ran a hand over his face. "Reichs could have come back with a knife or very bad friends. Think, Ginger, if he is Mariska's lover and if what the housekeeper Jean said is accurate, he could very well have killed Russo to keep him from stealing Mariska away from him, especially if she's his meal ticket."

I shivered. Okay, I hadn't thought of that.

"He's an artist; maybe Andre knows him," I said.

"Maybe," Harrison said. "But you don't go near him."

I felt myself bristle. I really don't like being bossed around.

"Don't have a wobbler," Harrison said. "We had a pact. Remember? No one does anything without a partner."

I supposed I could have protested again that today was an accident, but given that Harrison hadn't loomed over me or bellowed at me, I figured if he could let it go, so could I. Then I realized, much to my dismay, that I sort of missed his looming.

I must have looked fretful, because Harrison took my hand and gave it a squeeze.

"Don't worry, Ginger," he said. "Alistair is the best defense attorney in town. If anyone can help Ariana, it's him."

I squeezed his fingers back. It was a rare moment of connection between us, and it made me feel warm from the inside out. So, naturally, I had to ruin it.

"I know, Harry," I said. "I have complete confidence in Alistair."

"Harrison," he corrected me. "I'm delighted that you have such faith in my friend."

His tone was sarcastic and I knew I deserved it. I actually felt bad about it, but I was trying to maintain a healthy boundary. I had a long way to go to make it a year without a boyfriend, and I couldn't have Harry of the pretty green eyes messing that up for me.

"I also have faith in Ariana," I corrected him. "She's innocent. I just know it."

Harrison said nothing but his eyes were kind. I knew he was thinking the same thing I was. If she was innocent, why was Russo clutching a scrap of her blouse? If she was innocent, why was there a picture of her doing the nasty with Russo? I had no answers just a gut instinct. I hoped for all our sakes it was right.

The afternoon edition of the newspaper made my gut ache. There it was in all its black-and-white grainy glory, a picture of Ariana in bed with Anthony Russo. Page one. Despite the bad angle and lack of focus, it was obviously Ariana, wearing little more than a smile and a few black bars across her privates, courtesy of the censors. I felt a little queasy at the sight of it, but like everyone else in London, I read the accompanying article and my innards got more pinched and shriveled with each innuendo-laden word.

Stephen had been arrested for punching out an overzealous reporter—boy, could I relate—but he was let out pending further investigation. I hoped it was the same troll who had been pestering me. I could only imagine what his mother, Trudy, was thinking, given how much she adored Ariana.

Viv and I both called Harrison but we got no reply. I figured he was busy, trying to help Stephen. We left text messages but didn't expect to hear back from him anytime soon.

"This is a nightmare," I said.

"No doubt," Viv said. "But it's not over yet. Just because she slept with him doesn't mean she killed him. Relationships are complicated, and people sometimes do things we don't expect or understand."

I looked at her. Despite her three-hour nap, Viv was still pasty pale from our "tea" with Mariska Kravchuk. I supposed she could be feeling philosophical from our day's adventure, or perhaps there was a deeper meaning to her words. I didn't bother questioning her because I knew she wouldn't say more. Very annoying.

Instead, I wondered if Mariska had known the article was coming out today. Maybe she had cut her lover loose because she didn't want to share what she'd been paid for the photograph.

Perhaps the vodka and caviar with us had been her way of celebrating her ill-gotten gains and we'd just had the misfortune to be there to join her. Of course, the article in the paper did not name the source for the photo, but I knew it was Mariska and I planned to tell Inspectors Simms and Franks, if Alistair hadn't already.

I had no doubt that Harrison and Alistair were tracking down Jarrett Reichs. Being so close to Mariska, I imagined he had to have stories to tell, especially if she had dumped him. Another possibility would be to talk to Jean. I had a feeling she could talk more freely away from Mariska. I was tempted to try and get in touch with her, but Mariska would want to know why I was contacting her housekeeper, and it could get ugly if she thought I was trying to poach her, which if I made enough money, I absolutely would.

Where did that leave us? There were other ex-girlfriends we could go see, but given that Mariska had been meeting with Russo, she seemed the likeliest suspect of them all.

Compulsive cleaning is always an excellent way to manage a brain on overload, at least for me. While Fee and Viv worked on hats in the back, I cleaned the front of the shop in between customers. I was on my hands and knees cleaning out a low cupboard that was full of fascinators when Fee came up behind me.

"What did you find there?" she asked. She reached over me and lifted up one of the frothy confections to study it more closely. It was essentially a hair clip with purple feathers and a black poof of organza with purple crystals glued into a diamond shape in the center of the black fabric. It was very art deco.

"Oh, wow, these are the hats made by my predecessor," Fee said.

"There was an apprentice before you?" I asked. I hadn't even known about Fee until I'd gotten here.

"Yes, her name was Mara," Fee said. "She was the one who talked me into applying for the apprenticeship here, since she was leaving to move to Paris."

"How long did she apprentice here?" I asked.

Fee scooped up the three other hats I'd found tucked in the back of the lower cupboard and took them over to the main counter to look at them more closely.

"Just a semester," Fee said. "But she said that she learned so much from Viv that it was the best hat-making experience she'd gotten, including school. Naturally, I applied right away."

I stood staring at Fee, watching her blow the stray corkscrew curl out of her eye, as a thought formed slowly in the back of my mind, shifting on its feet until it could step into the front of my brain.

And then, just like that, I knew that the person to talk to about Anthony Russo was the woman who'd had Ariana's job before her. Whoever had been Russo's assistant would know who he had angered to the point of wanting him dead.

I left Fee with the hats and grabbed my computer tablet from the back room. Russo was an entertainment lawyer and in a weird way a sort of celebrity himself. It shouldn't be that hard to track down old articles that might mention who his assistant was.

An hour later I was still slogging through old news bits, looking for a name. Finally, the name "Naomi Ames" popped up in an article about Russo being arrested for trashing a hotel room with the rock band that was his client.

It said he was bailed out of jail by his assistant, Naomi Ames. There was no additional mention of her but I hoped it would be enough. I did a quick search on "Naomi Ames" but found nothing. There was, however, Naomi A. Hutchins listed. I called the number. I had no idea what I was going to say because it seemed highly unlikely that she was the one I was looking for.

"Hello," a woman answered. She had a soft voice with a refined accent.

"Hi, this is Scarlett Parker, I was calling to speak with Naomi Ames."

"Speaking," the voice answered. "Although it's Naomi Hutchins now."

I sucked in a breath. Could this be her?

"Mrs. Hutchins, did you once work for Anthony Russo?" I asked.

"Who are you?" she asked. Her voice was no longer soft but rather had grown so cold it could have blown in from the Arctic.

"Scarlett Parker," I said.

"I got that the first time," she said. "What I want to know is how did you get this number, and why are you calling me?"

"I looked you up on the computer," I said. "And I'm calling because my friend Ariana Jackson has been implicated in the murder of Anthony Russo, and I don't think she did it."

"You're not a reporter?" she asked. She sounded wary.

"Hell, no," I said. "I was the one who found Ariana with her boss's body. I don't think she's guilty but the evidence suggests otherwise."

"And you think I can help how?"

"Tell me about Russo," I said. "What sort of man was he? Who would want him dead?"

"You're not asking for much," she said. Her sarcasm was not lost on me. "The list of people wanting him dead is only slighter shorter than the list of people he shafted."

I heard a child crying in the background.

"Hold on," Naomi said. I heard her speaking softly on the other end. The crying stopped and then there was the sound of furniture being moved.

"All right then," Naomi returned. "My toddler is coloring now, so I have a minute or two. I have to say between keeping up with this one and the bun in my oven, I had no idea a body could get this tired."

I made sympathetic noises, but truly, I couldn't imagine it. Not even a little.

"When you said Russo shafted people, what did you mean?" I asked.

"Oh, all sorts of things," she said. "He used to have me bill people for phone calls he never made, motions he never filed; truly, he was an amoral bastard."

"Did any of his clients ever catch on?" I asked.

"A few," she said. "But whenever he got caught, he refunded the money and claimed it was a clerical error, blaming it on me in other words. I tell you, I couldn't wait to leave."

"Do you think he did the same thing to Ariana?" I asked.

"I'm sure of it," she said. "She called me a few times after she first started. I told her to get out of there, but she said she couldn't."

"Did she tell you why?" I asked.

"No," Naomi said. "I just assumed she needed the work."

I paced the shop, looking out the window to watch people walking up and down Portobello Road. A young couple was holding hands, laughing with each other, and I felt a pang of sadness. That should be Ariana out there, laughing with Stephen as they looked forward to their wedding.

"Why was he bilking his clients?" I asked. "Was he that desperate for money?"

"Gambling debts," she said. "He was a compulsive gambler. He bet on everything. He even lost his Jaguar once over the color of a woman's panties."

I was silent for a moment. I mean, there was no way I could unhear what she had just said. Not knowing what to say, I scanned my brain but came up with nothing.

I needn't have worried. Naomi had warmed up to her subject and started telling me all sorts of sordid details about Anthony Russo that quite frankly I could have lived without knowing.

"He was hooked on prescription meds," she said. "That was problematic with his drinking."

"Huh," I said.

"Also, he did enjoy shagging his clients, and it didn't really matter to him if they were married or not," she said.

She told a long story that involved a married woman, an irate husband, a bet for twenty thousand dollars on a horse race and Russo being found on the front steps of his house overdosing on pain pills for which he did not have a prescription. By the time she'd finished her story, I was convinced that someone had probably offed Russo to do the world a favor. Unfortunately, that brought Ariana and all of her substantial reasons to do him in to mind.

"Naomi," I interrupted her, stopping her from telling another story. "Who do you think killed Russo?"

She puffed out a breath and I knew she'd been giving the matter considerable thought.

"Assuming it's not Ariana," she said, "and I really don't think it's her, despite the unfortunate story in the paper."

"Unfortunate" being the nice term for a royal shredding in the press.

"Bruno O'Malley seems the most likely suspect to me," she said. "Despite the drama and chaos and lack of ethics, the only time I was actually scared on the job was when O'Malley showed up to collect payment from Russo, who didn't have it."

"He frightened you?" I asked.

"I really thought O'Malley was going to kill him," she said.

"Have you told the police this?" I asked.

"They haven't contacted me," she said. "You're the first."

"Well, if they do contact you, I'd appreciate it if you didn't mention that I had talked to you," I said. "They might construe it as me being . . ."

"Interfering?" Naomi supplied.

"I was thinking meddlesome," I said. "But same difference."

Naomi laughed and then I heard her toddler squawk about something.

"My adult time is over," Naomi said.

"Thanks for talking to me," I said.

"No problem," she said. "Feel free to call again if you think of anything else. And when you talk to Ariana, please give her my best."

"I will," I said. "I most definitely will."

I ended the call and strode back to the counter. Fee had taken the hats I'd found into the back room, and the shop was quiet. I continued my cleaning. It's good for what ails you.

Bruno O'Malley. His name kept coming up. Both Mariska and Naomi had mentioned him as being a threat to Russo. There had to be a reason. I was still chewing on this when Fee left for the night and Viv came out front to help me lock up the shop.

As I was turning the dead bolt on the front door, two faces appeared in the window and I started. Recognition hit right away, and I pushed the door open for my favorite neighbors, Nick and Andre.

"Dinner, my treat," Nick said. "And I won't take no for an answer."

I looked at Viv. "Do you think you're capable of holding down any food?"

"Are you sick?" Andre asked. "Is it contagious?"

"Only if it's possible to be a carrier for a hangover," I said. Viv gave me a dark look, and I laughed.

"Our Viv pissed in the middle of the day?" Nick asked. "Do tell."

"Over dinner," I said. The caviar had been hours ago, and I was starving.

"I don't know if I can eat," Viv said.

Nick eyed Viv's pallor. "Come on, love, a good meter of pizza at Portobello Ristorante will set you right."

"And they have wine," Andre offered with a wicked wink.

Viv groaned but we grabbed our coats and followed the boys out the door, locking it behind us.

On the walk over, I told them all about our visit with Mariska and then showed them the article in the paper.

Andre gave a low whistle, and even Nick looked serious for a moment.

As we sat at a cozy table for four, Nick looked at me and asked, "Are you quite certain that she's innocent?"

"Yes," Viv and I said together.

Nick and Andre exchanged a look.

"Let's order first," Andre said. "I'm going to need sustenance for the rest of this conversation."

We started with the antipasto to be followed by the Pizza Saltimbocca. Viv had a sparkling water while I nursed my glass of red wine.

Nick and Andre peppered us with questions throughout the meal, and the more we discussed the situation, the more I was convinced that Ariana was innocent.

I took a bite of my rolled pizza stuffed with pancetta and mozzarella and let myself enjoy the comfort of a crunchy crust filled with all that yummy goodness.

"What we need to do"—I paused to swallow before continuing—"is to find a way to interview Bruno O'Malley. If Russo owed him money and couldn't pay, then it stands to reason that he might have had reason to throw Russo off the roof."

"I can make that happen," Nick said.

Viv's head snapped up and we both looked at Nick.

"How?" Viv asked.

"I'll use my connections," Nick said with a careless shrug.

"You most certainly will not," Andre said. "Bruno O'Malley is a criminal and not a petty little thief criminal but a thug who would think nothing of twisting your body into a pretzel if you cross him."

Nick waved an unconcerned hand at Andre. "His bad reputation is overstated, besides off-course bookmakers aren't illegal in the UK. They're regulated. I wonder if I could meet him tonight."

Nick pulled out his phone and began to text someone.

"This is utter madness," Andre cried.

"Hush, it's no such thing," Nick said. He pressed his lower lip with his index finger. "I should dress the part, don't you think? Is a fedora too much?"

"Yes," I said at the same time Viv said, "No."

I gave her an exasperated look. "He is going to meet a bookie. He is not advertising the shop."

She gave me a sulky look, probably more due to her state of under-the-weatherness than my comments about the fedora.

"I can't believe you know Bruno O'Malley," I said to Nick.

"I fixed his girlfriend Dana's overbite," Nick said. He gave a delicate shudder. "Not to gossip about a patient but truly she was a mouth of horrors."

"Not your fault, the tooth hurts," Viv quipped.

"Well done." Nick laughed.

"Must have been quite the molar expedition," Andre said and Viv chortled.

"Be nice," I said. "I'm sure she has fillings, too."

They all turned to look at me with blank expressions. I swear they practiced this when I wasn't around.

"That was funny," I said. "And you know it."

"Scarlett, Scarlett, Scarlett," Nick said as he draped his arm on my shoulder. "Keep trying, love, you'll get it yet."

I rolled my eyes but then Nick's phone buzzed as it vibrated, drawing our attention to it.

"It's Dana," he said. His eyes scanned the small screen and then he grinned. He looked up at us and said, "Let's play."

Chapter 20

Yes, it did occur to me that this was the sort of thing Harrison expected to be informed about, but—there's always a but—since Nick and Andre were involved, it seemed less critical. Viv concurred.

The address of the meeting was for a place tucked away in West London on an inauspicious street that was made up of shops and restaurants with residences above them.

I kept a hand on the back of Andre's jacket for fear that if I let go, I'd be lost and never find my way home. It never ceased to amaze me how many tiny side streets were tucked in among the main roads, creating small neighborhoods that I had never known existed until I was led into one of them.

At the corner, we could see the place that Dana had indicated Nick should meet her and Bruno. I frowned. I had pictured a dimly lit, smoky pub. You know, the sort of place you walk into and it's so dark your pupils dilate into big black marbles, your feet stick to the floor, the bouncer looks like he wrestles bears in his off time, and the smell of cigarette smoke is so thick it coats your skin with tar and ash. Yeah, that kind of place.

"Are you sure you got the address right?" I asked Nick.

"Positive," he said.

"But that's a . . ." I hesitated. Maybe I was seeing things.

"Frozen yogurt shop," Andre said, clearly as bemused as I was.

"See? What can happen in a place called Snog?" Nick asked. "At worst, I'll get a brain freeze from slurping down my yogurt too fast."

Andre did not look relieved at all. If anything, he looked more suspicious.

"You're not actually going in there, are you?" Andre asked. "Bruno's probably on to you, and this is his way of toying with you, making you think you're okay while he's plotting your demise."

"Or maybe he just likes frozen yogurt," Viv countered.

"Who doesn't?" I asked. "Especially with the toppings. I always pile shredded coconut on mine."

"Blueberries and pineapple," Viv said. "It can't be beat."

"Too healthy." Nick made a face. "You have to pick the chocolate yogurt and then double down with chocolate chunks."

"You're seriously debating yogurt toppings when you're about to walk into a setup?" Andre asked.

"Relax," Nick said. He straightened his jacket and cuffs

and strode forward. "Come with me if you're game; otherwise I'll see you on the other side."

"Oh, no, don't . . . how do I get into these things?" Andre asked no one in particular.

He gave me a decidedly dirty look, as if this was my fault, before hurrying after Nick. It had been agreed that Nick and Andre would go in first and meet Bruno, while Viv and I followed a few minutes after, just to keep an eye on things and be backup if they needed it.

"Do you think this is a good idea?" I asked Viv.

"I don't see how it's a bad idea," Viv said. "Nick will chat up Bruno and Dana, maybe place a few bets, feel them out about Russo, and either he'll come out with some information or he won't."

I nodded. It seemed reasonable enough. Still, Bruno O'Malley did have a certain reputation. In a city where off-course bookmakers were legal, he seemed to like to bend the rules to his own advantage, which was the reason he seemed to keep landing back in jail. So long as bending the rules didn't include whacking my favorite neighbors, we were all good.

The night had turned cold and my coat was not nearly warm enough. I was hoping they served hot chocolate in the yogurt shop, but I wasn't betting on it. See what I did there? Betting when we were meeting a bookie? Hilarious, I know. Someday my friends would appreciate my wit.

Yeah, it was bad. What can I say? It had been an extremely long day. Starting at Mariska's with the fermented potato and domestic drama, facing Alistair and Harrison, seeing the bad news in the evening paper, interviewing

Naomi and now watching my friend meet the bookmaker. I was done in physically and emotionally. The lure of a hot cup of tea, a fuzzy blanket and a good book was almost more than I could bear. I had half a mind to turn and walk home, but I had no idea where I was or how to get back.

The streetlights illuminated our two friends as they ducked into the shop on the corner. Viv and I pretended to window-shop. There wasn't much to exclaim over. Then again my lack of enthusiasm could be nerves. Did I really think the boys were in danger? No, but then I hadn't expected to come across the dead body of Anthony Russo when I'd gone to his office either.

After what seemed like forever but was only five minutes by the clock on Viv's cell phone, we set off for yogurt or, in my case, hot chocolate.

We never made it into the shop. Viv reached for the door but it flew open, barely missing us as it slammed back. We both jumped and watched with our mouths hanging open as Nick and Andre raced past us.

I gaped at the man looming in the doorway. He was watching Andre and Nick run down the street while shoveling yogurt into his mouth as if afraid someone was going to snatch it away.

"You'll get a punch up the bracket if I catch you around here again!" he yelled after Nick and Andre, sending yogurt-covered spittle in all directions.

Viv and I backed up several paces while clutching each other close.

I figured this was O'Malley since there wasn't anyone else in the shop except the girl behind the counter, who was more interested in her smartphone than what was happening, and the woman standing next to Bruno, looking like she was about to give him a good scolding.

I gave her a lot of credit. O'Malley was shaved bald, had gauges in his ears, sported scruffy whiskers on his chin and was clothed in black—black leather jacket over a black shirt, black jeans and black boots. Very intimidating.

The woman next to him looked as out of place as a kitten in an alligator pit. She had her hand wrapped around his elbow and was frowning as she whispered something in his ear. Her hair was red like mine, but had more blond in it, and she wore it up on her head in a tidy twist. She wore a tailored blouse and skirt with tights and high heels. She looked like a bank teller. They made a perplexing couple.

"Bruno O'Malley, that was absolutely uncalled for," she said. It might have been more effective if she didn't say it in a singsong baby voice.

Bruno hung his head. Then again, it seemed to work.

"Do you think she thinks she can tame him?" Viv asked me.

"Housebreaking might be the place to start," I said.

"I'm sorry, Dana," he said. He had yogurt dripping off his chin and onto the sidewalk. Dana used a napkin to swab his chin.

"Maybe she fancies him as her big baby," Viv said.

"Shh," I said. I realized Bruno had noticed us and I didn't want to have whatever had happened with Nick and Andre happen to us, mostly because I really hate running.

"Are we done here?" Viv asked.

"Yes," I said. "After all, we did promise not to talk to anyone without taking Harrison with us."

"And we definitely don't want to break our promise twice in one day," Viv said.

Together we started backing away. Bruno took one stomping step toward us, and both Viv and I squealed and turned and ran down the sidewalk after Nick and Andre.

I was wheezing by the time we reached the corner but I kept going. When we were rounding a building to dash up another side street, a hand reached out from the alley and grabbed my arm. It might have been my adrenaline, but I punched out with a fist, connecting with an arm and the person connected to the arm yelped.

I recognized that yelp. It was Nick. I stopped, grabbing Viv and slowing her down.

"Wait!" I cried.

Viv stumbled to a halt. We were both breathing hard. Nick was doubled up, while Andre stood beside him, not breathing heavy but definitely hysterical.

"He's going to kill us and Scarlett will find the bodies," Andre whined. "I can see the headline now, *Young photographer Andre Eisel struck down in the prime of his life.*"

"What am I, a footnote in the story?" Nick asked. "*Meanwhile his lover, a dentist of no importance . . .*"

"Enough, you two!" I cried. "What happened back there? Why did you run out? Did Bruno threaten you? Are you all right? What did he say?"

"Take a breath, Scarlett," Andre said.

"I can't," I gasped.

I bent over next to Nick, trying to catch my breath.

"We had barely walked into the place when Bruno charged us," Andre said.

"That's not what happened," Nick argued. "Dana introduced us. It was going well. Bruno even complimented the job I did on her overbite, and then you"—he paused to jab a finger at Andre—"blurt out that he's so much nicer in person than we thought he'd be and clearly he couldn't have whacked Anthony Russo."

Viv and I both turned to look at Andre.

"You didn't," Viv said.

Andre raised his hands in a dramatic gesture. "It was meant to be a compliment."

"How is backhandedly accusing someone of murder a compliment?" I asked.

Andre stepped up to the corner to peer around the edge of the building as if he expected Bruno to show up and finish what he'd started.

"I tried to apologize," he said.

Nick snorted.

"Worse?" I asked.

Nick bobbed his head.

"I was trying to appeal to his masculinity," Andre said. Now he was beginning to look put out.

"By telling him you bruise easily?" Nick asked. "Honestly."

"Did you get any information about Russo?" I asked.

Nick pushed off his knees and met my gaze. "Yes. He did manage to yell that the police had already asked him about the blighter and that of course he didn't throw him off the roof because how would he get the money Russo owed him if Russo was dead?"

"Oh, that does make sense," Viv said.

"It does, unless the fall was an accident," I said. "Maybe Bruno and company were just trying to scare him."

"Then there would have been a record of the killer coming in," Viv said. "Because they'd have nothing to hide, they'd be on camera."

"Oh, and Bruno also yelled that he had an alibi," Nick said. "But I didn't catch what it was because I was too busy running for my life."

"The police must have verified it, or else he'd be behind bars by now," Viv said.

"What a disaster," I said.

"I'm sorry," Andre said. "I panicked."

"Not your fault," I said, although clearly it was.

Nick snorted so I knew he was thinking the same thing I was. We meandered back to Portobello Road. To make up for missing out on frozen yogurt, we stopped by Zaza, a gelato spot near our shop.

Not that gelato makes everything better, but we'd gone only half a block when the entire Bruno O'Malley episode struck me funny and I couldn't stop the giggle fit that erupted.

"All right, Scarlett?" Nick asked.

I nodded. My red hair was hanging over my face. The harder I tried to squelch the laugh, the more it slipped out sideways, making it sound like someone was stepping on a duck.

"Dear God, she's having a fit," Andre said.

Chapter 21

I did have a fit, a laughing fit, which was contagious. We were all in much better spirits when we reached the hat shop. Nick and Andre bade us a good night and continued on home.

Viv waited while I fumbled with my key. She was watching the street around us and said, "It's much quieter at this time of day. You know, that lull between the shopping and everyone coming home from the pub."

I opened the door and hurried inside to deactivate the alarm. Viv followed.

"I suppose all streets are quiet at this time of day," she said. As subtle as a brick to the temple, she is.

"What are you thinking?" I asked.

"Nothing," she said. She shrugged as if that emphasized her lack of a point.

"Yes, you are," I said. "Spill it."

"Do you suppose if two very bright women were to go to Ariana's place of employment and just take a casual look around, they might find something of interest?"

"The two bright women being me and you," I clarified.

"We are extraordinarily bright," she said.

"Yeah, except for when we come up against fermented potatoes," I said.

She nodded. "Even Superman has kryptonite."

"We can't go tonight," I said. I gestured for Viv to go upstairs so I could reset the alarm. She headed in that direction and I hurried after her.

"I wasn't suggesting tonight," she said as we climbed the stairs to our flat.

"Good because, unlike someone who had a three-hour nap today, I am done in," I said.

"Tomorrow night will do," Viv said. I followed her through the sitting room on to the main kitchen, dining and living area of our flat.

"We have to find out from Ariana how to get in, assuming the police don't still have it cordoned off," I said.

"True," Viv said. "So we visit the jail tomorrow?"

"Yes, I wanted to today but I couldn't manage it," I said.

Viv paused in front of her bedroom door, while I turned to go upstairs to my room. I considered Viv for a moment.

"What could we possibly expect to find that Inspectors Franks and Simms didn't?" I asked.

"I don't know that we'll find anything," Viv said. "I was thinking it more likely that we'll get a feel for what happened."

"Are we claiming to have psychic abilities now?" I asked.

We were both quiet. Viv's blue eyes, which mirrored my own, were wide as we both waited for it, the scent of lily of the valley, which came to us both at the oddest times. It was Mim's scent and I think we both felt that it signified there was some part of her that was still here.

Tonight she did not grace us with her presence, however. The apartment was scent free aside from the lavender sachets Viv used here and downstairs in the shop to keep us all calm. I thought she might need to up the pungency because I hadn't felt much calm since I'd arrived four months ago.

"No, just intuition," Viv said.

I nodded. My intuition had been faulty, especially in the man department for the past few years, but I believed that my moratorium on men might be strengthening my bull cheese detector.

"All right, Cuz, it's a date," I said. I jogged up the stairs, thinking how much my life had changed given that dating used to mean dinner and dancing with handsome men and now was breaking and entering with Viv.

We were dressed all in black, naturally. This was one of the few times that the color suited me better than Viv. She attributed it to my red hair, and she was right. Blondes can wear black but it needs to be accessorized; otherwise the black overpowers. Viv was out of luck as there were no accessories allowed on this mission.

From our black boots to our black knit caps, we were stealth all the way. Luckily, living in a city, no one batted an eye at us or called us cat burglars to our faces, which frankly, I'd been expecting.

Ariana had been pitifully grateful to see us today. She didn't talk much about the fallout from the newspaper article, but I was pleased to see that both Stephen and his mother, Trudy, were there. They seemed determined to stand by Ariana to the end. She was a lucky girl.

Alistair had been going over the next steps of the process with them. He seemed particularly delighted to see Viv, which she ignored and I found fascinating. Alistair was a fine hunk of man, and had I been on the prowl, I would have flirted with him until my flirter gave out. Not Viv. She barely even acknowledged his existence, which come to think of it, seemed to make him even more interested in her. When I did start dating again, that was definitely something I needed to add to my arsenal.

As Viv and I turned onto Russo's street, I was mulling over her resistance to Alistair's charm when a thought struck me. Maybe she wasn't interested in Alistair because he wasn't her type.

"Viv, we're close, right?"

"Don't you know?" she asked. "You're the one who's been here before."

"No, I don't mean to the office," I said. "It's right up there on the left. No, what I meant was, are we, as in you and me, close?"

"Like sisters," Viv said. She did it without hesitating, which gave me the warm fuzzies.

"Well, I want you to know you can tell me anything," I said.

"Oy, you're not going to start harping on my love life again, are you?" she asked.

"You'd have to have one for me to harp," I said. "And no, I was merely going to say that if there is something you care to share, I am one hundred percent nonjudgmental."

"What do you mean?" she asked. Clearly, she was not getting where I was going.

I went for being blunt. "If you prefer girls, that's okay with me."

Viv stopped walking and turned to stare at me. She looked at me as if I had three heads.

"What?" I asked.

"Are you asking if I'm a lesbian?" she asked.

"I'm just saying it's okay if you are," I said.

"Well, that's rude," she said.

"What do you mean?" I asked. "I'm being nice and understanding."

"No, you're not," she said. "You're being horribly nosy, and if I am a lesbian, it is certainly okay whether you say so or not."

"Well, of course it is," I said. "You're intentionally mis-understanding me."

"No, I'm not," Viv said. "You think you get to approve of my lifestyle, well, you don't. It is none of your business if I like boys or girls or—and here's a shock for you—maybe I just like being alone."

"I just wanted you to know you could tell me anything and I would love and support you," I said. It came out in a mumble as I examined the toes of my boots, feeling good and duly chastised.

"I know that," Viv said. "And you know I feel the same way about you. But here's the thing: If you choose to keep your private life private, even from me, I'll respect that and I expect you to do the same."

"Are you mad at me?" I asked.

"Yes. No," she said. "A little."

"I'm sorry," I said. "I just want to see you happy."

"I know that," Viv said. She took my hand and gave it a squeeze. "But you need to stop thinking about my personal life, which is fine, and think about something else."

"But I can't think about men for me," I said. "So I transfer those thoughts to you."

"Well, stop," she said. She began to walk down the sidewalk and then spun around to face me. "And don't start thinking about women for me either. I'm fine just as I am."

She turned back around and followed the address numbers to Russo's house. The feeling that Viv didn't want to talk about her life for a specific reason was dogging me. I didn't think she was fine the way she was; otherwise she'd be happy, right?

I considered her back as I followed her. The stiff set of her shoulders could be due to anxiety given that we were about to enter a place we definitely shouldn't and it might be because we hadn't called Harrison like we said we would. I fully intended to text him on our way out of the building as a sort of cover-my-butt move, I'd already written the text, in fact, and it was just waiting to be sent, but I didn't think that was it. I really felt that Viv was tense because she was hiding something.

Trying to keep a secret or pretending things were a certain way just to save your pride never worked. I know because I lived it. When I look back at the years I dated the rat bastard, I remember that I always had a stomachache.

He would dazzle me with a fancy dinner, a surprise weekend in Jamaica or a sparkly bauble, and I'd think I was crazy to have pangs of unease. I would push my anxiety way down deep, where it would fester into a bellyache that I would soothe with moon pies.

Did Viv have comfort food like mine? That would be a tell, but I couldn't think of anything specific. Was she imbibing more than she used to? Other than yesterday, I hadn't noticed any significant increase, but it was definitely worth watching. How about spending splurges? Maybe she was compulsively shopping. Then again, the way she bought supplies, in bulk, for the hat shop, it would be hard to tell.

"Hurry up," Viv hissed as she reached Russo's building.

As soon as I stepped beside her, she slipped into the shadowy alley and crept along the wall of the building toward the back. Once there, we waited. We didn't know if the police had assigned someone to watch the house or not, but since it was midnight, we knew most of the residents would be asleep while the pub crawlers wouldn't be coming home for a while yet.

From what Ariana had told us, Russo's house was accessible from the back through a security keypad; she'd given us the code. Viv and I agreed that her willingness to help us look through the office just made her seem all the more innocent in our eyes. Of course, it could all be one giant setup and she was going to sic the cops on us and Viv and I would end up in the slammer, but hey, it was worth the risk, right?

"It looks quiet," Viv whispered.

I scanned the alley. It looked dark. Period. Lights were on at a few of the buildings surrounding us but most everyone's curtains were drawn, giving us more of a suggestion of light than any actual illumination.

Viv stretched up on her toes and grabbed the latch on the back gate. Ariana had said that Russo locked his back gate only when he was out of town. I sighed in relief when the latch clicked and Viv was able to pull it open just enough for us to slip through into the yard.

She closed it softly behind us and we stood there, our breath misting around us on the cold, damp air, while we waited to hear a shout or footsteps or something that indicated someone had caught us. There was nothing but the occasional rumble of a bus, the siren of a police car or the muted murmur of someone's television.

"How long should we wait?" Viv asked.

"I don't know," I said. "I'm not exactly an expert at this sort of thing."

I couldn't see her in the dark but I sensed her narrowed gaze aimed in my general vicinity.

"Oh, I'd say you've got skills of the criminal kind," Viv said.

"How do you figure?" I asked. "I've lived an exemplary life."

Again, thanks to the dark, I couldn't see her eyes boring holes into me but I sure could feel them.

"You were sixteen, I was eighteen, and you made me stalk James Thrushgood and his date, Tilly Simpson," Viv said.

"I didn't make you," I said. "You demanded to go with me when I said I was following them to the movies."

"Well, I couldn't let you go by yourself," Viv said. "Who knows what you might have done?"

"Exactly what I did, which is exactly what I planned to do," I said. "I dumped my soda and popcorn over James's head, just like he dumped me for Tilly."

"Isn't that assault?" Viv asked.

"With buttered popcorn," I said. "Which is much less than he deserved."

Viv chuckled. "I've long admired that about you. You always do what you think is right."

"Even when it isn't," I added.

We were both silent, taking in the sounds of the night. I realized that I was across the small backyard from where Russo's body had been found. I was relieved that I couldn't see more than shadows in the dark. I really didn't want to remember the sight of his body broken and bloody on the cobblestones beneath it.

"He died right there," I said.

Viv pressed closer to me, and I felt her hand reach for mine in the dark. Her fingers were icy cold, and I shivered even as I tried to warm her hand with mine.

"Let's get this over with, shall we?" Viv asked.

"Yes, let's," I agreed. Suddenly I was feeling spooked. Not that I thought Russo was haunting the place of his death or anything like that, still I had no interest in lingering.

We went to the back door together. The keypad was just to the right under a small lid. I flipped the cover up and then entered the code that Ariana had given us. I heard the lock pop on the door, and Viv and I exchanged a quick look before I opened the door and pushed it in.

We were in the small kitchenette. I didn't think we'd find anything here so I pushed on through and up the short flight of stairs. We went down the hallway, passing a bathroom, again not really a place I felt the need to check, and into the main part of the house.

"Where should we start?" Viv asked.

"Let's go upstairs," I said. "Russo lived up there; maybe we'll find some connection to Mariska."

We crossed the sitting room and went through the door that led upstairs. It looked like someone had left the hall light on, probably for security, which made it easy to climb the stairs.

Russo's apartment was pretty much exactly what you'd expect of a confirmed bachelor and player: black leather furniture, a large bar along one wall and an enormous television. There were no pictures or personal effects. It could have been a hotel room, except a hotel would be warmer and more welcoming.

We did a cursory check of drawers but there was nothing. Even his magazines were scrupulously maintained with no back issues stuffed in nooks and crannies. His kitchen looked as if no one ever actually used it.

We hurried upstairs to the bedrooms. One was overdone with black satin sheets and a mirror for a headboard. Ew.

The other was clearly a guest room. We concentrated on the icky bedroom. The closet was as meticulously kept as the rest of the house. No pictures, no mementos, no indication that an actual person lived here.

"Gah!" Viv made a gurgling noise from beside the big bed.

"Did you find something?" I asked as I hurried over.

She slammed the drawer on his nightstand before I could glance inside it.

"His porn and sex toy collection," Viv said. Her upper lip was curled in distaste.

"Ew," I said.

"Well, it's the first thing we've found that indicates a person actually lives here," Viv said. "A perverted person but a person nonetheless."

"I don't think all porn is perverted," I said.

Viv gave me a long look. "No."

"What?" I asked.

"I'm not getting into a discussion with you about what is acceptable and what is unacceptable porn," she said.

"What discussion?" I asked. "I'm just saying some porn is not that bad."

"Because you've seen so much porn," Viv said.

"I've seen my share," I said.

"Well, I think it's safe to say we Brits are a little bit more open minded sexually than you Americans, so if I think his porn drawer is unseemly, then you can trust me," Viv said.

This just made me all the more curious.

"Do you have a porn drawer?" I asked. Yes, I was just teasing her.

To my surprise, her face went bright pink, yes, so pink I could even see it in the dim lighting.

"I am not discussing this," Viv said. "Let's go check the offices."

She stomped out of the room, leaving me to follow her.

"I have a porn drawer," I called after her. It's mostly made up of a collection of my favorite erotic novels, but she didn't need to know that.

"Shut up, Scarlett," she said.

When I joined her in the offices below, it was easy to see that the police had done a thorough search of both Ariana's and Russo's offices. Their computers were gone and so were any papers off the tops of their desks.

"I'll take Russo's office," Viv said. She disappeared through the door and I saw her switch on his desk light.

I turned back to Ariana's office. Her windows were right on the street so I didn't dare turn on the desk lamp. Instead, I used the face of my cell phone to illuminate the immediate area.

I sat in her chair and began opening her desk drawers. There wasn't much, and I had a feeling the police had probably taken anything of note, but still it felt like there had to be something—some clue.

Several minutes passed and I became more and more discouraged. Viv appeared in the doorway between the two offices.

"There's nothing," she said. "Nothing that indicates any connection between Russo and Mariska."

"I suppose it was too much to hope for," I said. "Why

couldn't it be a Cinderella story where we find a shoe and the only one it belongs to is Mariska?"

"And what?" Viv asked. "The heel of the shoe matches a puncture mark in Russo's behind where she booted him off the roof?"

"Exactly," I said. "Is that asking so much?"

Viv checked the time on her phone. "The bars will be closing soon and there might be more foot traffic in the neighborhood. We should go."

"All right," I agreed. I closed up Ariana's desk, feeling disappointed.

I followed Viv out, making sure the room looked just as we'd found it. Hanging on a rack by her office door was the blue raincoat Ariana had been wearing when she first came to see us. I took it off the hook and draped it over my arm. At the very least, I could return her jacket to her and the night wasn't a total loss.

Unless, of course, she ended up being convicted of murder and I never got to give her the jacket. Yeah, sometimes I go to the darkest of places.

Viv and I stepped outside and I quickly reset the alarm. Although we hadn't been inside for that long, it was definitely colder out now. I shrugged on Ariana's jacket. I was sure she wouldn't mind.

I tripped on a cobblestone and stumbled into Viv. She caught me and held my hand.

"Easy does it," she said.

We felt our way to the gate and Viv reached up to unlatch it.

She opened it just enough to be able to peek out into the alley.

"It's clear," she said.

I followed her out and quickly shut the gate behind me. We began to work our way down the alley when an angry voice broke through the quiet like a fist pounding on a table.

"What the devil do you two think you're doing?"

Chapter 22

I'm not sure who shrieked louder, Viv or me; probably it was me. Clutching each other, we scrambled backward until the wall was at our backs. I let go of Viv and assumed a fighter's stance.

"Run for help!" I ordered Viv. She looked at me as if I were mental. Not terribly off base of her, was it?

Then Harrison stomped out of the shadows and I felt a surge of really freaking mad blast me right between the eyes. I stepped forward and slapped his shoulder with my right hand while checking my heart rate with my left.

"Damn it, Harry," I cried. "You scared me half to death."

"Harrison," he said. Then he rubbed his shoulder. "Nice punch."

"It was a slap," I said. "A deserved one."

"Really?" he asked. "Because correct me if I'm wrong

but didn't we three agree to tell each other if we went off to do some investigating?"

"I wrote you a text," I said.

"No, you didn't," he said.

"Yes, I did," I argued. I pulled out my phone to prove it to him and found the text message sitting there unsent just as I'd left it. I turned the display to face him so he could see my intentions had been good. Thank goodness I'd had the sense to write the text earlier and save it.

"It helps if you actually send it." He crossed his arms over his chest and frowned. I got the feeling he doubted me and I didn't like that one bit.

"I meant to!" I protested.

"Uh-huh," he said.

"Do you suppose you two could lace into each other elsewhere?" Viv asked. "I don't think loitering around here is very wise."

"Come along then," Harrison said. "I have my car. You can explain yourselves on the drive."

I might have been annoyed with him but I was thrilled that he had his car. I was dead tired and the thought of hoofing it back to the shop didn't work for me.

Harrison helped Viv into the passenger seat and then held the door to the back open for me. I briefly wondered if this was a statement on the hierarchy of our friendship, Viv getting the front because they'd been friends longer, before I realized that I was so tired, I didn't even care.

Okay, I did care but not enough to let it show. I rested my head on the seatback and listened while Viv recounted our night's adventures. Harrison was much more civil with her than with me. He actually sounded admiring of her putting herself in jeopardy to help Ariana any way she could. It made me want to kick the back of his seat, but I resisted.

Instead I buried my hands into Ariana's coat pockets to warm them. There was a single knit glove, odd, and a crumpled bit of paper in the pocket. Curious. I pulled the paper out. I smoothed it on my lap and tried to read it under the passing streetlights. Finally, Harrison stopped at a light and I pulled out my cell phone to illuminate the paper.

It took me a moment, but I realized it was a dry cleaner's receipt. It listed two suits, several men's shirts and a woman's blouse. The name on the receipt was "Anthony Russo."

Now why would Ariana have a dry-cleaning receipt for Russo? I supposed it wasn't out of bounds for her to have to pick up Russo's laundry but it did seem an awfully twentieth-century girl Friday sort of chore. Then again, Russo was a bit of an asshat, so I supposed he might have made her do it for him.

"All right, Ginger?" Harrison asked from the front seat.

I glanced up from the paper. He was just pulling up in front of Mim's Whims. Without waiting for him to get my door, I popped out of the car.

"Never better," I said through the open door. "I just found a clue."

I shut the car door and strode into the shop, barely breaking my stride to unlock the door and deactivate the alarm.

Viv came hurrying after me, but Harrison took his time, obviously not in any rush to hear my news. Well, it would serve him right if I didn't tell him what I'd found.

Harrison locked the door behind him when he entered

the shop. He was looking at me in amusement and it was then that I realized he didn't think I had a clue at all. He thought I was teasing them. Well, I'd show him.

We all moved into the back workroom. Viv grabbed a bottle of Jameson that we kept in the workroom for just such emergencies and three small glasses.

"My nerves are shot," she said. "I need to fortify before we hear about your clue."

She uncapped the bottle and splashed a finger into each glass.

"Your health," she said, and without waiting to clink glasses or anything, she threw the shot back. She sputtered and choked and blinked watery eyes at us, but the color came back into her pale face.

Harrison and I both followed suit with our glasses. I didn't down mine in one swallow but rather sipped at it. I was too excited to share my find to need a drink to calm my nerves.

Viv stared at the bottle as if considering another shot. I moved the bottle away from her.

"Do you really want to repeat yesterday?" I asked.

She shuddered. "No, you're right. I'm good."

"Good, then look at this," I said. I pulled the receipt out of my pocket and put it on the counter.

Harrison and Viv both leaned over and studied it. Viv looked at me first with a frown.

"What does it mean?" she asked.

"That Ariana was picking up his cleaning," I said.

"Not out of order for an assistant," Harrison said. I frowned at him and he added, "Not that I would ever ask someone to do that for me but it's not unheard of."

"It's more than that, though," I said. "Look at the items. It says one woman's blouse."

"Still not following you," Viv said with a shake of her head.

"We have to find out who the blouse belonged to," I said. "It could link Russo to Mariska in a more intimate manner than she's admitting to, which would give her or her boyfriend a motive for murder, and would draw suspicion away from Ariana. Or it could be a new woman altogether, which would give us a whole new direction to go."

"Go?" Harrison asked. "Where are we going? This is a receipt for a blouse. There are a million reasons why Russo had a woman's blouse mixed in with his things."

"Well, tomorrow I'm going to find out the one reason," I said. I didn't know why but I felt sure that this was important.

"How do you propose to do that?" he asked.

"I am going to—" I began but was cut off when Viv plopped her head down on her arms at the table, a soft snore sawing from between her parted lips.

I looked at Harrison and lowered my voice. "I'm going to the dry cleaners first thing tomorrow and I'm going to ask them about the blouse."

"And you think out of the thousands of blouses and hundreds of customers they have, they'll remember this one."

Okay, that was an annoyingly good point.

"It's worth a shot," I said.

Harrison studied me for a moment. Then he looked at the receipt. He looked back at me. "Eight o'clock. I'll meet you out front and we'll go together, you remember, like we agreed."

"You're coming with me?" I asked.

He just stared at me.

"All right," I said. I tried not to wince when I added, "Eight o'clock."

"Do you need help getting her upstairs?" he asked.

I glanced at Viv. She was still snoring but it was more an exhausted sleep than a passed-out stupor so I figured I could rouse her.

"I think I can manage her," I said. "But thanks."

He nodded. Without another word, he turned and left the workroom. I knew he had a key and could lock up after himself, but he hadn't said good-bye, so I assumed he wanted me to follow him.

We navigated around the furniture and shelves of the dimly lit shop. To display the hats, Viv was partial to rounded metal hat stands. She felt that the mannequin head stands were too creepy, and in the shadowy room, I had to admit they would have given me the willies.

We stopped by the front door. Harrison turned the dead bolt and had his hand on the knob. He glanced at me over his shoulder, and asked, "Why?"

"You're going to have to give me more to go on there," I said. "Why what?"

"Why are you and Viv so determined to help Ariana?" he asked. "You don't know her. By all accounts, she is guilty and you have nothing to gain."

It was a fair question. From the outside looking in, there really was no reason for Viv and me to help Ariana. We could give her hat back and wash our hands of the whole unfortunate incident, except I had been the one to find her with Russo. I had seen the horror on her face. I couldn't explain it, but I knew she was innocent. I just knew it.

Then, of course, there was the fact that Viv and I had both sensed Mim's presence when we'd taken the hat from Ariana, and we had both assumed that it meant we should take on Ariana as a client. Was it Mim? Were we having a mass—and by "mass," I mean the two of us—hallucination? Was it just wishful thinking?

Then again, I had seen the way Viv's eyes had lit up at seeing the old hat of Mim's. To refurbish a hat of our grandmother's was such a gift for Viv. I knew how much it meant to her to bring the hat back to its former glory and to have Ariana wear it on her special day. Well, that was the point of the whole endeavor, wasn't it?

"I don't know if I can really explain it," I said. "There are so many reasons to want to help, but the most important is that I truly believe Ariana is innocent."

Harrison gave me a small smile. "I'm glad to hear it. I think the same and I know Stephen believes it all the way down to his core."

"He's standing by her then?" I asked.

"Yes, and his mother, Trudy, is, too," Harrison said. "Which makes up for her own family a little bit."

"Her father and stepmother?" I asked.

"Haven't shown up to check on her or anything," he said. He sounded disgusted.

I thought about my own parents and how they were always there for me even when I made a mess of things. As much as I love London, I had a sudden pang of homesickness for my parents, and the ocean between us seemed awfully big.

"All right, Ginger?" Harrison asked.

The nickname made me smile. Yes, my parents were far away but I had Viv, Fee, Andre and Nick, and yes, I had Harry, too.

"I'm fine," I said and I meant it. I reached around Harrison and pushed open the door. I gave him a shove into the doorway and then I surprised us both by standing up on my tiptoes and kissing his cheek. "Eight o'clock, Harry, and don't be late or I'll go without you."

Then I shoved him all the way out the door, pulled it shut and locked it. I heard him whistling as he walked down the street, and it made me smile.

Chapter 23

When you're not a morning person, eight o'clock is an ugly hour to be functional. I had set my alarm for six thirty and then slept through it. Okay, I shut it off, until some internal clock woke me up at seven forty-five and I had to scramble out of bed in a blind tangle of sheets, twisted jammies and bed head. Not my best look.

Knowing Harrison most definitely would not be late, I threw on a sweater and jeans and lace-up boots. Then I braided my hair and jammed a knit hat on my head. A quick stop in the bathroom for the necessaries and I was jogging down the stairs at seven fifty-nine on the button.

I glanced at the front door and saw Harrison striding toward it, looking disgustingly showered, shaved and suited up like the business mogul he was. He was as heart-stoppingly handsome as always, and I wasn't sure I could bear to have him see me looking like a college kid on a bender, but really, what choice did I have?

I sighed and crossed the room to unlock the door and let him in. If he was surprised by my appearance, he didn't say anything. Instead, he gave me a smile that I took to mean he knew I had just woken up.

Then he hammered the lid on my vanity coffin shut by saying, "You look cute."

Cute! Puppies were cute. Gerbils were cute. I was pre-coffee. I was not cute.

As if reading my mind, Harrison opened the paper sack in his hand and lifted out a cardboard tray that had two hot coffees on it. If I hadn't still been smarting from being called cute, I might have kissed him on the mouth. Good thing I can hold a grudge, yes?

"Thank you," I said.

I pried the lid off the coffee and took a deep inhale. The steam and pungent coffee aroma did more for my sleepy synapses than anything else could have. I glanced at the brew. It was just the right shade of pale brown. I took a sip. It had just the right amount of sugar in it. I gave Harrison a curious glance.

"I pay attention," he said. There was more awareness in his gaze than I was prepared to deal with at the moment so I glanced away.

"This was very kind of you," I said. "Thanks again."

"Not kind at all, Ginger," he said. His voice was teasing. "I know better than to go out there and face the world with a noncaffeinated Scarlett Parker on my hands. It'd be like going out there with a loaded gun."

I laughed because, yeah, it was true.

"Are you ready?" he asked.

I took another long sip. Then I nodded. I had Ariana's receipt in the purse hanging off my shoulder. My sweater was thick enough to keep out the late September chill. I was as ready as I'd ever be.

It took us a short trip on the Underground and a fair bit of walking to reach the dry cleaners in Russo's neighborhood. When we arrived, there were two people ahead of us picking up garments. I finished my coffee while we waited.

The first woman looked to be a housekeeper, wearing a camel overcoat on top of a plain black service dress and sensible black shoes. She wore her hair in a knot on the back of her head and reminded me of Mariska's housekeeper, Jean. She left with an armful of clothes after charging the amount due to her employer's account.

The next person in line was a young businessman, or so I assumed from the navy suit with the slim-cut trousers and pointy-toed shoes. I looked at his hands, manicured; his eyebrows, waxed; and his hair, highlighted. If the word "fop" were still in fashion, he would definitely be one. Now I think they go with the kinder term of "metrosexual." So lame.

Call me crazy, but a dude should look like a dude. I glanced at Harrison beside me. He was handsome, yes, but he had big callused hands, broad shoulders, and a certain knuckle-dragging charm that I found very refreshing. Maybe it's just me, but I think a man should be big and hairy and barely housebroken; otherwise what's the point of opposites attracting?

"Do you have hair on your chest?" I asked him.

Harrison had tipped his head back to finish off his coffee, and I caught him on the inhale. He sputtered and choked, hacking into one fist until the go juice was out of his airway.

"Beg pardon?" he asked.

"Hair on your chest," I said. "Do you have any?"

He glanced around the shop as if trying to figure out where this question had come from. I gestured at the man ahead of us. He was texting on his smartphone, and I could see the man at the counter getting irritated when he didn't stop texting to hand over his claim receipt.

"I'm betting he does a full body wax," I said. I made a face to make it perfectly clear what I thought about that. "So do you?"

Harrison grinned. "If you show me yours, I'll show you mine."

My mouth popped open in surprise. Then I laughed. Yes, he was definitely in need of domestication. No doubt he had hair on his chest. Thank God. Not that I was interested or anything at this juncture but it was good to know for future reference, of course.

"Please, sir, your receipt."

The man behind the counter spoke with an accent I couldn't place, but he looked ready to throttle the *GQ* wannabe in front of us. His thick brown mustache was positively twitching.

When the texter still didn't look up from his phone, the man behind the counter gestured us forward. As I made to move around the young man, he snapped his head up from his phone and shoved me back into Harrison, who caught me around the waist before I fell.

"Oy, I'm next, you cow," the texter snarled at me.

I was about to reply that maybe he should pay closer attention then, but I didn't get the chance. The man behind the counter started yelling at him in a language I didn't recognize, but it was clear he was incensed on my behalf. So sweet.

Harrison, clearly understanding the dry cleaner's language, grabbed the texter by the collar of his jacket and escorted him outside. The texter took one look at Harrison and the fight went out of him. As soon as Harrison let him go, however, the man let loose a volley of verbal abuse that was impressive for all that it was made out of rude hand gestures with no muscle behind them. Harrison made a show of picking some lint off his sleeve and then took two forceful steps in the skinny man's direction. The texter yelped and took off running.

Harrison rejoined us, and the man behind the counter gave him a grateful smile. "Thank you for your assistance, sir. What is wrong with young men today? Do they not know how to treat a lady? I am so sorry he manhandled you, Miss. You are all right?"

"I'm fine," I said. "Really, I didn't mean to cause a commotion."

"You had nothing to do with it," the man assured me. "It was all him." He waved a dismissive hand at the door as if to say good riddance. "Now how can I help you?"

I wished I had a pile of dry cleaning to dump on him. I

hated that a paying customer had run off, leaving just us here asking questions.

"I was wondering if you recognized this receipt?" I asked.

I held out the crumpled piece of paper that I'd found in Ariana's coat and the man took it from me, pulling a pair of reading glasses from his shirt pocket as he did so. He perched the glasses on his nose and scanned the receipt.

"This is one of ours," he said. "Anthony Russo was a longtime customer, but I'm not understanding. Are these items to be picked up, because it looks like they already have been."

"I believe they were," I said. "A few days before Mr. Russo died. What I am wondering is did he often have women's clothes in with his own?"

The man shook his head. "I can't remember. We have so many clients with so many clothes."

I didn't look at Harrison because I didn't want to get an I-told-you-so look from him.

The man scanned the receipt again as if looking for something on it that would trigger his memory. He frowned and glanced up at me.

"One moment," he said. Then he turned around and yelled, "Mahasti!"

"Coming, Father."

A few moments later a young woman came from the back. She was lovely with large brown eyes and long black hair and the same olive complexion and prominent nose as her father.

"Do you remember this order?" the father asked.

The young woman looked at it. She started to shake her head and then stopped.

"Wait. Yes, I do," she said. "There was a coffee stain on the woman's blouse and Mr. Russo was very insistent that I get it out."

"So Mr. Russo brought you the blouse himself?" I asked.

"Yes," she said. "Along with his regular clothing."

"Did he tell you who the blouse was for?" I asked hopefully.

"No," she said. "Only that it was important that it be perfect. It had a tear on the hem that needed mending and he paid me quite a lot to fix that as well."

Harrison and I exchanged a glance. I hadn't expected Russo to be the one dropping off the garments. It was blowing my theory that it was Mariska or another woman to heck.

"Can you describe the blouse to us?" Harrison asked.

Mahasti shrugged. "Sure. It was a pale blue silk with matching pearl buttons."

I sucked in a breath. Harrison looked at me.

"That's what Ariana was wearing the day Russo died," I said.

Harrison looked grim. If the blouse was Ariana's, it changed everything.

"Do you remember who picked up the blouse?" I asked.

"No, I wasn't here that day," she said. "Monday is my day off."

"It must have been Russo," I said. I looked at Mahasti's father but he shook his head and I knew he had no idea.

We thanked them for their time. Harrison spoke a few words of what I supposed was the man's native language because he perked right up and they talked animatedly for a few more minutes. Then I saw Harrison hand him some folded-up bills. The man waved him off, but Harrison insisted.

I glanced at Harrison as we left and asked, "What language was that?"

"Farsi," he said.

"Are you fluent?" I asked.

He shrugged. "I'm working on it."

He looked entirely too humble and I had a feeling he was, in fact, fluent. It was as attractive as it was intimidating. Smart men always are. I decided to go for broke. "How many languages do you speak?"

"Four or five," he said.

We continued on in silence as I absorbed the fact that I was palling around with a certified smarty-pants. As Harrison and I rounded the corner, I knew he wanted to talk about Ariana and the blouse, but I held up my hand.

"She didn't do it," I said. "I know it looks bad, but it really doesn't change anything. So the blouse is hers, so what?"

"So why was Russo dropping it off with his cleaning?" he asked. His voice was low and full of disappointment and I knew what he was thinking.

"You heard Mahasti," I said. "It had a coffee stain and a tear. Maybe Russo just took it to the cleaners as a favor to Ariana."

"Because he really seemed like the sort to do a favor for a person," Harrison said. "I think we have to face the facts."

"And what facts are those?" I asked. I started speed walking, and to my annoyance, Harrison was able to keep up just fine.

"That Ariana may have been sleeping with Russo, which

is why he had her blouse. Who knows, maybe she left it there after a tryst and he accidentally spilled coffee on it," Harrison said.

"You are such a man!" I snapped.

"A few minutes ago, that was a good thing," he said.

I rolled my eyes. "Well, a few minutes ago we were discussing body hair, not slandering an innocent woman."

"Slandering?" Harrison's eyes bugged out at the mere suggestion.

"Yes," I said. I paused at the entrance to the Underground. "Typical male, you just assume she must have slept with him. Well, I'm betting there is a much more reasonable explanation."

I turned to go into the station, and when he would have followed, I stopped him by holding up my hand.

"No, we're done," I said.

"Oh, come on, Ginger, don't be mad," he said. But not even the use of my coveted nickname would budge me. I turned and stomped into the station and stepped through the turnstile.

I was pretty sure I heard him offering to show me his chest hair as I stormed away but I didn't turn around and I didn't smile, at least not where he could see me.

Chapter 24

I blew into the shop with a hearty shove from the blustery wind at my back. No, it wasn't raining, but the bright blue sky and big fluffy clouds were accompanied by the sort of wind that ruined a perfectly good hair day. I was suddenly grateful for my hat and the fact that I had put no effort into my hair that morning.

The shop wasn't open for business yet, so I locked the door behind me and followed the sound of the music coming from the back room. Viv was there, using a steam iron on a length of wide dark brown ribbon. She glanced up when I came in and then frowned.

"How did it go?" she asked.

"Not good," I said. I slumped onto a seat at the table.

Viv pushed a plate of raisin scones and a jar of clotted

cream at me. Heaven. If there was one thing I had missed in the States, it was clotted cream on, well, everything.

I slathered a bit of the cream on the top of the scone. Viv continued ironing while I chewed. She is more patient than me; I don't know that I would have let her eat before telling me the news.

She pushed a cup of tea at me, and while I was still pretty amped from my coffee, I did need something to wash the scone down. I took a sip, and she took the half-eaten scone out of my hand.

"Tell me," she demanded. "What happened?"

I gave my scone a sad look and told her everything. If I spoke fast and left out some details, that's not really my fault since she was holding my scone hostage, right?

"Is that everything?" she asked.

"Yes," I said. I held out my hand and she handed over the scone.

I polished it off in three bites while she finished ironing her ribbon.

"What do you think about it?" she asked.

"Ariana is innocent," I said.

"Agreed," she said. "But why did Russo have her blouse?"

"That's the same detail Harrison couldn't let go of," I said. "There could be any number of reasons."

Viv stared at me.

"When does Fee come in?" I asked.

"In an hour," she said.

"Let's go see Ariana when Fee is here to watch the shop," I said. "She'll clear it all up. I'm certain of it."

"I can't run out of the shop again," Viv protested. "I have

orders that I'm falling behind on and you have a newsletter to write and you have to update our webpage."

I popped out of my seat. "The newsletter is almost done. I'll proof it now and send it out. You get to work and no more talking. We'll visit Ariana quickly and work late tonight if we have to."

Viv blinked at me. "Aren't you the motivated soul?"

"I want to help Ariana," I said. "I just feel like Mim would have wanted us to help the daughter of one of her own brides, you know?"

Viv and I both looked at each other and waited for the telltale smell of lily of the valley. There was nothing.

"Is that a sign?" Viv asked.

"Yes, that we're pathetic," I said. "Get to work."

I moved to the desk in the corner and opened up the newsletter I'd finished writing but needed to edit. It didn't take much. There were a few misspellings and I needed to replace the main picture of a holiday hat Viv had created for a clearer one. She'd done a forest-green wool cloche trimmed with a bright red ribbon with a cluster of holly leaves and berries. It pretty much yelled "Holiday Cheer" and I figured anyone who saw it would want it as a sure hit for holiday parties.

I brought up our list of newsletter subscribers. Since I had started including coupons, we'd had a surge of customers sign up and our number went from a paltry thousand subscribers to well over fifteen thousand. Of course, they lived all over the world but I figured it helped to give the shop buzz and build Viv's status as an elite designer.

Viv was a blur of motion. She worked on three different

hats at the same time, and when Fee arrived, she marveled at how much Viv had gotten done that morning.

"I'm so glad you think so," Viv said. "Scarlett and I have to go out."

"Again?" Fee asked. She gave us a distressed look. "I feel as if I'm working here alone."

"Which is how it was for me for years before I hired you. Loneliness is good for you. It builds character," Viv said.

I felt a pang of guilt. I had no idea Viv had been lonely. Then again, I'd been so self-absorbed with my own ridiculous life, even if I had known, I probably wouldn't have done anything. Yes, I was that awful.

"Character." Fee snorted. "I'd rather have a nice chin wag."

"We won't take very long, and I promise we'll come back with gossip," I said.

"The news today made it sound as if she was having an affair with her boss," Fee said. "They insinuated that she killed him because he was going to tell her fiancé about the affair."

Viv gave me a worried glance, and I knew she was thinking what I was thinking. Had the news media figured out something we hadn't? I refused to believe it was more than rampant speculation.

"They're just guessing," I said. "Come on, Viv, let's hurry."

Viv grabbed her jacket and we ran out of the shop, leaving it in Fee's capable hands.

"This has to be the last time we leave her alone," Viv said as we hurried down the street.

"Yeah, yeah," I said. I handed her my cell phone, which I had already dialed.

"What? What's this?" Viv asked.

"Just take it," I said. "It's ringing."

"I can hear that, Scarlett," Viv said. "But who is it calling?"

I didn't answer. I didn't have to as even I could hear the male voice answer the call on the other end.

"Oh, hello," Viv said. "This is Vivian Tremont and you are?" She frowned at me and then gave me an exasperated look. "Oh, hi, Alistair. Yes, I'm holding Scarlett's phone for her while she's fixing her hair. Here she is."

She practically threw the phone at me like it was a hot potato. I tried to hand it back but she tucked her hands behind her back and refused to take it.

"What?" I asked. "I thought you liked him."

"You've got me up a gum tree," Viv said.

"Why do you say that?" I asked. I lowered my voice to a whisper and asked, "You don't like him?"

Viv turned away from me and hurried down the sidewalk as if she could not put enough space between us.

"Hi, Alistair," I said into the phone, trying to make my voice sound cheery but my eyes stayed on Viv. The wind tugged at her long blond curls and the hem of her coat as she leaned into it, trying to keep her balance. It seemed metaphorical to me, but maybe I was reading too much into it.

"Scarlett, good to hear from you," Alistair said. If he'd heard any of our conversation, I couldn't tell from his tone of voice.

"Have you spoken to Harrison today?" I asked.

"No, why?" he asked.

"Oh, no reason," I said. "Listen, Viv and I were hoping

we could get in to see Ariana, well, right now, in fact. Is there any way you can help with that?"

"Absolutely," he said. "Meet me in front of the station and I'll escort you in. It'll do her a world of good to see some friendly faces."

I ended the call and hurried to catch up to Vivian. She didn't look at me when I began to walk beside her, so I figured for once I'd keep my yap shut, and if she wanted to talk, I would let her take the lead.

It was a very long, very quiet walk to the jail.

Ariana looked horrible. She was pale and thin. Her dark hair was stringy and her eyes were red and swollen as if she hadn't stopped crying in days. The sight of her made me desperate to break her out.

"Ariana, I know things look grim," I said.

She barked out a laugh that seriously lacked humor.

"That's an understatement," she said. "I'm probably going to prison for a crime I didn't commit and I'm going to lose my fiancé because I can't expect him to wait forever, now can I? Oh, and the media is making me out to be some sort of slut because of that damn photograph. And no one can tell me how they got it or where it came from."

"The police are working on it," Alistair said. "As am I."

Ariana's face softened. The custody sergeant let us use a small room in the back of the police station. Alistair was next to Ariana while Viv and I sat across from them.

"Ariana, why did Russo take your blouse to the dry cleaners?" Viv asked.

"Really?" I asked her. "No lead-up, no segue into the conversation? Just boom."

Viv glared at me. She was still hopping mad about the phone incident. I could tell because she barely looked at me and refused to look at Alistair. Only Ariana got her full attention.

"We don't have time for niceties," Viv said. She looked at Ariana, who looked confused.

"The blue blouse you were wearing on the day he died," I prompted her. "There was a bit of the fabric in his hand."

She blanched. "I didn't push him."

"We know," Viv said. She reached across the table and put her hands on Ariana's in a reassuring gesture. "But Russo took it to the dry cleaners recently. Why?"

Ariana stared at their hands and then she looked up. "He bumped into me in the kitchen one day, oh, it must have been weeks ago. He spilled coffee all down my blouse."

"Wait," Alistair said. "How do you know Russo took the blouse to the dry cleaners?"

"I found the receipt," I said.

"You did?" Ariana asked.

"In your jacket pocket," I said.

"Not the point," Viv said. "Ariana, when Russo took your blouse in, did you know there was a tear that he had mended as well?"

"A tear?" she asked. "No, I only knew of the coffee stain. I had a nasty burn on my belly from it."

"Did you go to a doctor?" Alistair said.

"Yes, I popped into an A&E," she said. "They gave me some ointment to help it heal."

243

Alistair looked from her to Viv and me. He looked cautiously optimistic as if he wasn't quite sure to believe this unexpected good fortune.

"How did you get this receipt out of her jacket?" he asked.

Viv and I both studied the tabletop. Now was the icky and uncomfortable moment where we had to admit to entering the crime scene, which we suspected was not going to go well.

"I asked them to stop by my office," Ariana said. "In fact, I asked Scarlett to retrieve my jacket for me. It's my favorite."

Ariana was such a horrible liar. She blinked repeatedly and her words trembled when she spoke as if they didn't have enough strength to stand on their own, as is the nature of lies.

"No, you didn't," I sighed. "Viv and I got the access code from Ariana so that we could go and snoop around the office."

Alistair lowered his head into his hand and squeezed his temples between his thumb and middle finger as if he were trying to keep his head from exploding.

"And you did this because two milliners are so much better at canvassing a crime scene than, say, a crime scene unit and two seasoned detective inspectors."

"It sounds so reckless when he puts it that way," I said to Viv.

"He sounds like Harrison," she agreed.

"Harrison knows about this?" Alistair asked. He pulled his cell phone out of his pocket. "So that's why he texted me three times telling me to call him. I thought it was about our upcoming rugby match."

"But this is good news, right?" Ariana asked. "I mean it helps, doesn't it?"

She looked so hopeful, we all leaned forward and reassured her that, yes, this was a good thing.

"We should tell the detectives, shouldn't we?" Viv asked Alistair.

He frowned. I could tell he was thinking the new information over. If Ariana was charged, this new information would be key in her defense, but if she wasn't charged, then this information could help the detectives find the real killer.

"Yes, let's tell Franks," Alistair said.

"Are you ready?" I asked Viv.

She nodded.

"I'll come with you," Alistair said. "In case it gets unpleasant."

I didn't like that his tone of voice indicated that he assumed it would.

Alistair knocked on the door and an officer came to lead Ariana back to her cell. I squeezed her hand as she went by.

"It's going to be okay," I said.

She nodded at me, and I noted that her dark eyes had something in them that they hadn't when we arrived. Hope.

Alistair led us down the hall. He rapped on the open door of what I recognized as Inspector Franks's office. Inspector Franks glanced up at us and I saw his mustache twitch. I wasn't sure if this was a good or a bad thing, but I decided to assume it was good.

"All right, Ms. Parker, Ms. Tremont?" he said. His look was much less friendly when he glanced at Alistair. "Turner."

"Franks," Alistair said. He sounded about as happy to talk to the detective as the detective was with him.

Franks leaned back in his chair. He stroked his mustache with a finger while he considered us. Viv cracked like a walnut under a hammer.

"We went to Russo's office," she said. "We know we shouldn't have but we were trying to help Ariana. We didn't find anything but it was cold out so Scarlett borrowed Ariana's jacket and she found a dry-cleaning receipt in the pocket, which had a woman's blouse listed. So Scarlett went to the dry cleaners and they said that the blouse had a coffee stain and a tear and it was the blouse Ariana was wearing the day that Russo was killed."

Inspector Franks sat forward at this but Viv had stopped talking, having run out of air. He turned to me. I twisted my fingers together. This wasn't exactly how I had pictured this going down.

"It's true," I said. "All of it. We just confirmed with Ariana that Russo had her blouse cleaned because he'd accidentally dumped hot coffee on her a few weeks back."

"Did you know about this?" Franks asked Alistair.

"First I'm hearing of it," Alistair said.

"The most interesting thing we learned from the dry cleaner was that Russo had them mend a tear in the garment. Mahasti, the seamstress, said it was right on the hem and Russo paid her quite a lot to make it perfect."

"Can I see the garment?" Viv asked.

Inspector Franks looked at her with wide eyes. I think he had been expecting anything but that.

"I'm a milliner," she said. "I know hand stitching and machine stitching. I'll be able to tell if the fabric found in his hand matched the repaired tear on the blouse."

"That's what's been bothering me!" Inspector Franks pounded his fist on his desk. We all jumped and he looked sheepish. "Sorry. But that has been needling me ever since we collected Miss Jackson's blouse. There is no tear. If Russo had grabbed her when he fell, there should have been a fresh tear and we could find no sign of a quick repair if she was trying to hide something."

Alistair stood straighter. He reminded me of a dog anticipating his ball being thrown. He was ready to chase it down.

"Will you let Ms. Tremont examine the blouse?" he asked.

Inspector Franks studied Viv for a moment and then nodded. "Follow me."

When Alistair and I made to go with them, Franks frowned at us. "You two wait here."

"Aw, what?" I protested.

"That's not right," Alistair argued.

"Do either of you sew?" Franks asked.

I thought about lying but really what was the point? I couldn't even thread a needle without stabbing myself half to death—only a mild exaggeration, I assure you.

"Sit," Franks barked.

Alistair and I both sat. Viv gave me a brave smile as she left with Inspector Franks.

"Where is he taking her?" I asked.

"Crime lab or possibly the property room and then the crime lab," Alistair said. "Depends upon where they stored the evidence for Ariana's case."

I stood up and began to pace. Franks's tiny office wasn't really conducive to pacing, so I awkwardly circled my chair a couple of times and then gave up and sat back down.

"About your cousin," Alistair said. He wasn't looking at me and I sensed that he was feeling awkward.

"Vivian?" I clarified, although she is the only cousin of mine that he knew about, so really who else could he be talking about? I have a few cousins on my father's side of the family but they are all much older and I seldom saw them unless there was a wedding or a funeral to attend.

"Yes, um, is she . . ." His voice trailed off.

He looked so adorably awkward, I just wanted to ruffle his hair, but I suspected that would not be welcome. I decided to help him out a little.

"Beautiful?" I asked.

He looked up at me and smiled. "I can see that. What I was wondering was whether she is . . ."

Again his voice ebbed.

"Brilliant?" I supplied. Might as well talk the girl up, right?

"I can see that, too," he said. Now his glance was rueful. "You know, I haven't had much opportunity to chase a woman before."

"They all fall at your feet, do they?" I asked.

He looked a bit embarrassed and then shrugged. "Yes."

I laughed. I liked his honesty. "But not Viv."

"No, she has me spinning," he said. "Much like you have Harrison turned upside down."

That wiped the smile off my face. "No, I don't."

"Please. I know my mate and he has never acted around a woman like he acts around you," Alistair said.

"And how is that?" I asked.

"Like a boor," he said.

Caught by surprise, I laughed again. "And here I thought that was his natural state of being."

"Harrison Wentworth?" he asked. "Oh, no, he's all polish and shine until he's around you. You make him . . . real."

I wasn't positive but I was pretty sure that was high praise. Then again, he may have just been buttering me up for information on Vivian. Mission accomplished.

"I'm sorry I've been teasing you, what did you want to know about Viv?"

"Is she not into dating or is it more that she isn't interested in dating me?" he asked.

"I don't know. I wish I could tell you more about what is going on in Viv's head," I said. "But the truth is, I've been trying to find out about her personal life for months, but she isn't sharing."

"Not even with you?" Alistair asked.

I shook my head. Admitting the emotional distance between Viv and me to Alistair made me feel even worse about it than I did before. Why was she shutting me out?

"I don't know if she's involved with anyone, although if she is, it must be long distance because she never goes out," I said. "And if it's long distance, she's never on the phone either so I have no idea how it could be working."

"Ah, maybe it is that she just isn't interested in me," Alistair said. "It's been known to happen—not often, but it's happened."

"I don't think that's it," I said. I thought of the way she refused to look at him or talk to him on the phone. That wasn't someone who was immune. That was someone who was attracted and trying desperately to ignore it.

"Well, if the opportunity presents itself, do let her know that I'd be interested in taking her out," he said.

"Done," I promised.

"Now, what can I say to sell you on my friend Harrison?" he asked.

I felt my face get hot and I turned away with a nervous giggle, yes, an actual giggle. It was galling. Mercifully, I was spared from answering when the door opened and Viv walked in with Inspector Franks behind her.

Alistair and I both jumped to our feet. "Well?"

"Ms. Tremont has confirmed along with our forensic specialists that the fabric in Russo's hand matches a piece taken from Ms. Jackson's blouse *before* it was mended at the cleaners."

I looked at Viv. "Explain."

"The seamstress at the cleaners did a wonderful job using a machine to fix the hem," Viv said. "But once I undid the stitches, the fabric in Russo's hand matched the missing piece perfectly."

"Inspector Simms is taking the garment to the cleaners to confirm that they did the repair," Inspector Franks said. "So there can be no suspicion that Ariana mended her blouse before we took it into evidence."

"She couldn't have," I said. "She was a wreck when I found her."

"And the stitches I removed from the blouse were

definitely from a professional sewing machine. There is no way they were hand stitched."

"Brilliant!" Alistair pumped his fist and swept Viv into a crushing hug that lifted her off her feet. She laughed a very un-Viv-like guffaw. When Alistair released her, their gazes met and then he kissed her.

Chapter 25

Inspector Franks and I stared at them and then we both looked away, studying the wall, the floor, the ceiling, repeat.

"Yes, well." Franks cleared his throat twice.

Alistair stepped back from Viv, and I noted that they both looked bemused and a bit breathless. Huh.

"I want Ariana released," Alistair said. He stepped away from Viv as if it took great effort on his part.

Viv turned away from all of us, seemingly to study the top of Franks's desk. It was a mess, littered with papers and old coffee cups. Honestly, the man needed a maid.

Inspector Franks held up his hands, giving Alistair the signal to slow down. "I need more than this."

"You'll get it," Alistair said.

It wasn't a threat, it was a promise, and I could see that Franks was okay with it.

"There's still her cell phone and the threatening texts she sent to Russo on it," Franks said.

"She allegedly sent. Remember, her phone was missing," Alistair argued.

"According to her," Franks said. "It was found in her flat when we did the search."

"But it's true that she didn't have her phone," I said. "She didn't answer our calls for a couple of days, which was why I went to see her."

Franks looked at me and rubbed his mustache. I gave him a closed-lip smile, you know, the one that says I'm just trying to help. Yeah, he didn't look overly grateful.

"Ms. Tremont, thank you for your help," Inspector Franks said to Viv. He didn't acknowledge Alistair or me, and it was clear we were being dismissed.

Alistair led us out the door. In the hallway, he paused. He looked at Viv, who did not meet his gaze.

"I'm sorry about just now," he said. "I got carried away."

He was so charmingly awkward, I was beginning to wonder if Viv was made out of stone, but then I remembered her face after he'd kissed her. No, not stone.

"It's fine," she said. "We're all a bit emotional."

"All right then," he said. "I'm going to see Ariana and tell her what's happening. I expect she could use some good news. I'll . . . be in touch."

We watched as he walked down the hall. Viv looked like she wanted to call after him, but she didn't. Instead, she turned and headed for the nearest exit. As soon as we stepped outside, I opened my mouth to grill her about the kiss. Particularly, was it as amazing as it had looked?

She held up her hand, shutting me down. "Not one word, Scarlett. Not one."

It was another very long and quiet journey back to the shop.

When we arrived, we found Harrison waiting for us. He and Fee were at the counter of the shop, looking over one of her homework assignments for her small business class. Harrison had been helping her with her studies, which I had to admit was very nice of him.

He took one look at Viv's face and asked, "What happened?"

I opened my mouth to answer but Viv interrupted, "Nothing!"

I looked at her like she was crazy, not unwarranted, and she made bug eyes at me that clearly said she would kick my behind if I breathed a word of what happened with Alistair and her. See, being cousins, I can register an unspoken threat especially when she makes the crazy face.

"Viv figured out that the fabric found in Russo's hand matches a piece from Ariana's blouse," I said.

"But you already knew that, yeah?" Fee asked.

"Yes, but Viv looked at the blouse in the crime lab and the piece in Russo's hand was from before Ariana's blouse was mended at the cleaners," I said.

Fee frowned and then shook her head. "I'm not following."

"Ariana is being framed," Harrison said.

"Exactly," Viv said. She looked at Fee. "Someone put a

piece of Ariana's blouse into Russo's hand either before or after he died, but he most definitely did not get it from snatching at her before he fell."

"So the only thing tying Ariana to his death now is the photograph and the nasty texts that came from her phone," I said. "We need to know who sent the picture and who had her phone."

"They found the phone in her flat when they searched it, so it has to be someone who was there the day Russo was killed," Viv said.

"Alistair had the police check the security cameras for her building for the days that her phone was missing," Harrison said. "Her building is large enough and with a young enough residency that there are all sorts of people coming and going at all hours day and night. They are trying to identify over thirty nonresident visitors to see if there is anyone with a motive to kill Russo and frame Ariana."

"I want to visit the roof of Russo's building," I said.

All three of them looked at me.

"I got lucky last time, maybe I'll get lucky again. Can you manage here?"

"Like you're giving me a choice," Viv said.

"Do you want to come with me?" I asked.

Viv shook her head. "No, I need to work."

I knew she meant that she needed to work like she needed to breathe. It was that much a part of her and I suspected it was the only thing that was going to help her level out after Alistair's unexpected display of affection.

"I'll go with you," Harrison said.

"What about me?" Fee asked. "I never get to go anywhere."

"And not today either," Viv said. "We've got to finish the hats for Philippe's fashion show. I promised him."

Fee sighed and waved her hand at us. "You're right. Carry on, detectives, without little old me."

Harrison looked at me and gestured to the door. "After you."

We left the shop and I could feel Harrison studying me as we walked. He waited until we were off Portobello Road and entering Notting Hill Gate before he said, "So what aren't you telling me, Ginger?"

I glanced at him out of the corner of my eye. He was frowning.

"I don't know what you mean," I said.

"Please, I saw the look Viv gave you," he said. "It was reflected in one of the shop's many mirrors."

We went through the turnstile and hurried to our platform. The wind in the tunnel and the crush of bodies as everyone headed to their train made it hard to hear. I took it as a reprieve while I tried to figure out what to say.

Once on the train, Harrison and I snagged two seats in a middle car. I could feel him watching me. Finally, I threw up my hands.

"What?" I demanded.

"You know what," he said. "What else happened at the police station?"

"Ask Alistair," I said. There. That was lobbing the problem off nice and neat.

"So it has something to do with Alistair and Viv?" he asked.

"You're worse than a gossipy old woman," I snapped. "Quit trying to get me to say something."

"I can't," he said. "Alistair won't say anything because he's a guy, and Viv looked like she'd rip my head off, so that leaves you."

"You're out of luck, Harry," I said. "These lips are sealed."

That was a poor choice of words as it made his gaze move to my mouth, which made me loosen my grip on my handrail. The train jolted forward and I fell against him. He smiled at me. It was a dangerous smile, the sort a lion gives an antelope right before he takes it down.

"Harrison," he corrected me.

We were entirely too close for comfort. I pushed off him before I did something dumb like kiss him the way Alistair had kissed Viv, because that most definitely would not do.

Mercifully, the train pulled into our stop and I shot out of my seat and out the door, nearly taking an older couple out with me on the way. Healthy boundaries must be maintained.

We didn't speak on the walk to Russo's office, and the one time I glanced at Harrison, I caught him looking at me. There was so much sizzle in the air between us, you'd think bacon was frying. Yowzers.

I led the way through the back gate into Russo's yard. It was quiet. No police or reporters at large. I glanced at the spot where Russo's body had been found. Unlike the night Viv and I had come here, it was daylight now and I could see the dark stains, bloodstains, where his body had been found broken beyond repair.

I glanced from the cobblestones up to the roof. It was a long drop onto the hard ground. I tried to remember Russo's face. Had his expression been scared or angry or surprised? I couldn't remember. Honestly, I hadn't looked too closely at his face. What I did remember was the smell of death, and the quiet stillness that shrouded his lifeless body.

"All right, Ginger?" Harrison asked.

"Yeah," I lied. "I'm good."

I led the way to the keypad, where I tapped in the code. The door clicked and we entered the house. It was dark and beginning to smell musty from being shut up.

Harrison took in our surroundings as I led the way to the stairs. We went up all the way to the top floor. After checking several doors, I found the one that led to the roof. Before it shut, I checked to make sure it didn't lock behind us. I didn't like the idea of being trapped on the roof where a man had been pushed to his death.

Harrison walked the perimeter of the roof. It was a flat roof with a slight tilt toward gutters along the edge to drain the rainwater. A short brick railing ran around the top of it. It was untidy, with a couple of broken chairs and a wobbly table. There was a weather-beaten shed, and some old soggy cigarette butts floating in a can full of rainwater.

"You don't suppose someone was living up here and Russo surprised them, do you?" I asked.

"No, the security cameras would have picked that up," Harrison said.

He wandered over to the ledge where Russo had fallen. It was the only spot of the roof without camera coverage. That had bothered me from the very beginning. The railing was knee high and it made my hands sweat to stand too close to it. I didn't like the way Harrison was leaning over it. One slight push and he would topple to his death just like Russo.

"Back up, Harry," I said. "You're making me nervous."

He turned and grinned at me. His green eyes were full of mischief as he pretended to lose his balance and start to fall. I grabbed him by the jacket and yanked him to safety.

"Nice catch," he said. We were just inches apart and his arms slid around me as naturally as if we were a couple.

"You could have fallen," I said. Good grief, I sounded like someone's mother. Oh, horror.

"But I didn't," he said.

"Well, Russo did, and I'd rather not repeat that," I said.

"Why, Ginger, I didn't know you cared so much."

He was teasing me. I could see it in the twinkle in his green eyes. He was too charming for my well-being and I stepped away from him. Of course I cared. He was my friend.

I thought about Russo. As far as I could tell, he had no friends. No one seemed to mourn his loss. How sad.

I walked around Harrison to the ledge. As I leaned over it, I felt him grab the back of my jacket. Ah, so he wasn't so calm when someone else stood by the edge.

I glanced down. I couldn't see the dark stains on the cobblestones from this high up. Still, it was a sheer drop and I felt that loopy feeling of vertigo and was glad Harrison had my jacket, because I also felt a weird desire to jump. I stepped back.

"What's wrong?" Harrison asked. He looked concerned and I knew he could see how rattled I felt.

"When you were looking over the edge, did you have a sudden urge to jump?" I asked.

"No," he said. Now he was frowning. "Did you?"

"Just for a second," I said. He gave me a horrified look. "What? It was just a weird psychological urge, but it made me wonder . . ."

"Yes?"

"Why do we think Russo was pushed off the roof?"

"Because he was a horrible human being with lots of enemies," Harrison said.

"But what if he wasn't?" I asked.

"Wasn't horrible? I'd say he clearly was."

"No, what if he wasn't pushed? What if he jumped?" I asked.

"Suicide? But there was no note," Harrison said. "Wouldn't he have left a note?"

"Maybe it was an impulse," I said. "Like I felt just now."

"Then why did he have a bit of Ariana's blouse in his hand?"

"He was in love with her," I said.

Harrison's eyebrows went up at that.

"Mariska Kravchuk said they broke up because he was in love with his mousy little secretary. She was very bitter about that," I said. "She also told me that she thought a photo was worth a million pounds; she has to be the one who leaked the picture of Ariana and Russo to the media."

"Then it makes sense that Mariska pushed him," Harrison said. "And tried to make it look like it was Ariana."

"But Mariska has an alibi," I said. "And so does her boyfriend."

"So we're back where we started," Harrison said. "Bloody maddening it is."

I looked back at the ledge. Anthony Russo had been in debt to a bookie who was definitely going to cause him some damage, he was in trouble with his clients for false billing, and he obviously had a substance abuse problem. In short, his life was in the toilet. Add that he was about to lose the woman he loved to someone else, and what did he have to live for? Not much.

Suddenly, it all made perfect sense to me. I knew who had killed Russo and why.

"Come on," I said. "Ariana is innocent and I know how we can prove it."

Chapter 26

"Are you sure about this?" Harrison asked me.

We were standing down the street from Mariska's apartment with Detectives Franks and Simms. They actually had me wearing a wire that was hooked into my bra. I felt very MI5.

Harrison and I had left Russo's building and gone to the station. I had told the detectives my theory, and to my surprise, Franks was willing to consider it. They were tracing the origin of the photograph of Ariana and Russo that had been leaked to the papers, but the reporter was refusing to cooperate in order to protect his source.

Then there was Ariana's cell phone. The crime lab was trying to track what cell towers had sent the threatening text messages to Russo's phone. If they could track the route the messages had taken, then they might be able to determine a point of origin that wasn't Ariana's home, which would mean someone else had used her phone to send the texts.

If none of that worked, the plan was to have me chat up Mariska while the police listened and hope she said something, anything, incriminating that they could use against her.

"I'll be fine, Harry," I said.

Instead of correcting me like he usually did, he leaned in close and whispered in my ear, "Please be careful."

I shivered, but not from the cold, and resisted the urge to hug him tight—barely.

"If you feel even the least bit in danger, get out," Detective Franks said. "Don't worry about a graceful exit, just go."

I nodded. Detective Simms gave me a wink and a double thumbs-up and I couldn't help but smile in return.

I left them all at the unmarked van on the corner and hurried down the sidewalk and up the walkway. This time I knew which apartment to buzz. I hit the button for Mariska's place and was relieved when it was Jean who answered.

"Good afternoon," she said.

"Hello, Jean, it's Scarlett from the hat shop Mim's Whims. Is Mariska in?"

Jean hesitated a moment and I wondered if Mariska'd had her quota of vodka and caviar for the day.

"Let me check, Miss," she said.

I waited on the stoop, wondering what I was going to do if Mariska refused to see me. Maybe I could cajole Jean. It would be worth a shot.

"Come right up, Miss," Jean's voice came back on the intercom and I almost sagged with relief. The door popped and I pulled it open quickly, half afraid Mariska would change her mind.

I was winded by the top steps. I really needed to start working out. I wondered if the detectives and Harrison could hear me huffing and puffing through the wire. The thought was mortifying. I tried to breathe as quietly and as shallowly as possible without passing out.

Jean opened the door before I reached it and I had the feeling she was relieved to see me.

"Come in," she said. She stepped back and waved her hand at me to enter.

I saw Mariska right away. She was sitting in the same spot I'd last seen her, reclined on the vibrantly printed chair. Sure enough, there was a decanter on the table in front of her.

"Vivian," she said. "So good to see you."

"Actually, I'm Scarlett," I said.

She waved her French manicure at me. "Who cares?"

I looked at Jean as if to say "Really?" and she shrugged.

"She's been like this all morning," Jean whispered.

"Someone should tell her it's very unattractive," I said. Yes, I know I sounded grumpy but I didn't think I was that unforgettable or unimportant.

"Hmm," Jean hummed noncommittally. "Can I get you anything, Miss?"

"No, thank you," I said. I took a seat across from Mariska.

"If you'll excuse me then," Jean said. She practically ran from the room.

I looked back at Mariska. It was then that I noticed she wasn't dolled up like she had been the last time I'd seen her.

Her hair was jammed into a sloppy knot on top of her head, she wore no makeup, and her robe this time wasn't sheer but big and fluffy. Honestly, I liked her better like this. She was more human and less mannequin-like.

"Is everything all right, Mariska?" I asked.

"No," she moaned. "Nothing is all right. My lover is dead and I . . . I . . . miss him."

Her overwrought tone was perfect for a B movie actress.

"The towel guy?" I asked. "He's dead?"

Mariska lifted her head to give me a look that stated quite plainly she thought I was too stupid to live. Really, this visit was doing wonders for my self-esteem.

"I can assure you I am very much alive." Jarrett Reichs entered the room and I started.

"Oh, is this a bad time to talk about modeling the hats for the shop?" I asked Mariska. I hoped I sounded sincere and not as scared as I suddenly felt. I really hadn't thought the ex-boyfriend, who was a bit scary looking, would be here. "I didn't realize you had company."

"Don't worry, as soon as I get what I want," Jarrett said, "I'm leaving."

Mariska rose from her seat with the decanter in hand. Jarrett barely had time to duck as it sailed over his head and exploded against the wall, sending glass shards and vodka all over the room.

"You get nothing!" she cried. Her accent was thick with her anger.

"But I helped, I deserve a cut," Jarrett said. His fists were clenched and I wondered if he was about to take a swing at her.

"You deserve nothing!" Mariska said. "He left everything to me."

A smart person would have left, no, would have run from the room right then and there. I did not. I am not smart.

"Is this about Russo's death?" I asked. I really hoped that the mic I was wearing was working. Even more, I hoped that the detectives had heard the decanter smash and were on their way. "Did you two kill him?"

"No!" they answered together. I did note that Jarrett looked outraged while Mariska looked guilty. Interesting.

"I didn't think so," I said. "Want to know what I think?"

"No!" Mariska said. "You are here about hats. That is all."

"Yeah, that was a big, fat lie," I said. "We aren't going to hire you as a model. I'm here because someone framed my friend Ariana, and I think it was you."

I swear I could almost hear Harrison yelling at me from down the street. This was not what we had discussed. This was not how I was supposed to play it.

"And you helped," I said to Jarrett.

He visibly paled. That was when I knew I was on to something.

"You're mad," he said.

"Which one of you sent the texts?" I asked.

"I don't know what you are saying," Mariska snapped.

"Well, let me explain," I said. "Ariana's phone went missing a few days before Russo's death. I think he took it and gave it to someone with instructions to send him some threatening messages."

Mariska and Jarrett were actively not looking at each other. Guilty!

"Here's the thing," I said. I was full-on bluffing now but what the heck? These two were already rattled. I just needed to shake them loose.

"The police are going to track the route of those messages, because you know they can do that, right? Text messages ping cell phone towers just like phone calls. Yeah, and they'll be able to pinpoint where those messages came from. So I wonder if it will be your place"—I paused to look at Mariska and then Jarrett—"or yours."

Jarrett didn't meet my gaze. "Then they'll finish sorting the security camera footage from Ariana's apartment building and see who returned her phone to her place the morning of Russo's death, and boy, will that person have some explaining to do."

Now Jarrett looked at Mariska in a blind panic. Gotcha!

"Damn it!" he yelled at her. "You told me this was easy money. You told me all I had to do was break in and leave the phone and that was it."

"Shut up, Jarrett," Mariska said. She glared at me. "You can't prove anything."

"Can't I?" I asked.

This might have been where I went too far. Mariska's face contorted in fury and she launched herself at me, taking me down to the hard floor. I had no time to prepare myself. She had me around the neck and was choking me while banging my head on the floor at the same time.

I tried to shove her off, but she was too heavy. Jarrett ran for the door, no doubt to leave before he witnessed my murder. The last thing I saw before I blacked out was Jean sneaking up behind Mariska with a broom clutched in her hand.

"Ginger, wake up." A hand was patting my face, and not very gently either. "Come on, love, you're scaring me stupid."

"Uh," I grunted and then I sucked in a deep breath, which caused me to hack and cough.

"She's all right!"

"Thank goodness!"

I squinted against the bright light. Harrison was leaning over me, looking worried and very, very dear.

"Did we get them?" I asked.

"Jarrett Reichs ran right into Inspector Simms's arms," Harrison said. He pushed a bit of hair out of my face, and I noticed his hand was shaking.

Jean was hovering behind him. "All right, Miss?"

"Did you clobber her with the broom?" I asked. My voice sounded gruff and it hurt to swallow.

"Didn't get the chance," she said. She clapped Harrison on the shoulder. "Your boyfriend here lamped her good."

I looked at Harrison in shock. "You hit her?"

He shrugged. "No one throttles my girl."

And if that didn't just make my heart go pitter pat.

"All right, Scarlett?" Inspector Franks peered down at me.

"Fine," I lied.

"Think you can sit up?" Harrison asked and I nodded.

He scooped me up as if I weighed no more than a basket of laundry and put me gently down on the couch.

"I'm going to brew you some tea for that throat," Jean said, and she left for the kitchen.

I looked across the room where Mariska and Jarrett were both seated on the floor and handcuffed.

"Well done," Franks said. "Jarrett Reichs just peeled open like a hot chestnut. He told us everything we needed to know. I've already called the station and your mate, Turner, is overseeing the paperwork to let Ms. Jackson out."

I sagged back in the seat. "Excellent. So it was suicide?"

Franks nodded. "Yes, Russo jumped off of the building on purpose. His plan was to frame Ariana for his murder, figuring if he couldn't have her, then he'd make sure she spent the rest of her life in jail to keep anyone else from having her."

"Whoa, that's sick," I said. "How do Mariska and Jarrett factor in?"

"Russo confided his plan to Mariska," Franks said. "And he left her a large sum of money to do as he asked upon his death, which was to release the photograph and put Ariana's phone back."

"She didn't send the threatening messages?" I asked.

"Just the last one," Franks said.

Jean handed me a cup of tea and I took a grateful sip. The warmth did help. "Thank you," I croaked.

A commotion at the door drew our attention. Several uniformed officers entered the room, no doubt to escort Mariska and Jarrett to the station.

"You need to go to an A&E to have your throat checked," Franks said. I was about to protest but he gave me a dark look. "That's an order."

"Fine," I whispered.

"I'll make sure she goes," Harrison said, and I knew it was nonnegotiable.

Inspector Franks put his hand on my shoulder. "When

you're up to it, come by the station and we'll file an official report."

I nodded and he gave my shoulder a solid squeeze. As he walked away, I could hear him singing, " 'It's Five O'clock Somewhere.' "

I exchanged an amused look with Harrison, who handed my tea cup to Jean and swept me up into his arms to carry me downstairs, presumably to his car, which we'd left parked at the corner.

"I can walk," I protested.

"I know," he said.

I glanced at his face and got lost in his bright green gaze. It was all there. He was letting me look right inside him, and I could see how scared he'd been and how relieved he was now and how he wasn't about to let me go anytime soon.

I gave him a small smile and rested my head on his shoulder. What I didn't tell him or let him see in my gaze was that when Mariska's hands were closing off my airway and I was losing consciousness, my one thought had been that I desperately wanted to see Harry again.

As I breathed in the calming bay rum scent of him, I let one tear trickle out of my eye. Just one because I was so grateful that he was here, holding me close.

Chapter 27

The ferret won. My dreamy blue-eyed boy lost *The Great British Bake Off* and now I was forced to make dinner for all of my friends. "Catastrophe" was not a descriptive enough word for how bad this was going to be. Adding to the pressure, of course, was the fact that our social circle had expanded quite a bit to include Alistair, Ariana and Stephen, as we were celebrating Ariana's release and their upcoming wedding. Oh, and Fee didn't have class tonight so of course she was invited, too.

Nine people! I was supposed to make a multicourse dinner for nine people. I wondered if there was a flight out of London that evening and how I could manage to be on it.

I was standing in the market, feeling like crying, when a woman waved to me from the produce section. I forced my tears back as it was probably a customer and I didn't want to shame the shop by being known as the weepy milliner.

"Scarlett, dear, how are you?" the woman asked as she joined me in front of the cheese case.

She had ash-blond hair that hung loose about her face and she was dressed in jeans and a wool coat. I had no idea who she was.

"It's Jean," she said, "from Mad Mariska's."

"Oh." I looked at her again. "Oh, wow, I didn't recognize you. You look amazing."

She wrinkled her nose. "Housekeeper uniforms and severe hairdos are very stifling."

"So you've left that career behind?" I asked.

"Yes, after Mariska was arrested, I realized I never wanted to work for one like her again," she said. "So I've opened up my own catering company."

"You don't say," I said. And then it hit me like a bolt of lightning, as all the best ideas do, and I asked her, "Do you have a job already lined up for tonight?"

"No," she said. "I'm still building my client base."

"Well, I think I might be able to help with that," I said. Together we made our way through the shop as I proposed my plan to Jean.

A table set for nine was a tight squeeze in the main room of our flat, but I managed it. I had pulled out all the stops and had linen tablecloths, fresh-cut flowers and Mim's best china, crystal and flatware all sparkly and shiny.

I had managed to sneak Jean in the front of the shop while

Viv and Fee worked in the back. She had spent the afternoon cooking up a storm in our flat, while I pretended to mind the store and run upstairs occasionally to check on "my dinner."

When Viv and Fee went to change, I snuck Jean out the back. The meal smelled delicious and I doubled her fee for working so hard on such short notice. Honestly, I would have quadrupled it if she'd let me. She didn't.

Before she left, she gave me the last bit of instructions. I was sure I could handle them. I raced up to my room and threw on the dress I had put aside for the evening. It was a red Nicole Miller sheath that ended just above my knees. I was wearing it with a pair of silver high-heeled sandals. I had put up my auburn hair in a French twist, leaving a thick strand loose that framed the right side of my face. I touched up my makeup and I was good to go.

I hurried downstairs to find Viv and Fee already entertaining Nick and Andre. I was relieved that no one was wearing the same dress as me—yes, it had happened before.

"Scarlett, dinner smells amazing," Nick said as he kissed my cheek and handed me a big bouquet of yellow and orange dahlias. "Is there anything I can do to help?"

I gave a careless shrug. "Thanks but I think I've got it."

Andre handed me a bottle of wine and kissed my cheek as well. "If I didn't know better, I'd say you've been holding out on us."

"Me?" I asked as I put a hand over my heart, the picture of innocence. "Don't be silly. I think it's just a matter of putting your mind to something."

"Well, I'm ready to put my fork to it," Nick joked, and I laughed.

Viv led them into the sitting room, and I hurried into the kitchen to check on things. I picked up the bib apron that used to be Mim's, but was now more of a decoration that hung on the wall beside the refrigerator, and pulled it over my head. This at least made me feel like a cook.

Jean had left most everything warming but she'd been very clear that I had to serve dinner shortly after everyone arrived; otherwise the roast beef would dry out. She had offered to do the dishes but I had insisted she leave them. That way no one could accuse me of ordering takeout and just reheating.

I was just tossing the salad like she had instructed when Harrison, Alistair, Stephen and Ariana walked into the room. Ariana was holding Stephen's hand and beaming up at him. They were getting married at the end of the week and they both looked as though they couldn't wait.

As soon as Stephen handed over his bottle of wine and Harrison and Alistair offered up a triple-layer chocolate cake, Viv grabbed Ariana by the hand and dragged her into her bedroom. Fee and I followed.

"Sorry, fellas, girl time," I said. "Harry, would you make sure everyone has a drink?"

"It's Harrison," he corrected me, but the corner of his mouth was turned up in a half smile. "Sure thing."

Once the bedroom door was shut, Viv held out a hatbox to Ariana. She gasped and clutched it close.

"Is it done?" she asked.

Viv nodded and Ariana put it on the bed to pull the lid off. She unpacked it from its nest of tissue paper, and a soft sigh escaped her lips. The discolored and torn parts had been replaced and the hat looked as glorious as it had on the day Ariana's mother had worn it in her own wedding.

"Let's see how it fits," Viv said. She moved to stand behind Ariana and helped her put it on her head.

Ariana walked to the tall standing mirror in the corner, and she put her hand to her throat as if trying to hold back the tears as she looked at her reflection.

"It's perfect," she said. "Thank you."

Viv gave her a wide warm smile. I knew the moment Viv caught the scent of lily of the valley that seemed to slowly seep into the room because her gaze met mine and tears were shining in her eyes.

"Here, let's see it all unfurled, yeah?" Fee asked and she spread the embroidered train out behind Ariana. It was gorgeous.

"You did a great job," I said to Viv.

"I had a lot to work with," she said.

The scent that reminded us so much of Mim flared and then began to dissipate.

"She approved," I said to Viv.

"I hope so," she said. She looked a bit forlorn and I wondered at it.

Wearing a pale blue chemise that shimmered when she walked and having her hair done in a half-up, half-down style, Viv had an almost otherworldly beauty about her. Then again, maybe that was just the distance I always felt with her these days. It made me sad and frustrated even as I tried to give her some space. I couldn't help but wonder why Viv seemed to be shutting me and everyone else out.

I almost started to grill her, but I didn't want to spoil the evening. Fee and Ariana were checking out the hat from all angles and Ariana looked so happy that it was impossible to stay in a bad mood.

A knock sounded on the door and then Harrison's voice called through the thick wood, "Ginger, not to alarm you, but there's a buzzer going off in the kitchen."

"Dinner!" I cried. "Box it up, girls."

I slipped through the door and back into the main room. Harrison was the only one there as the other men had gone into the sitting room to watch some sporting event on television.

"Would you call everyone to dinner?" I asked him.

He didn't say anything, just stared at me.

"What?" I asked.

"Nothing," he said. Then he gave me a slow smile that had wickedness in every dimple. "Just taking it all in. You're like a domesticated wild animal in that apron."

"Be careful, Harry, I still have claws," I said.

He laughed. "I'm counting on it."

He turned and left the room and I blew out a breath. The man could seduce the common sense right out of a girl if she let him. Luckily, I was made of sterner stuff or so I kept telling myself.

Once everyone was seated, Viv helped me haul the dishes out to the table and bus them as needed. She sat at one end of the long table with Alistair on one side of her and Nick on the other. I sat on the other with Harrison on one side and Andre on the other. Stephen and Ariana squeezed in between Alistair and Harrison while Fee sat across from them. It was definitely snug but no one seemed to mind. As far as hostessing went, thank goodness Viv and I had dined at Nick and Andre's often enough to know what we were doing.

We got through the soup and salad course. Jean's roasted vegetable soup with walnut and sage pesto wowed them, but yes, I was happy to take the praise.

Then it was potted shrimps with pickled cucumber. Amazing. Everyone had their own little casserole dish and I was pleased to see them all scraped clean.

Andre and Nick were in rare form entertaining everyone with their latest bits of gossip. Ariana and Stephen talked about their upcoming wedding, to which we'd all been invited. And Alistair updated everyone on Mariska's arrest. Her partner, Jarrett, had been able to work out a deal for testifying against her. Although she had nothing to do with Russo's death, she had hampered the investigation, let an innocent woman be wrongly accused and had assaulted me. She was definitely going to be doing some time. I put my hand to my throat, remembering the feel of her fingers cutting off my air, and I knew I didn't feel sorry for her, not even a little.

Lastly, we settled in for the roast beef with individual Yorkshire puddings and rosemary roasted potatoes. Again, I basked in the compliments. A girl could really get used to this, let me tell you.

I began to clear away the last of the dishes and the others went back to the sitting room. Harrison stayed behind to help me. Once the table was cleared, he set to making tea and coffee.

"So how are you feeling, Ginger?" he asked.

"I'm fine," I said. "You heard the doctor at the A&E; no permanent damage was done."

"I was thinking more along the lines of how you're feeling right now," he said. He gestured to the kitchen's piles of dishes. "This must have taken you most of the day."

"Yes, it was quite an undertaking," I said. Then I grinned at him. "But when I lose a bet, I pay up."

He turned away from the teapot, which was steeping, and the coffeepot, which was brewing. He stepped closer to me but I refused to back up.

He looked down at me, and his green eyes sparked with mischief. "How is Jean by the way?"

"She's go—" I sucked in a breath. "How did you know?"

"I came by earlier to tell you that you didn't have to go through with it," he said. "I was worried it was too much for you after . . ."

His voice trailed off and his fingers traced the place on my neck where the bruises from Mariska's fingers had finally faded. His touch almost made me lose my power of speech but I cleared my throat and forged on.

"You saw me sneak her in, didn't you?"

"Yes," he said. Then he laughed. "Very clever."

"Are you going to tell the others?" I asked. I really hated to lose my kitchen cred so fast. I knew full well that with my lack of culinary prowess, time would out me soon enough.

He considered me for a moment. "Well, I might be persuaded to work out an alternate payment on the wager."

"Oh," I said. He was staring at my mouth, and I felt my ears start to ring as my blood pressure spiked. I think he intended to kiss me, and there was not a single part of me that was against this payment option.

"I'm sorry, Alistair, but I can't," Viv said.

It took all of my brain capacity to look away from Harrison to where Viv had just stormed into the room. Alistair was right behind her, looking bewildered.

"It's just dinner, Viv," he said. "I'm not asking for a lifetime commitment here. But I know what I felt when I kissed you and I know you felt it, too."

I grabbed Harrison's arm. I glanced at him and knew he was thinking the same thing I was. Which was mostly that their timing was lousy but also that we didn't want to witness whatever this was and how could we get out of there without them noticing us.

"Yes, it was an amazing kiss," Viv said. She sounded like she was going to cry and I felt my chest clutch. "But here's the problem—I'm married."

I gasped. Viv turned and saw Harrison and me standing there. With a cry, she ran into her bedroom and slammed the door.

I turned to look at Harrison. The first thing I noted was that he did not look surprised. I let go of his hand and stepped away from him.

"Oh, my God, you knew, didn't you?" I asked.

His silence, as the expression goes, spoke louder than words.

Be on the lookout for more Hat Shop Mysteries,
coming soon from Berkley Prime Crime!
In the meantime, turn the page for a preview of
the next book in Jenn McKinlay's *New York Times*
bestselling Cupcake Bakery Mysteries . . .

DARK CHOCOLATE DEMISE

Available April 2015 from Berkley Prime Crime!

"He looks really good in there," Angie DeLaura said. "Peaceful even."

"You can't say that about everyone," Melanie Cooper agreed.

"It's all about the casket," Tate Harper said. "You want to choose a lining that complements your skin tone in the post mortem."

Mel and Angie turned and gave him concerned looks.

"How could you possibly know that?" Mel asked.

"The funeral director at the mortuary told me," he said. He threw an arm around Angie. "Since we're engaged and all, maybe we should pick out a double-wide so we can spend eternity snuggling."

Angie beamed at him and giggled. Then she kissed him.

It did not maintain its PG-13 rating for more than a moment and Mel felt her upchuck reflex kick in as she turned away.

She was happy for her best friends in their coupledom, really she was, but sometimes, like now, it was just gag worthy.

"Really you two, how about a little decorum, given the gravity of the situation?" she asked. She knew she sounded a bit snippy but honestly, some days they were just too much.

"Of course, you're right," Tate said. "Sorry."

He and Angie untangled themselves from one another. He smoothed the front of his shirt and straightened his jacket while Angie fluffed her hair and shook out her skirt. Duly subdued, the three of them stood beside the casket that held their friend and employee Marty Zelaznik.

Marty looked particularly spiffy in his white dress shirt and his favorite bold blue tie. His suit was black and Angie had tucked a blue pocket square into his breast pocket so that just the edge of it was visible. His features were relaxed and his bald head was shiny as if it had been waxed to a high gloss.

"Hey." Oscar Ruiz, a teen known as Oz, who worked alongside Marty in the bakery Fairy Tale Cupcakes that Mel, Angie and Tate owned, joined the trio by the casket. "So, we're going with an open lid, huh?"

"We think it's for the best," Mel said.

"His tie is crooked," Angie said. "We should fix that."

"Yeah, and his makeup is a little on the heavy side," Tate said. "He has angry eyebrows."

"Anyone have a handkerchief?" Mel asked. "A little spit will take care of that."

At this, Marty's eyes popped open and he sat up in his coffin and glared. "What am I five? You are not spit-shining me!"

"Ah!" Angie yelped and leaped back with her hand clutching her chest. "Gees, Marty, you scared me to death!"

"Nice one." Tate laughed as he and Oz high-fived and knuckle-bumped Marty.

"What? Did you think I was really dead?" Marty asked, sounding outraged.

"No!" Angie snapped. "I thought you were napping. You had a little drool in the corner of your mouth."

"I was, but that doesn't mean you get to swab my decks," Marty said as he shifted around and rubbed the dried spittle off of his chin. "You know, I have to say it's pretty comfy in here. I may have to look into putting a deposit on one of these for the future."

"*Way* in the future," Mel said.

Marty glanced at the four of them. "So when do we leave for the zombie walk? I want to catch a few more Z's. Oh, and by the way the undead look you've all got going, yeah, I don't want to wake up to that ever again."

Mel glanced at her friends. Tate and Angie were doing the undead bride and groom. In requisite tux and white wedding gown, they had topped off their look with gray makeup and faux partially rotted flesh. Tate had a fake knife lodged in his skull while Angie had an axe sticking out of her back. They had already taken bogus wedding photos that Angie was seriously considering making their official wedding portrait.

Being single and thinking this was going to become a permanent state, Mel had decided to go as an undead chef complete with her toque, double-breasted white coat and checkered pants. She wore her pleated hat back on her head to enhance the amazing latex scar Oz had adhered to her forehead. It was pretty badass.

Oz had decided to wear his chef whites as well, but had changed it up by making the side of his face appear to be rotting off. Every time Mel saw his fake putrid skin flap in the breeze, she had to resist the urge to peel it off.

Being the body in the casket, Marty had chosen to be less undead than the rest of them. He was pasty pale and sunken eyed but that was about it. Mel suspected because he was closer to his actual expiration date than the rest of them, dressing up as a dead man had less appeal for him. Overall, she had to admit, they were fabulously gruesome.

"Sorry, Marty, but no napping," Mel said. She grabbed him by the elbow and hauled him out of the casket, which was sitting on a trailer on the back of the cupcake van. "We've got to load up the van and get over to the Civic Center Park and set up our station before the undead descend upon us."

"Ooh, that sounded nice and grisly." Angie shuddered.

"It did, didn't it?" Mel said. She let go of Marty, ignoring the look of longing he gave the coffin. "Let's move, people."

She hurried to the back of the bakery, where she'd left her rolling cart. Loaded with boxes of cupcakes, she pushed it beside the service window of the van and began to hand them off to Oz, who was inside.

"What flavors did you create for zombie cupcakes?" Tate asked.

"No new flavors," Mel said. She flipped open the lid of one of the boxes to show off the cupcakes. "Just new names. In place of the usual suspects we have the Marshmallow Mummy—"

"Hey, you made the frosting look like bandages on a mummy's head," Oz said from the window. "Cool."

"And it has a marshmallow filling," Mel said. "We also have Vanilla Eyeballs, Strawberry Brains, and Dark Chocolate Demise just to round out the flavors."

"The eyeball one is staring at me," Marty said. "I don't think I could eat that."

"How about the brains?" Tate said. "How did you pipe the frosting in the shape of a pink brain?"

"Fine pastry tip," Angie said. "It was fun."

"Are those little candy coffins on the chocolate ones?" Oz asked. "I dig those. Get it?"

"Aw, man, that stunk worse than rotting flesh," Marty said. He closed the lid on the box, took it from Mel and handed it through the window. The others stared at him and he asked, "What? I'm just getting into the spirit of things."

"Fine, but please keep the rotten flesh remarks to a minimum when selling the cupcakes," Mel said.

"This from the woman who ruined a perfectly good cupcake by putting a bloodshot eyeball on it," he said. He shook his head as if he couldn't fathom what she'd been thinking.

Mel lowered her head to keep from laughing. She didn't want to offend Marty as he took his vanilla cupcakes very seriously.

"Melanie!" a voice called from the bakery. Mel glanced up to see her mother Joyce Cooper stride out the door. Joyce took three steps and stopped, putting her hand to her throat. "Oh, my!"

"We look amazing, right?" Mel asked. She spread her arms wide to include her entire crew.

"*What* are you?" Joyce asked.

"The baking dead," Oz said from the van.

"Niiiice." Tate nodded.

"Yeah, I'll give you that one," Marty agreed and exchanged a complicated handshake with Oz.

Mel approached her mother who only flinched a little when she drew near. "Thanks for watching the bakery so we could work the zombie walk, Mom."

"No problem," Joyce said. "But, honey, really I just have to say that white foundation you have on, well, it's really not terribly flattering and now that you're single, you really might want to consider a little blush and maybe a less prominent eye shadow."

"I'm supposed to look like a zombie," Mel said. "I'm pretty sure they don't wear blush or eye shadow."

"Lipstick?"

"No," Mel said.

Joyce heaved a beleaguered sigh, turned and walked back into the bakery.

"Really?" Mel said to Angie. "She's worried about my pasty foundation but she blithely ignores the fact that I have a gaping wound on my head."

"She's just looking out for you," Angie said. "Maybe you'll meet a nice undead lawyer at the zombie walk and she'll stop worrying."

"There's only one lawyer I'm interested in," Mel said. "And as far as I know he is alive and kicking."

Angie gave her a half hug as if trying to bolster her spirits. The love of Mel's life was Joe DeLaura, the middle of Angie's seven older brothers. A few months ago, Joe had rejected Mel's proposal of marriage even though he had already proposed to her and she'd said yes. As Mel explained to her mother, it was complicated.

The truth was that Mel had gotten cold feet at the "until death us do part" portion of the whole marriage package, but she had worked through it. Unfortunately, when she had gotten over her case of the wiggins and proposed to Joe, he'd just taken on the trial of a notorious mobster, who was known for wriggling off justice's barbed hook by murdering anyone who tried to lock him up.

Joe had walked away from Mel to keep her from being a target. To Mel it still felt like rejection. She didn't handle that sort of thing well and in the past three months had gained fifteen pounds from comfort eating. For that alone, she hoped Joe brought his mobster to justice.

"Come on, ladies, it's 'time to nut up or shut up'," Tate said as he dropped an arm around Mel's and Angie's shoulders and began to herd them to the van.

"*Zombieland*," Mel and Angie identified the movie together.

The swapping of movie quotes was one of the foundations of their friendship. Mel and Tate had met first in middle school but then Angie had come along and the three friends had spent weekends in Tate's parents' home theater watching old movies and eating junk food. Ever since they had played a game of stumping one another with movie quotes.

These days just the memory of those happier times made Mel glum. Why did it seem like everything was so difficult now?

"Chin up, Undead Chef," Tate said. "We're going to go

sell cupcakes to the shambling masses and make an arm and a leg in profit."

"*Ba dum dum*," Angie made the sound of a drummer's rim shot.

Mel rolled her eyes. "I guess that's better than making a killing."

"That's the spirit," Angie said with a laugh.

"Aw, come on. It's a zombie walk finished off with an outdoor big screen showing of the *Night of the Living Dead*," Tate said. "How could we have anything but a good time?"

From *New York Times* Bestselling Author
Jenn McKinlay

Cloche and Dagger

THE FIRST IN THE BRAND-NEW HAT SHOP MYSTERIES

Not only is Scarlett Parker's love life in the loo—as her British cousin Vivian Tremont would say—it's also gone viral with an embarrassing video. So when Viv suggests Scarlett leave Florida to lay low in London, she hops on the next plane across the pond to work at Viv's ladies' hat shop, Mim's Whims, and forget her troubles.

But a few surprises await Scarlett in London. First, she is met at the airport not by Viv, but by her handsome business manager, Harrison Wentworth. Second, Viv seems to be missing. No one is too concerned about it until one of her posh clients is found dead wearing the cloche hat Viv made for her—and nothing else. Is Scarlett's cousin in trouble? Or is she in hiding?

"A delightful new heroine!"
—Deborah Crombie, *New York Times* bestselling author

jennmckinlay.com
facebook.com/TheCrimeSceneBooks
penguin.com

M1340T0613

From *New York Times* Bestselling Author

Jenn McKinlay

DEATH OF A MAD HATTER

A HAT SHOP MYSTERY

Scarlett Parker and Vivian Tremont, co-owners of a London hat shop, are creating the hats for an *Alice in Wonderland* themed afternoon tea. The tea is a fund-raiser hosted by the Grisby family, who wants a new hospital wing named after their patriarch.

When the Grisby heir is poisoned, evidence points to Scarlett and Viv, and the police become curiouser and curiouser about their involvement. Now the ladies need to find the tea party crasher who's mad enough to kill at the drop of a hat...

"A delightful new heroine."
—Deborah Crombie, *New York Times* bestselling author

jennmckinlay.com
facebook.com/TheCrimeSceneBooks
penguin.com

FROM *NEW YORK TIMES* BESTSELLING AUTHOR

JENN MCKINLAY

~~~~~~

THE CUPCAKE BAKERY MYSTERIES

Sprinkle with Murder
Buttercream Bump Off
Death by the Dozen
Red Velvet Revenge
Going, Going, Ganache
Sugar and Iced

INCLUDES SCRUMPTIOUS RECIPES!

~~~~~~

Praise for the Cupcake Bakery Mysteries

"Delectable . . . A real treat."
—Julie Hyzy, *New York Times* bestselling author
of the White House Chef Mysteries

"A tender cozy full of warm and likable characters
and...tasty concoctions."
—*Publishers Weekly* (starred review)

jennmckinlay.com
facebook.com/jennmckinlay
facebook.com/TheCrimeSceneBooks
penguin.com

M1212AS1013

FROM *NEW YORK TIMES* BESTSELLING AUTHOR
JENN MCKINLAY

-The Library Lover's Mysteries-

BOOKS CAN BE DECEIVING
DUE OR DIE
BOOK, LINE, AND SINKER
READ IT AND WEEP
ON BORROWED TIME

Praise for the Library Lover's Mysteries

"Fast-paced and fun...Charming."
—Kate Carlisle, *New York Times* bestselling author

"A sparkling setting, lovely characters, books, knitting, and chowder! What more could any reader ask?"
—Lorna Barrett, *New York Times* bestselling author

"Sure to charm cozy readers everywhere."
—Ellery Adams, *New York Times* bestselling author of the Books by the Bay Mysteries

jennmckinlay.com
facebook.com/TheCrimeSceneBooks
penguin.com

M1145AS0514